Books by Tom Hoffman

The Eleventh Ring

The Thirteenth Monk

The Seventh Medallion

Orville Mouse and the Puzzle
of the Clockwork Glowbirds

Orville Mouse and the Puzzle
of the Shattered Abacus

Orville Mouse and the Puzzle
of the Capricious Shadows

Orville Mouse and the Puzzle
of the Last Metaphonium

Orville Mouse and the Puzzle
of the Sagacious Sapling

The Translucent Boy and
the Girl Who Saw Him

The Translucent Boy and
the Cat Who Ran Out of Time

Available online at Amazon and Barnes & Noble

The Thirteenth Monk

by Tom Hoffman

Cover design by Tom Hoffman Graphic Design
Anchorage, Alaska

This book is a work of fiction. Names, characters, places, and incidents either are products of the author's imagination or are used fictitiously. Any resemblance to actual persons, living or dead, events, or locales is entirely coincidental.

Tom Hoffman
Visit my website at thoffmanak.wordpress.com
Printed in the United States of America

First Printing: January 2016

ISBN-13: 978-0-9971952-1-7

With lots of love for
Molly, Alex, Sophie, and Oliver

A very special thanks to my wonderful editors
Debbie, Alex, Amanda, Molly, Beth, and Karen
for their invaluable assistance
and excellent advice.

Table of Contents

"The universe begins to look more like a great thought than like a great machine. Mind no longer appears as an accidental intruder into the realm of matter; we are beginning to suspect that we ought rather to hail it as a creator and governor of the realm of matter."

– Sir James Jeans, British physicist (1930)

"For the simplicity on this side of complexity,
I wouldn't give you a fig. But for the simplicity
on the other side of complexity,
for that I would give you anything I have."

– Oliver Wendell Holmes Sr.

Bartholomew the Adventurer
Trilogy • Book Two

The Thirteenth Monk

Chapter 1

Falling

Edmund was falling. He wasn't falling for a lovely female Rabbiton, he wasn't falling for one of the Tree of Eyes' juvenile pranks, and he wasn't falling for the persuasive banter of a fast talking door-to-door sales-rabbit. He was instead falling through churning gray clouds at precisely one hundred and twenty miles per hour, terminal velocity for an object of standard air resistance.

Edmund the Rabbiton was a ten foot tall, six hundred and ninety-four pound silver robot created by the former inhabitants of the Fortress of Elders. He had been created over fifteen hundred years ago, shortly before the mysterious Elders had abandoned their fortress and moved to Mandora, a peaceful new world of their own creation.

For the last fifteen hundred years Edmund had been known only as a 'Model 9000 Rabbiton with the optional A7-Series 3 Repositorian Module'. That meant he was the caretaker for the Central Information Repository, a gigantic library containing the collective knowledge of the highly evolved and enigmatic Elders. It was Morthram, the Penrith Shapers Guild Master, who had suggested Edmund choose a shorter name for himself. He chose the name 'Edmund', naming himself after a long forgotten Elder known as Edmund the Explorer. Even though Edmund was a robot he had always wanted to be an adventurer and felt an inexplicable connection to Edmund the Explorer.

Edmund had helped Bartholomew bring to a close the reign of the dastardly Grymmorian King Oberon, then taken on the role of Master of Rabbitons to the Fortress of Elders. As Master of Rabbitons, Edmund was responsible for the nearly fifteen thousand robotic Rabbitons abandoned by the Elders. He was also given the task of returning the Fortress of Elders to its original state, including a full restoration of the underground gravitator transportation system. Only the Rabbitons possessed the highly advanced technological expertise to perform this monumentally complex task.

As Edmund was plummeting towards the ground below, he had only one moment of panic. That was when he thought he had lost his cherished adventurer's hat to the one hundred and twenty mile per hour wind. The hat was a gift from his dear friends Bartholomew and Clara. In the days following King Oberon's overthrow, Bartholomew had been exploring the expansive transportation system beneath the Fortress of Elders and spotted a hat in one of the ancient shops. It was a traditional adventurer's hat made from brown felt with a wide brim and a tightly woven straw band. The right brim folded up to the crown and a single purple feather was tucked into the straw band on the opposite side. Bartholomew remembered Edmund mentioning he had always wanted to wear a hat, so he and Clara presented it to him before their return to Bartholomew's home in Lepus Hollow. Much to Edmund's great relief he found his beloved hat still strapped tightly to his head.

"Oh my, that was rather a fright. A real adventurer would never lose his hat."

Edmund eyed the large gleaming ship falling alongside him, also plummeting towards the ground at one hundred and twenty miles per hour.

"I hope Oliver isn't too distraught over the potential loss of the *Adventurer II.* I know he spent a great deal of time and effort on its design and construction, and he does seem especially proud of his creation. I suppose we could enlist the robotic A9 Engineering Rabbitons to help rebuild it. That should cheer him up." Edmund cupped his hands to his mouth and hollered across to the sleek silver craft.

"Oliver, no need to fret! We'll be able to repair the *Adventurer II* with help from the A9 Engineering Rabbitons back at the Fortress!"

Two heads, both possessing very wide eyes, popped up from behind one of the cabin seats. The heads belonged to Bartholomew Rabbit, also known as Bartholomew the Adventurer, and to Oliver T. Rabbit, former head of research and material acquisitions at the Excelsior Electro-Vacuumator Corporation, the largest manufacturer of electric powered household cleaning appliances in Lapinor.

The extraordinary series of events in which the three adventurers were now deeply immersed had begun quite innocuously, nearly three months earlier at the Excelsior Electro-Vacuumator Corporation headquarters in New Fendaron.

Chapter 2

The Meeting

Senior Engineer Alexander J. Rabbit strode down the long hallway, a sheath of technical drawings tucked beneath his arm. Alexander was employed at the Excelsior Electro-Vacuumator Corporation in the great Lapinoric metropolis of New Fendaron, and was on his way to meet with Oliver T. Rabbit, head of research and material acquisitions. This would be the first time Alexander had ever seen Oliver T. Rabbit in the flesh, but he had heard plenty of stories, each one more outlandish than the previous one.

It was said Oliver had inexplicably vanished, returning many months later with fantastic tales of a talking tree covered with eyes, the daring rescue of his long lost sister Clara, who he claimed was a mystical shaper, the dethroning of an evil Grymmorian king named Oberon, and even a mysterious valley inhabited by prehistoric pterosaurs. He also spoke of a rabbit named Bartholomew the Adventurer who possessed shaping skills that beggared the imagination.

Alexander muttered to himself as he padded briskly

down the hall. "Unadulterated poppycock – ridiculous stories told by rabbits ignorant of the most basic scientific principles. He may once have been a great scientist, but Oliver T. Rabbit is now nuttier than my Aunt Molly's fruitcake."

Reaching the end of the corridor, Alexander stopped and eyed the ornately carved wooden door adorned with a brass plaque reading *Oliver T. Rabbit.* With a dismal shake of his head, he knocked loudly on the door.

There was a garbled sound from within which sounded vaguely like, "Umber!"

Correctly assuming the word he had heard was 'enter', Alexander swung the door open and was met by the sight of a rather plump rabbit leaning back in his chair, both feet resting on his desk. In one paw he held an éclair from which he had just taken a substantial bite, the now obvious reason for his nearly unintelligible response.

"Éclair?" Oliver pointed to a plate of the delicious pastries sitting on his desk.

"No thank you, sir. I don't want to take up too much of your time. As you had requested, I am here to show you the revised drawings for the Mark VII Commercial Series 2 Electro-Vacuumator."

"Ah, yes, the new commercial Electro-Vacuumator designs." Oliver removed his feet from the desk and set the half-eaten éclair on the window sill behind him.

Spreading the drawings out in front of Oliver T. Rabbit, Alexander began his presentation. "As you can see here, sir –"

"Oliver. Please do call me Oliver."

"Yes, sir... Oliver. As you can see here, I have made four changes to the existing design of the Mark VII commercial model – here, here, here, and here. These relatively minor alterations have increased the total output of the duplonium engine by twelve percent, all with no increase to the current manufacturing costs. It's rather exciting if I may say so... Oliver."

"Yes, quite exciting indeed. Twelve percent at no additional cost." Oliver reached for the half-eaten éclair, pausing to gaze out the window at the busy streets below. "Not quite as exciting as facing Zoran the Emerald Shaper in the Fortress of Elders though. Now that is a day I will not soon forget."

"Zoran... I'm afraid I'm not familiar with him. He was someone you worked with?"

"Ha! Indeed, he was my boss for two days until he threw me into a dungeon and then tried to vaporize us all. If it wasn't for a fifteen hundred year old robotic Rabbiton named Edmund, I'd be a pile of purple glowing ashes."

"Ah, a pile of glowing ashes. Well, thank you for your time, Oliver. I'll just leave these drawings with you, and at your leisure you may make whatever changes you wish, or approve them as they are."

Oliver glanced at Alexander with an apologetic smile. "Pay no attention to my fantastic tales, young sir. These are well crafted, thoughtful designs and you are to be highly commended." Oliver quickly initialed each of the drawings and handed them to Alexander. "Your drawings are approved as they stand."

"Thank you, Oliver, it is an honor to receive such praise from a great scientist such as yourself." With a quick nod to Oliver, Alexander walked out the door, closing it carefully behind him.

Senior Engineer Alexander J. Rabbit strode back

down the hall, muttering to himself. “It’s all true. Oliver T. Rabbit is as mad as a bag of frogs.”

Chapter 3

Oliver Takes a Holiday

"Drat. Bartholomew was right, I must refrain from telling tales of our adventures to rabbits who possess no understanding of the science behind them. That's one more engineer who thinks I'm quite mad, and I'm afraid there aren't many left who would disagree with him."

With a long sigh, Oliver T. Rabbit turned his attention to the stack of unanswered letters sitting on his desk. "I suppose a year ago I wouldn't have believed my stories either. If someone had told me there were rabbits who use their mind to create thought clouds, then convert those clouds to solid objects, I would have laughed louder and longer than most." He smiled, remembering the first time Bartholomew had shaped an object in front of him. A molasses cookie had blinked into existence right in Bartholomew's paw. Rabbits with this ability called themselves shapers, and some shapers could blink themselves almost instantly to other locations, or transform themselves into the physical form of other creatures. Bartholomew called that formshifting, and was quite adept at it himself.

It had been a slow, painful process for Oliver to come to the realization that these seemingly miraculous events had a solid foundation in certain esoteric principles of physics. Unfortunately, most of these principles lay outside the current boundaries of general scientific knowledge. As a result of his research and experimentation, Oliver now understood more about the science of shaping than any other living rabbit. To his great dismay, however, his theories regarding these phenomena had been soundly rejected by his peers, many quickly distancing themselves from Oliver T. Rabbit and his preposterous new ideas. Even with an abundance of proof, a good number of these scientists still did not believe in the existence of shapers, claiming the objects created by them were only 'illusions'".

Oliver pulled a letter off the top of the stack and began to read. One of their suppliers was raising the price of cast wheel assemblies. For no particular reason he flipped the letter over and wrote, '*The Adventurer*'. It was this seemingly insignificant event which would eventually lead to Edmund the Rabbiton's spectacular fall from the sky.

The Adventurer was the name of the vessel Bartholomew and Oliver had sailed up the Halsey River towards Penrith during their search for Oliver's long lost sister Clara, who had also been Bartholomew's dearest bunnyhood friend. *The Adventurer* was tragically torn apart on jagged rocks, disappearing forever beneath the roaring river. Bartholomew and Oliver had barely escaped with their lives.

Ever the perfectionist, Oliver meticulously sketched the craft. He had originally designed it as a three-wheeled duplonium powered wagon to carry their supplies, later converting it to a power boat for their excursion up the Halsey River. Duplonium is an extraordinarily rare element, and a source of unlimited power. A piece the size of a small marble could drive a massive steam generator for hundreds of years. Since Bartholomew's discovery of a huge duplonium deposit in the Swamp of Lost Things, all the Excelsior Electro-Vacuumators were now powered by this rare element. His discovery had incidentally made Bartholomew an exceedingly wealthy rabbit.

Oliver eyed the completed drawing with a wistful smile, then turned the drawing sideways and slid it into his outbox, reaching for the next letter. His paw stopped in mid air, however, his eyes filled with the brilliant light of realization.

"Good heavens! I am a complete dunderhead! Why have I not thought of this before?" He grabbed another letter and flipped it over, scribbling madly, his pencil racing across the paper. "Yes, yes, this is quite elegant, it will certainly work. It is simple physics and nothing more. This will change *everything*." He leaped to his feet, grabbed the drawing and dashed out of his office.

Ten minutes later Oliver T. Rabbit unceremoniously barged into the plush offices of Augustus C. Rabbit, president of the Excelsior Electro-Vacuumator Corporation. Oliver held the drawing up in front of Augustus. "You are looking at the future, sir. This is the beginning of a great revolution in the world of rabbits and muroidians."

Augustus C. Rabbit looked at the drawing curiously,

then at Oliver, then back at the drawing. He slowly removed his gold rimmed glasses, pausing for a moment to brush away a speck of dust. "Oliver, I hope you know I have nothing but respect and admiration for you. Your reputation as one of Lapinor's foremost scientists is beyond question, and the Excelsior Corporation has been extraordinarily lucky to count you as one of its employees."

Exactly thirty-four minutes later Oliver flew out of the office, banged the door shut behind him and dashed out the front door of the Excelsior Electro-Vacuumator Corporation headquarters.

The following morning, Senior Engineer Alexander J. Rabbit was strolling down the hallway to his office, a large porcelain mug of steaming coffee in one paw. He stopped to peruse the bulletin board, one notice in particular catching his attention.

NOTICE FROM PRESIDENT
AUGUSTUS C. RABBIT
Please be aware as of yesterday afternoon
Oliver T. Rabbit, head of Research and Material
Acquisitions will be on extended holiday.
Acting head of R&MA will be selected
later this week.

Alexander snorted. "Knew it. Mad as a bag of frogs, and they finally chucked him out on his ear."

Chapter 4

The Fortress of Elders

Oliver T. Rabbit stood at the border crossing, a bulky leather valise in one paw, a roll of freshly drawn technical drawings in the other. After his sudden departure from the Electro-Vacuumator headquarters, Oliver had returned to his home on the outskirts of New Fendaron. One week later he emerged with these new drawings – plans for a remarkable invention he was certain would revolutionize travel for rabbits and muroidians alike.

The neighboring country of Grymmore was primarily inhabited by muroidians, creatures resembling large wild rats. After the defeat of evil Grymmorian King Oberon, Grymmore and Lapinor had opened new lines of communication which dramatically improved relations between rabbits and muroidians. Grymmore's newly crowned King Fendaron, who Bartholomew and Oliver knew as 'Fen', had played a significant role in King Oberon's overthrow.

Oliver stepped across the border and was met at the white wooden gate by a stern faced Grymmorian border guard. A small freshly painted sign reading "WELCOME TO GRYMMORE" hung from the gate.

"Name, please?"

"Oliver T. Rabbit."

"Are you in possession of any vegetables or invasive insects?"

"I am not, sir."

"Are you a member of the New Grymmorian Shaper's Guild?"

"No, I–"

"Wait, what did you say?"

"I said I'm not a member–"

"No, your name, what did you say it was?

"Oliver T. Rabbit."

The guard's stern demeanor melted away. "I beg your pardon, sir. I do apologize for not recognizing you. There's a carriage waiting to take you to the Fortress of Elders. King Fendaron sends his best regards and wishes you a safe and pleasant journey. He also wishes to inform you that Edmund the Rabbiton is anxiously awaiting your arrival."

"Ah, thank you, good sir. Would it be possible to make a slight detour to Madame Beffy's Pastry Shop in Grymmsteir?"

"Indeed, sir, it is on the way, only a few miles past the mouth of the Farlo River. If I might add, it is an honor to meet one of the rabbits who helped bring about the downfall of King Oberon, may he be infested by angry fleas and rot for all eternity in the deepest and darkest of Malgraven dungeons."

"Good heavens, I did nothing more than anyone else

would have done in such a desperate situation. Oberon was planning to transform all the rabbits in Lapinor into mindless slaves with his infernal shaping machine and he had to be stopped. It was Bartholomew Rabbit who defeated Zoran and nearly lost his life destroying Oberon's insidious device. He is the true hero, not me."

"Spoken like a true hero, sir." With a smile, the guard held open the door of a highly polished maroon carriage and a flustered Oliver T. Rabbit stepped inside.

The guard waved to the driver and the carriage lurched forward on the first leg of its journey to the Fortress of Elders. Oliver recalled only one year prior he had been riding in a similar carriage with Zoran the Emerald Shaper, who at the time was formshifted into Master Scientist Tarami. Oliver shuddered at the memory. He had met many rabbits and muroidians in his life, but none as chillingly evil as Zoran.

"Enough of these dreadful thoughts. Time to get cracking on the final plans for the *Adventurer II*." He unrolled the sheath of technical drawings and spread them out in front of him, grinning like a bunny on his birthday. "Whatever will Bartholomew think when he sees this astonishing new craft?"

The carriage ride to the Fortress was long and uneventful, something which pleased Oliver immensely. Although he had accompanied Bartholomew on a number of extremely perilous adventures, he was by nature not very adventurous and rather averse to risky situations. They stayed at comfortable inns along the way where Oliver sampled generously the fare offered by each, often having lengthy discussions with the chef regarding the cuisine and its preparation. Oliver's culinary skills were almost as highly developed as his expertise in the scientific arena.

The afternoon of the fourth day found him kneeling on the carriage floor, studying several dozen mechanical drawings now peppered with red penciled comments and diagrams.

"With some assistance from Edmund's A9 engineering Rabbitons, I believe this will be a rousing success."

Oliver felt the carriage slowing down and peered out the window. They came to a rattling halt in front of the monumentally massive Fortress of Elders. There was not another structure in all of Grymmore or Lapinor that even came close to the sheer enormity of the Fortress. The huge bronze colored metallic doors leading into the Fortress were over forty feet tall. The angled sand colored walls of the Fortress rose up several hundred feet above that. During his first visit to the Fortress Oliver had closely examined it's construction and found the doors and the walls to be composed of unknown synthetic materials far more durable than stone and metal.

The carriage door swung open, the driver nodding politely to Oliver. "We have reached the Fortress, sir. I do hope you had an enjoyable trip."

"Yes, all quite delightful, I assure you, especially Madame Beffy's Pastry Shop in Grymmsteir. Excellent éclairs, just excellent, and Madame Beffy herself was quite charming."

"Very good, sir. I will bring your bags into the Fortress. I understand you are eager to see your friend Edmund the Rabbiton. I must confess I've never seen a Rabbiton before. Are they really ten feet tall?"

"Indeed they are, good sir. Ten foot tall silver robotic rabbits created by the Elders over fifteen hundred years ago. They are also absolutely indestructible, completely resistant to shaping, and incomprehensibly strong. The mechanism of their fabrication is still a mystery, of course, but one day I hope to unlock those secrets."

The driver's eyes widened as he turned towards the Fortress.

"Great Fendaron's ghost, it's one of those metal Rabbitons!"

A wide grin spread across Oliver's face as he recognized his old friend Edmund.

Edmund strode across the gatehouse bridge towards the carriage. "My old friend Oliver! It has been three hundred and forty-five days since I last saw you, and at times your absence seems to have negatively affected the processes of my synthetic neuronic brain."

Oliver laughed. "Are you saying you missed me?"

"Well, yes, I suppose I am saying that." Edmund looked puzzled. "It's very curious. I'm not certain Rabbitons have the innate capacity for such feelings, but time and time again I find myself wishing to be in the presence of my old adventuring friends."

"Edmund, stop all the talking and give me a hug. I missed you too. Life at the Excelsior Corporation pales in comparison to my thrilling adventures with you and Bartholomew."

Edmund leaned down, giving Oliver a great hug. "I have not hugged anyone since I hugged Clara and Bartholomew soon after Oberon's infernal device was destroyed. The other Rabbitons have no interest in such behavior."

"I've always said you were one of a kind, my friend. How have you been? Have you reactivated many of the Rabbitons which were left in storage?"

"Indeed so. Thirteen thousand two hundred and twenty-nine have been activated so far, and they are currently working on the restoration of the Fortress and the underground gravitator transportation system. Many of the shops have opened, and a growing number of muroidians and rabbits have been visiting the Fortress. It is quite evident they are losing their fear of Rabbitons, and I have personally noticed they seem especially fond of the food synthesizers."

"Excellent news. Have you any word of our old friend Morthram?"

"Morthram is the New Grymmorian Shapers Guild Master and is extremely busy since Fen declared shaping to be lawful in Grymmore. He said they are opening new Guild centers all across the country."

"I'm ever so glad to hear he is doing well. I haven't seen Bartholomew and Clara since the wedding in Lepus Hollow. They honeymooned on the Isle of Mandora and I have received a number of lovely letters from Clara since then. They sound wonderfully happy, but Clara did mention Bartholomew seemed to be pining somewhat for the adventuring life. They sold their homes and moved to Penrith, where Clara replaced Morthram as Guild Master. She has been well received there, and I hear Guild membership has nearly doubled. Parfello is still with them, of course."

Edmund gave a muffled little laugh.

"What is it?"

"Oh dear, they wanted it to be a surprise, but Bartholomew and Clara are coming to the Fortress in thirteen days for a visit. I have missed them also."

Oliver's face broke in to a grin. "That's wonderful! I can't wait to see them. I'm certain they have missed you too, Edmund. They count you among their dear friends, as do I. Now, shall we pay a visit to those A9 engineering Rabbitons of yours? I would like to have the *Adventurer II* completed and fully operational before Bartholomew's arrival. If he thought *The Adventurer* was miraculous, just wait until he sees this!"

Chapter 5

The Ant

"No, no, put those parts back in the storage bin. We won't need them until after we have installed the Mark VII Commercial Prototype Electro-Vacuumators."

"As you wish, sir."

Oliver watched as the A9 Series 6 Engineering Rabbiton gingerly picked up a stack of wooden crates filled with parts, each box weighing over six hundred pounds.

"I shall return these to the proper storage bins, as you requested."

Oliver's gaze turned to the thirty foot long metal alloy frame sitting in the center of the room. With its long graceful curves, the ship held a certain resemblance to a traditional Lapinoric fishing vessel. Eight A9 Engineering Rabbitons were busily molding and shaping sheets of metal and welding them to the framework.

"Excellent work, my friends, we are well ahead of schedule. You are doing a fine job and should be proud of yourselves."

None of the Rabbitons acknowledged Oliver's compliment.

"Once the outer shell is complete we can add the Mark VII Vacuumators. They arrived only yesterday from the Excelsior Corporation and are even more efficient and powerful than I had expected. It looks as though Senior Engineer Alexander J. Rabbit managed to bump up the output of the Mark VII by almost sixteen percent."

Again the A9 Rabbitons said nothing.

Oliver eyed the Rabbitons with a slight frown, then chuckled. "How many Rabbitons would like to go out for a glass of wine and a delicious éclair once we've completed the outer shell? Perhaps we could even take in a play afterwards, one filled with adventure and romance."

One of the A9 Rabbitons stood up, his silver face expressionless. "Rabbitons do not eat or drink. We are not powered by the ingestion of organic matter, but by Cross Dimensional Energy Transference Spheres, more commonly known as CDETS, created by the Elders. We do not attend plays of any kind, romantic or otherwise, and we require no sleep. Consequently, we will continue working on the fabrication of the vehicle until it is complete, if that is your wish."

"Ah, thank you my good Rabbiton, for your most enlightening comments. With that in mind, we shall forego such frivolous activities and instead proceed with the assembly and installation of the Mark VII Vacuumators." With another chuckle Oliver turned to the technical drawings spread out before him. Only seconds later he was interrupted by a familiar voice.

"Good afternoon, Oliver. It looks as though the A9

Rabbitons are on schedule with the fabrication of the *Adventurer II.*"

Oliver spun around to see a smiling Edmund. "You are quite perceptive, my friend. The A9s are well ahead of schedule. I feel quite certain she'll be ready by the time Bartholomew and Clara arrive. We'll have to run extensive operational tests before our maiden voyage, of course. Better safe than sorry, I always say."

"I would be happy to pilot the craft during those tests. As you know, I am quite indestructible, so if anything were to go awry, there would be no injuries. I have just now done the necessary computations, and have determined the eight Mark VII Vacuumators will provide more than enough power for the craft. My current calculations indicate the ship can safely operate using only five Mark VII Vacuumators."

"That's excellent news, Edmund. Your ability to solve such complex mathematical problems so rapidly is truly amazing. It would have taken me at least half a day to come up with a proper solution."

"Yes, the synthetic neuronic brain which the Elders created for the Model 9000 Rabbitons is capable of over six hundred and fifty million–" Edmund stopped in mid sentence, his eyes focused on something across the room. Without a word he turned and walked towards it.

Oliver watched with a puzzled expression. It was quite unlike Edmund to walk away in the midst of a conversation, and he had no idea what Edmund was looking at. The two hundred foot wide room on sub level 2 of the Fortress was empty save for the construction of the *Adventurer II.* Edmund stopped about fifty feet away and sank down to his hands and knees, peering at some invisible object on the floor.

"Good heavens, what is that Rabbiton up to?" Oliver walked across the room to Edmund. "Did you lose something? Whatever are you looking at?"

"I am observing an ant. They are quite miraculous creatures. Did you know some ants can lift over one hundred times their own body weight? It's quite remarkable when you consider a Rabbiton can only lift ten times its body weight. It's almost frightening how strong ants really are."

"That's... remarkable indeed. I had no idea you were interested in ants, Edmund. The study of entomology has always been a favorite–"

Edmund abruptly stood up. "I have not previously had an interest in ants, and I am unable to explain my sudden urge to examine this particular one. The urge has passed now, so I will return to my original task, assisting the engineering Rabbitons in their preparation of the Mark VII Vacuumators."

"Ah... all right. Yes, that would be a great help. Thank you, Edmund." Oliver watched Edmund walk back across the room towards the *Adventurer II.* "That may be the strangest conversation I have ever had. Quite peculiar, even for Edmund."

The A9 engineering Rabbitons worked around the clock as promised, and ten days later the *Adventurer II* was ready for its initial testing. Oliver stood in front of the gleaming craft, paws on his hips and a smile on his face. This was a far more complex vehicle than the original *Adventurer,* and Oliver foresaw this as the future of transportation for rabbits and muroidians.

Edmund climbed into the craft, calling out to Oliver, "I will begin testing the Mark VII Electro-Vacuumators, first making certain they all function properly. Once I am satisfied with their performance I will push this yellow lever to send the air stream through the sixteen custom designed air release nozzles."

"Excellent. Please activate the first Vacuumator." Oliver put his paws over his ears. He remembered very well the earsplitting roar created by the old Vacuumators. Edmund stepped over to the ship's center console, holding his paw above a row of eight small red levers, then flipped the first one.

The was a slight humming noise.

"What's wrong with it? Is it not working properly?"

"It is working perfectly. These Mark VII Vacuumators have a radical new sound deadening mechanism built into them, courtesy of Senior Engineer Alexander J. Rabbit." He flipped the second red lever, then one by one all the rest. The room was filled with a deep and powerful droning sound, but nothing even remotely resembling the terrific shrieking roar of the old Mark III models.

Oliver lowered his paws. "This is wonderful, we'll be able to talk while the ship is operating! Do the nozzles rotate properly?"

Edmund pushed one of the large green levers at the center of the console and with a whirring noise all sixteen nozzles swung into position. "They work perfectly. Shall I activate the nozzles?"

Oliver took a deep breath. All their calculations had led to one inarguable conclusion, but as he was so fond of saying, 'the proof is in the pudding'. "Push the lever!"

Edmund flipped the yellow lever and all sixteen nozzles throttled open. He inched the number one green lever forward and the low droning noise rose to a deep throaty roar. He glanced over at Oliver and gave the number two green lever a gentle push.

Oliver's jaw dropped. The pudding was tasty indeed. "We've done it! We have done it! Great heavens, Edmund, we have really done it!"

Chapter 6

The Adventurer II

"I believe I have packed everything you and Clara shall need for your trip to the Fortress of Elders, sir." Parfello set down two oversized leather valises in front of Bartholomew. Bartholomew looked at the two highly polished bags and gave a mock frown.

Bartholomew was remembering his first visit to the Cavern of Silence. "Parfello, with shiny new bags such as these, everyone will surely think this is my first adventure. We can't have that. I'll need a pack with some age to it."

"Indeed so, sir. Perhaps I could fetch a tattered old canvas sack from the dust bin behind the fish market, one which has been used to convey rotting fish entrails. Would that be satisfactory?"

Bartholomew laughed. "After some further thought I have decided these two valises will be quite adequate, Parfello."

Parfello gave the faintest hint of a smile. "Very good, sir, I shall postpone my excursion to the fish market. Will you be riding the train to the border and then traveling by carriage to the Fortress?"

"I think not, Parfello. Clara and I have decided to blink to the Fortress. The trip will take only four jumps at the most, so we will arrive shortly after we depart."

"Oh dear, you're going to do *that* again? Perhaps you might wait until I am otherwise occupied in the kitchen before you perform your blinking business. It's most alarming to see you and Clara vanish into thin air. It doesn't seem natural, if you don't mind my saying so, sir."

"I understand completely, my friend. We will wait until you're safely out of sight."

There was a flash of light and Clara blinked into view in front of Bartholomew. "Are you packed? I'm quite eager to see Oliver and Edmund again. It seems like it's been ages since we've seen them."

Parfello staggered back a step, putting his paw to his chest, but quickly regained his demeanor. "I beg your pardon madam, your appearance was... rather unexpected. If you would be so kind as to give my regards to Oliver T. Rabbit when you see him, I would greatly appreciate it. And perhaps to your new friend Edmund the Rabbiton, though I have never met him." He mumbled under his breath, "Or any other ten foot tall mechanical rabbit."

Much to Parfello's embarrassment Clara gave him a hug, saying, "Have a lovely relaxing time while we're away, Parfello. Bartholomew will return after two weeks, and I shall be back in three, following a week long initiate quest. I will be guiding four new members of the Penrith guild on a hunt for Night Blossoms in the Brycin mountains."

Bartholomew picked up both satchels. "Ready to

blink?"

Parfello scurried out through the doorway, disappearing into the kitchen.

"We'll see you in a few weeks, Parfello!" With a brilliant flash of light, Bartholomew and Clara blinked and were gone.

It was Morthram who had taught Bartholomew how to blink, after their narrow escape from the terrors of King Oberon's ferillium mine. Blinking involved converting the physical body into a thought cloud, traveling at enormous velocity for no more than two seconds, then converting the thought cloud back to its original physical form. If the shaper remained in cloud form for more than two seconds it became impossible to convert back to their physical body. They were technically still alive, but no longer able to interact in the world. This time limitation was a harsh reality of shaping and put a deadly restriction on the distance they could travel with each jump.

Three minutes and four jumps later they blinked into the main foyer of the Fortress of Elders. A smiling Rabbiton greeted them warmly. "Good afternoon...." The Rabbiton's eyes glowed brightly, scanning their faces. "...Bartholomew and Clara. I will take your bags and you may head down to sub level two. Please note we have recently numbered all the rooms in the Fortress for the convenience of both our visitors and resident Rabbitons. Your two friends, Oliver T. Rabbit and Edmund the Rabbiton, are waiting for you in room 2810 on sub level two. Oliver has mentioned a number of times how anxious he is to see you."

"Thank you, it's wonderful to be back in the Fortress." Bartholomew and Clara walked along the main corridor down to the first sub level. They walked silently past the room where Oberon's infernal shaping machine had once stood. Bartholomew had come very close to losing his life there. Clara looked away when they walked past.

"That dreadful room. You almost died saving my life."

"I would do it again in an instant."

"I know you would, and I would do the same for you."

Bartholomew took Clara's paw as they walked through the long corridors. "This is where we defeated Zoran. I was not at all certain my plan would work, you know. So many things could have gone wrong."

Clara nodded but said nothing. She did not like reliving the memories of those dark days when she had been held captive by King Oberon. They continued on until they spotted the massive stairway leading down to sub level 2. After another ten minutes of walking they reached room 2810. Clara touched a violet disk on the wall and the door silently slid open, revealing a vast chamber and a long, graceful silver ship.

"There they are!" Oliver's great voice echoed across the room. Bartholomew and Clara's faces lit up the instant they spotted Oliver and Edmund.

There were hugs for everyone, especially Edmund. Before Bartholomew could say a word, Oliver pointed to the gleaming craft and said, "Allow me to introduce my latest creation, the *Adventurer II*, the future of transportation for all rabbits and muroidians. What do you think? Is she as miraculous a creation as the duplonium wagon we used to outrun those dreadful pterosaurs?" He laughed loudly.

Bartholomew studied the craft carefully, but appeared perplexed. "I realize you are a renowned scientist and inventor, Oliver, but it seems you may have unwittingly neglected to put wheels on this sleek silver wagon."

Oliver slapped his paw to his forehead. "Oh, great heavens, I thought something looked off about it! I know, I shall dash back to the Excelsior Corporation and requisition four Model B12-A heavy duty wheel assemblies." He strolled over to the gleaming ship and climbed a small ladder to the cabin. Taking a seat at the main console, he flipped all eight red levers, then the yellow lever. A low and powerful humming noise filled the room. Bartholomew and Clara looked at each other with clear concern, backing away from the craft. Oliver waved to them, then pushed the number one green lever. The nozzles rotated in unison, and were now directed towards the floor. He pushed the number two green lever and the hum changed to a deep roar.

Bartholomew and Clara watched in astonishment as the *Adventurer II* gently rose up from the floor until it was hovering twenty feet in the air. Oliver nudged the number two green lever and the craft circled the huge room. Moments later he brought it softly down to the ground.

"What do you think?? Are you ready to take her out on a real adventure?

Bartholomew was plainly dumbstruck. "Good heavens, Oliver, this is amazing. You have created a flying vehicle! You are a miracle worker, my friend. I have only one question. How soon can we leave?" He turned to Clara. "What do you think? Shall we take the *Adventurer II* on a quest to find Bruno Rabbit's mystery house in Pterosaur Valley?"

Clara laughed. "Count me in. I've always wanted to see a real pterosaur."

Oliver beamed with pride. "It's settled then, we're off to Pterosaur Valley. Edmund, you'd better pack your bags – I'll be needing a trusty copilot on this adventure, and I can't think of a better one than you."

Edmund was already backing up towards the door, his eyes locked on Oliver. "Do *not* leave without me. I'll be right back – *right back*. I have to get my adventurer's hat!"

Chapter 7

Edmund's Curious Question

After giving it more thought, Oliver decided to conduct three full days of rigorous flight testing on the *Adventurer II* prior to their departure for Pterosaur Valley. This would additionally give him time to teach Bartholomew the proper operating procedures for the craft, in the event he should ever have to fly it. Clara chose to take advantage of these three extra days by exploring the underground gravitator transportation system, and Edmund had graciously volunteered to be her guide.

Their first stop was the vast Central Information Repository where Edmund had spent over fourteen hundred years as Master Repositorian, a vast library of knowledge containing several million books and countless crystalline storage centers.

"Weren't you lonely spending so many years by yourself, Edmund? The Elders left for the City of Mandora shortly after you began your position here as repositorian. What was it like when the Elders left, and what made you decide to remain here in the Fortress?"

"To answer your first question, I had no concept of loneliness during those years. It was only when Morthram asked me to choose a name for myself that I began to feel a sense of self-awareness. It was not until after my adventures with Bartholomew, Oliver, Morthram, and you that I found myself wishing to be in the presence of others, specifically the four of you. Since I had never had anything resembling a friend before, I had no reason to feel lonely. It has proven to be a bewildering transition for me, at times quite unsettling. Oliver seemed pleased when I said I missed him and he did say that he also missed me. It is readily apparent that rabbits enjoy the attention and affection of others, as do muroidians, but this quality seems to be lacking in Rabbitons. More precisely, all Rabbitons but me.

"To answer your second question, I remember when the Elders left, but I did not take much notice of it. I was the Master Repositorian and that was my sole focus. The Elders are in some ways quite different from you and Bartholomew. I spoke with them on a regular basis, but I don't believe they ever thought of me as anything other than a Model 9000 Rabbiton with the optional A7-Series 3 Repositorian Module. I do have a faint memory of meeting Edmund the Explorer, which for some reason has stayed with me all this time. Perhaps even then part of me wanted to become an adventurer, just as Bartholomew always did.

"I have no ready explanation as to why I remained here in the Fortress." Edmund paused. "I simply could not leave, but I do not know why."

"Thank you for telling me all this, Edmund. I count you among my dear friends, and it is well accepted among rabbits that friends can discuss with each other their concerns and worries. If there was something I was worried about, I would feel quite comfortable sharing it with you. Now, to lighten the mood a little, Bartholomew mentioned some wonderful food synthesizers down in the gravitator tunnels. Could we visit them? I'm quite hungry and Bartholomew had nothing but good things to say about the food there."

"Of course we may go. We can ride one of the vertical gravitators down to the underground tunnels right now."

Edmund led the way across the repository to the vertical gravitator. He tapped the violet disk and the door quietly slid open. Once inside the gravitator he tapped a blue disk and the door closed behind them. The transparent cylinder descended rapidly for several seconds then came to a gentle halt.

They exited into a vast tunnel, at least three hundred feet wide and several hundred feet tall. Clara watched as any number of gravitator cars shot past, floating several feet above the long rows of sparkling silver tracks. One of the cars had come to a halt at a nearby platform, a steady stream of rabbits and muroids pouring out of the seventy foot long glass cylinder. The extensive system of platforms paralleling the tracks were filled with muroids, rabbits and Rabbitons walking this way and that, many of them carrying brightly colored shopping bags. Wide stairs led up to the main shopping areas.

"Oh my, why have I not been here before? This is quite marvelous. I've never seen anything like it."

"The food synthesizers are farther down the platform, if you would like to visit them before we see all the shops in the upper levels."

"Thank you, Edmund, that would be wonderful."

A half hour later Edmund and Clara were sitting at a table by a wall of brightly lit panels filled with moving images of rabbits eating all manner of tasty delights. As rabbits and muroids approached the synthesizers, the panels would talk to them, describing in great detail the various types of food available at each machine.

"This looks delicious, Edmund. Thank you for showing me how to use the food machines – they are quite miraculous. Bartholomew always shapes his food, but I'm a little more adventurous and like to try food I'm unfamiliar with. I never know what I'll find."

"Clara, I would like to speak to my inner voice. Can you tell me how to do this? I have watched Bartholomew speak to the Cavern of Silence, but I lack a clear understanding of the process."

Clara's fork stopped in mid air. This was the last question she had expected to hear from Edmund. "You wish to speak to your inner voice?" She repeated the question, trying desperately to think of an appropriate answer.

"Yes. From what I understand, my inner voice will be able to tell me more about who I am. I have begun to question my sense of self."

"You wish to know more about who you are?" Clara repeated the question, her mind racing. Did Rabbitons have inner voices? Perhaps they did. A rabbit's physical body is just an organic machine, so why couldn't a Rabbiton have an inner voice? The difference was that rabbits were filled with life force, as were all living creatures. She would not tell Edmund he had no inner voice, as she had no idea how that might affect him. He might be indestructible, but she could clearly see there was also a very fragile bunny-like side to him. Besides, to be truthful, she didn't really know if he had an inner voice or not.

"Indeed so. I have recently become interested in understanding my place in this world."

An answer finally came to Clara. "Edmund, the process is quite simple. You need only find a quiet spot where you can be alone, away from all distraction. For Bartholomew, that place was in the Cavern of Silence. It was really only an ordinary cavern, but it gave him a silent refuge where he could close his eyes and listen to the voice inside him. He was looking for the answer to a specific question. There was something missing from his life and he wanted to learn what it was. It took several days before he finally heard the answer to his question. Often times the answer is not entirely clear – you may only get a feeling, or an image, or a sound, but don't be disappointed if you receive no answer at all. Many rabbits have gone an entire lifetime without speaking to their secret voice within. It may simply not be the right time for you, and there is no shame in that."

"Thank you, Clara. I will follow your instructions. Because I am a mechanical creation of the Elders, it is logical to assume I do not possess an inner voice. That being said, I am quite certain I do have one."

Clara reached across the table and put her paw on Edmund's hand. "Whether you have an inner voice or not, Edmund, you are always my true friend, and in this world true friends are what matter above all else."

Chapter 8

Maiden Voyage

"Is everyone ready?"

"Edmund is wearing his adventurer's hat, so I know he's ready!" Bartholomew laughed, giving the thumbs up sign to Oliver. One by one, Oliver flipped the red levers and the eight gleaming Mark VII Vacuumators began their low, steady humming.

"Amazing! I can hardly hear them. Remember how jarringly loud the old Mark IIIs were?" He flipped the yellow lever and powerful streams of air blasted out of the sixteen high pressure exhaust nozzles.

Edmund called out to Oliver, "Rotating nozzles to 90 degrees."

Oliver inched the green levers forward and the Mark VII Vacuumators roared to life. Clara could feel the ship vibrate briefly as it lifted off the ground. "Three cheers for good Captain Oliver!"

Oliver gave a great guffaw, giving Clara an exaggerated salute. He then turned to Edmund saying, "Once we've reached an altitude of five hundred feet, head us due south southeast. We'll take it slow for a while – twenty miles per hour should do it."

The *Adventurer II* rose smoothly into the air, Edmund's watchful eye on the altimeter. "Five hundred feet." Edmund pulled back imperceptibly on the number two green lever and the ship held steady. He adjusted their speed and direction. "South southeast at twenty miles per hour." The craft turned gently and began to accelerate.

"Look at the Fortress down there! It's massive. I can't imagine how the Elders engineered such a gargantuan structure."

Clara cried out, "Look how far you can see! And how small the trees look. We are seeing what the birds see when they fly – it's breathtaking!"

For almost an hour the only sounds were the steady roar of the Vacuumators and the rushing wind as the *Adventurer II* sped forward through the clear blue skies. The adventurers watched in silence, mesmerized by the ever changing kaleidoscope of landscapes passing below them.

Their peaceful reverie came to a sudden end when Edmund sprang to his feet, frantically skittering back from the control panel. "An ant! Oliver, there's an ant on the console! What should I do? It might damage the controls and crash the ship!"

Clara and Bartholomew spun around towards Edmund, confused by his sudden outburst about an ant.

Oliver remembered well Edmund's inexplicable fascination with the ant back at the Fortress, but this was different – Edmund seemed to be afraid of this ant. Oliver strode over to the console and spotted a single ant walking up the side of the number one green lever.

"It's all right, Edmund. The ant won't interfere with

the ship's operation. It's true they're very strong for their size, but they are far too small to cause any problems with the ship. I will toss it over the side – it's so light it will float safely down to the ground below."

Edmund nodded, but kept his distance from the ant. Oliver let the ant walk onto his paw, then stretched his arm over the side of the craft and the wind carried the ant away. "It's gone now."

Returning to the console, Edmund was his old self again. "Current speed is twenty-five miles per hour. Shall I boost it to forty? Everything is running smoothly."

Oliver nodded. "Make it so, my friend."

A gentle nudge to the green lever and the *Adventurer II* sped forward, now cruising through the skies at an amazing forty miles per hour.

Oliver called out to Bartholomew. "We're traveling faster than when we were being chased by the pterosaurs, but this time there's no wild and terrifying ride!"

"This is fantastic, Oliver! You were right, this ship is the future of transportation. You've created Lapinor's first flying carriage!"

Nobody mentioned Edmund's unusual reaction to the ant, but several minutes later a puffy blue thought cloud floated out of Bartholomew's ear and over to Clara. She pulled it to her and heard Bartholomew's voice in her thoughts.

"Why do you think Edmund reacted to the ant like that? He seemed to be truly frightened of it."

Clara thought for a moment, then sent a cloud back to Bartholomew.

"I honestly don't know. There's something

happening here that I don't understand yet – it feels like a transformation of some kind. I can't pull any thoughts from him though. When he was showing me around the Fortress he asked me how to speak with his inner voice. You can imagine my surprise. I was as gentle as I could be with him, and truthfully I have no idea if he has an inner voice or not. This new fear that ants hold for him is quite mystifying, but I know in time its meaning will become clear. Events are unfolding and we can only watch and wait."

"I think he will be all right. I don't have a bad sense about it."

"Neither do I. Lately I have been having the feeling there is much more to Edmund than we are aware of – and much more to him than he is aware of."

"Who's hungry besides me?" Oliver held up a very substantial picnic basket he had prepared for their voyage to Pterosaur Valley. He pulled out an oversized panel at the stern of the ship which unfolded to a table for four. "Oh dear, I hadn't thought about this wind. I'm not certain we can set a proper table while racing along at forty miles per hour."

Bartholomew approached the table. "I believe I may have a ready solution to your problem." With a flick of his paw the entire ship was surrounded by an impenetrable protective sphere, the wind instantly vanishing.

"I always seem to forget your wonderful shaping abilities. This is perfect. I knew there was a reason we brought you along." Oliver's grin abruptly changed to a look of concern. "Do you think your protective shield will be strong enough to protect us from those frightful pterosaurs?"

Bartholomew glanced over at Clara. She raised her eyebrows questioningly. He had never told Oliver about Bruno Rabbit or the Eleventh Ring which Bruno had given him.

"Oliver, I have not told you any of this, but when I took Oberon's ferillium crystal to the Isle of Mandora, the Great Tree was there waiting for me."

"Good heavens, you met the Great Tree? You talked to him?"

"I did. He is not really a tree, however. His real name is Bruno Rabbit. He has since moved to the City of Mandora to be with the Elders, but before he left he gave me this ring." Bartholomew held out his paw for Oliver to see."

"That's just your ruby Shapers Guild ring. I see nothing new."

"Oliver, look very, very carefully. Focus on the ring, seeing not only with your eyes, but also with your mind."

Oliver frowned slightly, staring intently at Bartholomew's paw. "It looks just as I– hold on, the ruby is gone! It just vanished into thin air. I see the Guild's symbol of the single eye, but there is no stone on the ring."

"It is called the Eleventh Ring and you must never mention it to anyone, not even Morthram. The same goes for you, Edmund. There are not ten Shapers Guild Rings, there are eleven. Like the Emerald Ring, there is only one Eleventh Ring in each world, and it is worn by the most powerful shaper in that world. Bruno Rabbit told me one day I would hold that distinction, though the chances of that happening seem remote to me. The ring grants certain powers to the wearer, most of which

I have yet to discover. The point is, Bruno told me as long as I wear this ring the pterosaurs will not bother us." He waited for Oliver's reply.

"That's excellent news indeed, Bartholomew, and quite a feather in your cap. It's also a great relief to me. I honestly don't believe I could have faced those ferocious pterosaurs again, not after our last experience with them. Now, shall we be seated for lunch? As a special surprise I have a lovely box containing one dozen of the most delicious éclairs you will ever taste, straight from Madame Beffy's Pastry Shop in Grymmsteir. Take your seats, everyone."

Bartholomew looked across the table to Clara. She shrugged and smiled. "I can't wait to try one of those éclairs, Oliver."

After lunch the four adventurers once again became entranced by the breathtaking scenery below. From time to time they sailed over small villages, watching as the inhabitants gaped at the extraordinary craft flying overhead. Some waved and shouted, beckoning for the ship to land, others ran terrified to the safety of their homes. The first time they passed over one of these villages Edmund looked down and murmured, "They look like ants."

Finally, as the sun began to set, Oliver announced, "It's time to put her down and set up camp for the night." He pointed to a lovely open pasture directly beneath them.

"All right, trusty copilot, reduce speed to zero and bring us down."

Edmund pulled the green levers back and the *Adventurer II* gently descended to the pasture below.

Chapter 9

Voices Within

Bartholomew shaped their campsite in the center of the beautiful grassy meadow. Edmund, however, became very concerned that ants might invade his tent during the night, so Oliver agreed to move their tent back into the ship. Bartholomew and Clara's tent was on the crest of a long sloping hill, giving a marvelous view of the distant countryside. Bartholomew shaped a blazing campfire, and Oliver and Edmund soon joined them. Oliver had successfully convinced Edmund that ants sleep during the evening and they would not be making an appearance. They were treated to a spectacular sunset, and there was much speculation about the nature and location of Bruno Rabbit's mysterious house. As the fire died down they bid each other good night and retired to their tents. It had been a long day and they were ready for sleep.

Bartholomew was woken abruptly during the night by the sound of heavy footsteps approaching his tent. He instinctively flicked his wrist and a defensive sphere silently shot up around him and Clara. The footsteps moved past the tent, then stopped. He peered outside into the darkness. There was a partial moon in the sky, its light reflecting off a glimmering figure about thirty feet away. There was no doubt it was Edmund. Bartholomew watched curiously as Edmund sat down on the soft grass and gazed up at the moon. Then Edmund lowered his head, resting his hands on his knees.

"What in the world is he doing?" Bartholomew peered though the tent at Edmund for several more minutes. Finally he drew the tent flaps closed. He lay back down, speaking silently with his secret voice. "Cavern, do you know what Edmund is doing?"

"He is doing the same thing you once did in the Cavern of Silence."

"He's trying to talk to his inner voice? Clara did confide in me that he had asked her how to do that."

"I am aware of everything Clara says and thinks. A rabbit may have only one inner self, but I may have more than one outer self. Clara is one of my outer selves, just as you are. That is why the connection between you is so strong."

"Sorry, sometimes I forget. Do you know if Edmund does have an inner voice?"

"I cannot speak of this now. Many events must unfold in their proper order before you will understand the truth that lies beneath his actions."

"Is this transformation Edmund is going through a good or bad one?"

"That is a question to be asked by a young bunny, not by you, Bartholomew. You are certainly aware by now there are no bad events. There are only events where the goodness within goes unrecognized by the creature experiencing it. Many painful experiences result in a near miraculous deepening of our self-awareness and our understanding of the world's true nature. Think how profoundly you were changed by your ordeal in the Swamp of Lost Things. This was a trying time for you, but it led to the discovery of your Great Gem and your awareness of a deeper self within you."

Bartholomew held out his paw and a glowing translucent white gem appeared in it, filling the tent with its invisible light, and filling him with a great warmth and comfort. "You're right of course. I just worry about Edmund. He is a dear friend of mine and I do not wish to see him so troubled."

"This is as it should be. Clara has the same thoughts. I will tell you this much. If you do as you have done in the past, and act upon the voice within you, there will come a day when you will see Edmund happier than you have ever seen him."

"Thank you, Cavern. That's really all I needed to hear."

Bartholomew lay his head down on the pillow. Half an hour later he was woken again by Edmund's footsteps as he strolled back to the ship.

Bartholomew and Clara rose the next morning to warm sunlight shining through the walls of their tent. After packing their gear they returned to the *Adventurer II*, the aroma of breakfast greeting them well before they reached the ship.

"Ah, there they are. Are the two sleepyheads ready for breakfast?"

"Sorry, Oliver, I didn't sleep very well last night. I woke up several times and couldn't seem to get back to sleep."

Edmund rose from his seat at the console. "I hope I didn't wake you. I walked to the center of the pasture and spent an hour attempting to communicate with my inner voice. The moon was quite lovely."

Clara studied Edmund's face for any clues which might indicate his success or failure. "That's marvelous Edmund. I wish you the very best of luck, but do remember it can take years before you find your secret voice within."

"Yes, that is certainly true for many rabbits and muroidians."

Clara blinked. "What do you mean? Are you saying you spoke with your inner voice?"

"I'm afraid I am unable to discuss that now."

"Why can't you discuss it?"

"I'm afraid I am cannot tell you why I can't discuss it."

Clara put her hand on Edmund's arm. "Then I will not ask you again. Just know that everyone here cares deeply about you and wishes only the best for you, Edmund."

"Thank you, Clara. I will continue my preparations for the day's journey to Pterosaur Valley."

Clara looked over to Bartholomew and a small blue cloud floated out of her ear. Bartholomew drew the cloud to him and heard Clara's voice. "What in the world is going on with Edmund?"

Several hours later breakfast was cleaned up, the ship packed, and they were ready to go. Oliver and Edmund sat at the console, Bartholomew and Clara sat comfortably in the stern of the ship.

"Activating Mark VII Vacuumators."

"Rotating nozzles to 90 degrees."

"Let's take her up to one thousand feet, Edmund, then south southeast at forty miles per hour."

"According to my calculations we should arrive at Pterosaur Valley in approximately four hours."

With a low roar the *Adventurer II* once again took to the skies.

Chapter 10

Pterosaur Valley

"There it is! Pterosaur Valley, straight ahead!" Bartholomew stood at the bow of the *Adventurer II* pointing towards the long narrow valley that sliced through the Landorian mountain range. Before Bruno Rabbit made the City of Mandora his new home he had bequeathed both the Eleventh Ring and his mysterious house in Pterosaur Valley to Bartholomew. Finding this house was the purpose of their trip, although it was also a very good excuse for taking the *Adventurer II* on its maiden voyage.

The ship sailed on towards the valley while Oliver kept a wary eye out for pterosaurs.

"Bruno said I might have a little trouble finding his house, so look for anything that even vaguely resembles a dwelling. Knowing Bruno, we will have more than a little trouble finding it. With his shaping skills there's no telling how he may have camouflaged it."

Oliver looked at his map and said, "It seems logical it would be located near the cave where the pterosaurs live, as their main purpose was keeping away unwanted visitors."

"There's no arguing with your logic, Oliver. Head the ship over that way and we'll take a look."

Soon the ship was directly above the area where Bartholomew and Oliver had first encountered the pterosaurs. Oliver brought the ship to a standstill, hovering five hundred feet above the entrance to the pterosaur cave. For half an hour they studied the side of the mountain, but spotted nothing out of the ordinary. Oliver's anxiety over the pterosaurs was beginning to fade, as they had not made their expected appearance. "I don't see anything that looks like a house. Not a door or window in sight."

"Let me try something." Bartholomew held his paw out and a wide blue beam shot out towards the mountainside. He scanned the beam back and forth across the rugged terrain, then shook his head, the beam flicking off. "There's nothing obvious – no invisibility shaping or secret doorways."

Clara had been silent during the search, but now spoke. "I think we should land the ship and go inside the cave where the pterosaurs live. I believe the entrance will be found there."

Oliver frowned. "Do you think that's advisable? What about the pterosaurs?"

Bartholomew nodded. "Remember, Bruno said they would not bother us as long as I wear the Eleventh Ring."

Oliver looked dubiously at Bartholomew. "It's certainly reassuring to know they won't eat Bartholomew the Adventurer and his marvelous Eleventh Ring, but what about the plump, juicy scientist who happens to be standing next to you?"

Clara burst out laughing, quickly covering her mouth with her paw.

Edmund said, "I have a solution. I am quite indestructible, so I will accompany Bartholomew and gauge the pterosaurs' reaction to my presence."

"Good idea, Edmund. Oliver, also, don't forget the last time we were in the cave I was not the shaper I am now. I can easily create an impenetrable defensive sphere that will protect us from them."

"Ah, that is all I needed to hear. Very well, I will join your excursion. Let's take the ship down, Edmund. It's time to meet a couple of ferocious prehistoric monsters with a yearning for rabbits."

Edmund grinned, and the ship began to descend. With a barely noticeable thump they touched down on the valley floor. Oliver switched off the vacuumators, the only sound now was a brisk northerly wind whistling through the valley.

"Let's head up through the trees, then climb the slope to the cave entrance."

A half hour later they stood eyeing a thirty foot wide circular opening in the side of the mountain. When they peered in, all that was visible was darkness and shadows.

Bartholomew turned to Clara and said with a wink, "Say, Oliver, why don't you lead the way and keep an eye out for those ferocious pterosaurs?"

"I shall be quite happy to let you have that dubious honor. I'm afraid I am highly allergic to pterosaur claws and teeth."

"Very well, then, if you insist." Bartholomew stepped into the shadowy tunnel, the other adventurers following close behind. He flicked his paw and a bright orb of light floated up to the ceiling. The orb followed them as they moved deeper into the cave. "Here's the bend in the tunnel, Oliver. Remember this?"

"I do indeed. Thank you so very much for reminding me."

"Shhhh. Listen!" They stood motionless, ears standing straight up. There was a snuffling noise coming from around the curve in the tunnel.

Bartholomew held up his paw for them to stop, then padded silently ahead. Peering around the bend he was met by both a familiar and terrifying sight. A gigantic pterosaur lay sleeping on the tunnel floor, its long beak tucked under one leathery wing. It made a slight snorting noise and rustled its wings. Oliver poked his head around the corner, his eyes growing wide at the sight of the pterosaur.

Bartholomew crept closer to the beast, which proceeded to do four things. It opened one eye and looked at Bartholomew, gave a great yawn which revealed a row of vicious looking teeth, closed its eye again, and went back to sleep.

Oliver whispered excitedly, "Great heavens, it didn't try to eat you!"

"The Eleventh Ring worked just as Bruno said it would."

Clara stepped closer to the pterosaur. "It's rather cute in a terrifying, prehistoric sort of way." She moved next to the sleeping beast, gently scratching the top of its head. An odd chirping noise came out of the pterosaur's prodigious beak.

Bartholomew grinned. "I think it likes you."

"Are you jealous?"

"Well, you never scratch *my* head like that."

Oliver interrupted their conversation with a mildly disapproving frown. “Perhaps we should begin our search for the entrance to Bruno’s house?”

“Excellent idea, Oliver. Let’s head to the rear of the cave.”

They continued on through the tunnel, passing the second sleeping pterosaur, which took no notice of them. The tunnel grew wider the farther back it went. At the end of the tunnel they found themselves facing a fifty foot wide wall of solid granite. Bartholomew moved the glowing orb of light back and forth across the rocky barrier, but it revealed nothing of interest. It appeared to be no more or less than a wall of solid granite.

“I don’t see anything.” A blue beam of light shot out from Bartholomew’s paw, scanning the wall for any sign of invisibility shaping. “Nothing.”

“What should we do?”

“I’m not sure, Oliver. Clara, what do you think? Are we missing something?”

Clara closed her eyes and held her paws out in front of her. “She walked slowly forward, veering to the right, sensing the subtle directions being sent to her by the universe. She continued on until her paws touched the wall. She opened her eyes. “Here. Send the orb over here.”

The orb zipped over to Clara, hovering several feet above her head.

“Look here. I think you’ll recognize this symbol.”

Bartholomew moved next to Clara and examined the wall. There was a tiny symbol cut into the granite, right where Clara’s paw had touched the wall. It was an indentation in the shape of a single eye.

"You found it!" Bartholomew pressed the eye symbol with his paw. Nothing happened. "How does it work?"

Clara though for a moment. "Try touching your Eleventh Ring to the eye."

Bartholomew touched the symbol of the eye with his ring. The embossed eye on his ring fit precisely into the eye on the wall. With a small blink of light, a wide expanse of the granite wall began rippling.

"What is it doing? Is it a doorway?"

Clara cautiously touched the shimmering wall with her paw. Her arm moved easily into the rippling granite. "We can walk through it."

Oliver's response was immediate. "Do you really think that's a good idea? We have no idea where it goes or what will happen to us if we step into it. It could be some kind of deadly trap."

Bartholomew turned to Oliver and grinned. "If we knew what was going to happen, it wouldn't be an adventure. Wait here." He disappeared into the rippling granite. A minute later he reappeared, stepping out from the wall. He waved his arm. "This way everyone. Welcome to Bruno Rabbit's house of mystery!"

Chapter 11

Bruno's House

One by one the adventurers stepped through the granite wall, emerging moments later on the other side. The view was stunning. A vast cavern had been hollowed out, forming a chamber approximately two hundred feet long and fifty feet tall. The outer wall was completely transparent, giving a breathtaking panoramic view of Pterosaur Valley and the Landorian mountain range.

Bartholomew gazed at the invisible wall of granite. "The cavern should have been visible through that window as we hovered overhead, but we didn't see it." He walked over to the wall, running his paw across the rough invisible surface. "It's definitely solid granite. It appears Bruno made the side of the mountain transparent when viewed from the inside, but opaque when seen from the outside. I have no idea how he accomplished such a feat."

They roamed through Bruno's house, discovering a large number of side rooms connecting to the main cavern, including an elaborately furnished kitchen, a game room with a large billiards table, four bedrooms, and an extensive shaping library surpassing that of the Penrith Shapers Guild. The furnishings in the house were exquisite, more than likely all shaped by Bruno.

Oliver emerged from the kitchen with a slice of apple pie on a sparkling crystal dish. "I found this pie sitting inside an odd looking contraption in the kitchen. Bruno has been absent for over a year, yet the food stored within the device is still perfectly crisp and fresh. I will have to examine it more closely – after I finish this pie, of course."

Bartholomew heard Clara calling to him from another room. "Bartholomew! In here, there's something you should see." He followed her voice to a small alcove at the far end of the cavern.

"Look at this." Sitting in the center of the alcove was a rectangular block composed of a black glossy substance that appeared to be obsidian. The block was approximately eleven feet long, three feet wide and three feet tall. Across the top of the block were twelve key-shaped depressions, eleven of them containing gold keys. The seventh indentation was missing its key. Bartholomew kneeled down and examined the keys, being careful not to touch anything.

"Look here. Each of these gold keys has an embossed single eye on it, and clearly the keys are not all identical. Each one must fit a different lock."

"What are they for? Do they have something to do with the Shapers Guild?"

"I have no idea. I haven't noticed any locks around here, and there's nothing like this at the Penrith Guild."

Clara reached for one of the keys. "I can't move it – it's stuck to the block somehow, more than likely

Bruno's handiwork."

"Edmund! Could you help us for a minute?"

Moments later Edmund appeared in the doorway. He eyed the keys curiously. "What are these for?"

"We're not sure. Can you pick one up?"

Edmund attempted to pluck one of the keys from the obsidian block, but when he lifted his arm the block rose up also.

"How odd." Edmund set the block of keys back down again.

Bartholomew shrugged. "Bruno does love a good puzzle. Perhaps we can only take a key when we truly need one." He turned to leave the room, then stopped. Clara watched as he walked back to the block, reached over and picked up one of the keys.

"It's the Eleventh Ring. Only the wearer can pick up the keys. Bruno did not want these keys stolen, but he did want me to have access to them."

Edmund murmured, "These keys remind me of something. Perhaps if I review some of my–" He froze, his eyes glowing with a pulsing red light.

"What's happened to him? He's not moving."

"I don't know. I've never seen his eyes do that before." Clara placed her paw on Edmund's arm. "I still can't read his thoughts."

Edmund's body twitched slightly and he began moving again. "What was I saying?"

"Edmund, are you all right?"

"Yes, I am functioning perfectly, thank you, but I have forgotten what we were discussing."

"The keys. You were saying they seemed familiar."

"Yes, of course, the keys. Those are World Door keys and open the twelve doors in the Hallway. No key is necessary to reach the Isle of Mandora, but the other twelve doors require a key. As you can plainly see, the Seventh Key is missing. I suppose we should look for it."

Clara was intrigued by Edmund's curious revelation. "Edmund, how did you know these were World Door keys?"

"I am uncertain how or when I gained that particular piece of knowledge. I suppose I read about them in the Central Information Repository and the image of the keys triggered a neuronic connection in my synaptic network. Well, I am off to help Oliver in the kitchen now. He requires my assistance in unraveling the technology behind Bruno's mystifying pie box."

Bartholomew's eyes were fixed on the World Door keys. Everything Bruno Rabbit did, he did with purpose, and he most certainly had left the keys here for a reason. Bartholomew felt himself being drawn towards the missing key, sensing the universe wanted him to find it. Something was afoot, and it had to do with Edmund's aberrant behavior and now with the missing Seventh Key. Edmund had said it himself. "*I suppose we should look for it.*"

When Edmund reached the kitchen he found Oliver studying a glass case containing an assortment of food, still fresh after sitting in the case for over a year.

"Ah, there's my old friend Edmund. Take a look and tell me what you see. I have no idea how Bruno could preserve food in such a manner as this. I see no mechanical contrivances or a power supply for the box, and yet there is some force at work which prevents the food from spoiling."

Edmund stepped over to the case. His right eye

glowed brightly, a holoscreen blinking up in front of him. He flicked through a series of pages until a group of pulsating red and blue concentric circles appeared, which he aimed at the glass case. He watched patiently as the circles changed size and color, then turned to Oliver.

"You are quite correct in saying there is no external source of power to the case. The box itself is not the source of the phenomenon. There is something affecting the contents of the box, but it exists outside this physical world, outside of the space and time you are familiar with. Are you currently carrying a watch?"

"I am, and a very accurate one at that. In fact, this pocket watch was presented to me over ten years ago by the president of the–"

"Any watch will do. Please place it inside the glass case."

Oliver removed the heavy gold watch from his vest pocket, carefully detaching it from its long gold chain. He set the watch down on a shelf inside the glass case.

"There. What are we looking for?"

"Pay close attention to your watch."

Oliver leaned over, gazing at his pocket watch. His eyebrows raised slightly. "That's odd. The second hand has stopped moving." He picked it up and gently shook it. "Ahh, now it's working again." He placed the watch back on the glass shelf. Once again the second hand stopped moving.

"The watch stops when I place it in the box. Is there some kind of magnetic field interfering with the watch's movement?"

"There is not. I believe time has slowed down within the glass case. I know you are familiar with the Isle of

Mandora, where there is no time. This is quite different. Time still exists within the box, but it is passing at a far slower rate than it does outside the box. If you watch and wait you will see your watch is still functioning properly."

Oliver eyed the watch for over a minute, but saw nothing.

"Nothing's happening. I don't think the watch is working."

"Wait."

Oliver gazed at the watch for another three minutes, shifting his weight from one foot to the other, a frown forming on his face. "I don't think you are correct in your assessment of–"

With an audible tick the second hand on Oliver's watch moved forward one notch.

"Good heavens, you were right, Edmund! This is quite astonishing. Bruno has managed to slow time to a crawl within this confined space. The food will eventually spoil, but at this rate it will take years. Do you have any idea how he did this?"

"I do not. The elders are quite capable of altering the passage of time, but not in such a manner as this. I can only assume Bruno used shaping to produce this phenomenon. If you remember, Bartholomew utilized a similar skill to defeat Zoran."

"You're right, I had forgotten about that." Oliver put the watch back in his vest pocket. "Perhaps it's best that knowledge such as this remains a mystery. I'm afraid to think what some rabbits might do with the ability to alter time."

Chapter 12

Edmund's Creation

Oliver, Edmund, Bartholomew and Clara were sitting comfortably in the *Adventurer II* as it hovered high above Pterosaur Valley. Oliver was passing a large wooden bowl of salad across the table to Clara. "Oh, drat, I forgot to bring the tin of molasses cookies I baked in Bruno Rabbit's marvelous kitchen. Or more correctly, I should have said *your* marvelous kitchen, Bartholomew, since the house now belongs to you. Did Edmund tell you about the astonishing glass case that preserves food by slowing the passage of time?"

"He did indeed. Even in his absence Bruno Rabbit still continues to amaze me. I would like to see him again one day, but with time passing so quickly in Mandora that doesn't seem very likely." He smiled at Oliver. "You forgot the cookies? You also once again forgot about my shaping abilities." With a blink of yellow light a colorful rectangular tin appeared in front of Oliver.

"Oh dear, it's still quite startling to see objects appear out of thin air." He quickly opened the tin, however, revealing several dozen freshly baked molasses cookies. He inhaled deeply and said, "Ahhh.... I might forget your shaping abilities, but the smell of freshly baked molasses cookies is something I will never forget."

After everyone had finished lunch, Clara said her good-byes. "Finding Bruno's house was a marvelous adventure, but it's time for me to blink. My four new initiates are quite anxious to begin their first quest as members of the Penrith Shapers Guild. Bartholomew, enjoy your visit with the Tree of Eyes and give it my best regards – I have such fond memories of the Tree from when I was a bunny."

Clara leaned forward and put her arms around Bartholomew. A blue thought cloud floated out of her ear and was drawn into him. Bartholomew heard Clara's voice in his mind. "I am quite certain something will happen soon after I leave – something which will prevent you from returning home for several months at least. Our voice within has told me this. There will be unimaginable obstacles, but the result will be a great and wonderful change. I know you will remain safe if you listen to your secret voice and do what you know to be right. My thoughts will be with you, as always."

A thought cloud emerged from Bartholomew's ear and Clara quickly drew it to her. "I have sensed this also. Whatever is happening to Edmund will take a sharp turn. I wish you were going with us, but apparently the universe has other plans for you. I love you always."

Clara gave Oliver a hug, then put her arms around Edmund. "Have a safe trip, my dear Edmund."

Edmund put his long silver arms around Clara.

"Thank you, Clara. I am quite indestructible, so there really is no need to worry about my safety. I'm certain our visit with the Tree of Eyes will be most enjoyable. Oliver has told me much about the Tree, including the story of how it was created by Bruno Rabbit."

Clara smiled gently. "I know you're indestructible, Edmund. It's just my way of saying I care for you." She turned and waved to Bartholomew, then vanished in a flash of light.

Oliver stood up, gazing southward. "Shall we head the ship towards the Tree of Eyes? It shouldn't take long to get there – several hours at the most."

"That sounds like a fine plan to me, Oliver."

Oliver called out to Edmund, "Let's take her up to a thousand feet. South southeast at thirty miles per hour."

Edmund nodded, taking his seat at the console. "Bartholomew, I am now at liberty to tell you why I was unable to answer Clara's question."

"What question was that, Edmund?"

"When she asked me if I had talked to my inner voice that night in the meadow, I told her I could not discuss it."

"Oh." A sudden chill ran through Bartholomew.

"That night I did speak with what I believe to be my inner voice. It sounded familiar, but I was unable to clearly identify the speaker. It told me I must find the missing Seventh Key, and made me promise not to discuss it with anyone until we were on our way to the Tree of Eyes."

"How could it have known about the Seventh Key before we did, or know we would be visiting the Tree of Eyes?"

"I do not know. Perhaps my voice within has access

to information existing outside of space and time, as does your inner voice."

"Mmm... perhaps. Did it tell you where to find the missing key?"

"I believe at one point it did, but I have forgotten what it told me to do or where I am supposed to go. There was a complex task I was supposed to perform, but again I have no recollection of what the task was, which is unusual for me. I feel as though lately I have not been my normal–" Edmund abruptly stood up, his eyes filled with unspeakable fear. He pointed to the back of the ship, his long silver finger shaking. "GET THEM OFF! GET THEM OFF THE SHIP! OLIVER! GET THEM OFF!"

Bartholomew could see nothing at the stern of the ship. "Edmund, what is it? What do you see?"

Edmund's voice was low and raspy. "I see ants. There are ants on the ship."

Oliver stepped quickly to the stern of the ship, spotting four small ants walking along the railing. One by one he let them walk on his paw and tossed them over the side. "They're gone Edmund. They can't hurt you. Ants are far too small to hurt you."

Edmund's face was still twisted with fear. "They're so strong... they can lift one hundred times their weight. Their mandibles can..." Edmund closed his eyes, unable to continue.

Bartholomew looked at Edmund with grave concern. "It's all right Edmund. The ants are gone, and I will make certain no more board the ship. I will use a defensive shaping skill to prevent them from climbing into the ship." Bartholomew was confounded – where was Edmund's irrational fear of ants coming from, and what did it mean?

Moments later Edmund was acting as though nothing had happened. “Thank you. I shall be perfectly fine as long as I don’t see any more... any more... of those small insects we were just discussing.” He stepped back to the console and sat down. “South southeast at one thousand feet. Velocity set to thirty miles per hour.”

Bartholomew watched as Edmund deftly manipulated the green levers, sending the ship towards the Tree of Eyes. Bartholomew sank down into one of the padded cabin chairs, calling upon his secret voice within. “Cavern, Edmund’s condition is increasing in severity. Can you tell me anything more? Why does he need to find the Seventh Key?”

“Bartholomew, all transformations are chaotic events, but within this chaos a deeper order may be found, just as you found order within your bouncing marbles. You realized that each careening marble was obeying precisely the laws of physical motion, and you were witnessing perfection, not chaos. The same principal applies to the events of your life. You see wild chaotic events, but hidden beneath them lies order. Just as there is perfection in the wildly bouncing marbles, there is perfection in each and every moment of your life.”

“Hmm.,. that sounds as though it should be reassuring, but I still don’t like not knowing what is going to happen.”

“Didn’t you once say, ‘If we knew what was going to happen it wouldn’t be an adventure’?”

“If I may have everyone’s attention for a moment, I remember now what I am supposed to do.” Edmund pushed away from the console and rose to his feet, turning towards Bartholomew.

The chill in Bartholomew's body was now intense. "What do you mean, Edmund?"

"I remember now what my voice within told me to do. I have no choice but to obey it, for as you said, our inner voice speaks absolute truth."

Edmund extended his long silver arms, cupping his hands together to form a bowl. He stood motionless, his red eyes flickering brightly. Bartholomew watched as a diaphanous wavering sphere the size of an orange formed above Edmund's cupped hands. The sphere began to grow more substantial, changing to a translucent blue green color, pale clouds swirling about inside it.

Bartholomew's insides turned to ice. This was most certainly what Clara had warned him about. "Edmund, you need to stop and tell us what you're doing."

The sphere grew larger, tiny blue sparks shooting out from its periphery. It rose up from Edmund's hands and was now hovering above the ship.

"Edmund, what is that? What did you make?"

"I am not precisely certain how I am doing it, but I believe I am creating something called a spectral doorway."

"A spectral doorway? What is that? Where does it go?"

"I'm afraid I don't know."

"Edmund, you have to stop this right now!"

"That's quite impossible. I have no idea how to undo what I have done."

Bartholomew and Oliver rushed to the stern of the craft. Edmund's creation was expanding with increasing speed and was now enveloping the *Adventurer II.* Ghostly gray clouds within the sphere swirled wildly while miniature bolts of lightning created scenes of ethereal dancing light and shadow. In one fractional instant the sphere exploded with a monstrous blast, the concussion rattling the ship and leaving only a world of madly churning clouds and brilliant thunderous flashes of light. The wind howled and shrieked like an unchained demon, tossing the *Adventurer II* violently about, threatening to flip her over at any instant.

"What have you done??" Bartholomew's cry went unheard, drowned out by Edmund's terrifying creation.

Chapter 13

Song

As the *Adventurer II* twisted and bucked in the ferocious screaming winds of Edmund's nightmarish vortex, several events occurred in rapid succession. The duplonium powered Mark VII Vacuumators all ceased functioning simultaneously, rendering the ship powerless. What was once a miracle of engineering became a thirty foot long projectile. A monstrous fist of wind caught the ship and flipped it over, throwing Edmund out into the clouds. Oliver and Bartholomew were hurled beneath a deck table. And lastly, the *Adventurer II* began plummeting towards the ground, soon reaching a velocity of precisely one hundred and twenty miles per hour.

Edmund cupped his hands to his mouth and called out,"Oliver, no need to fret! We'll be able to repair the *Adventurer II* with a little help from the A9 engineering Rabbitons!"

Bartholomew and Oliver popped up from beneath the table top. The ship had flipped upright again, and they spotted Edmund about thirty feet away from the craft, the speed of his descent matching theirs.

Edmund hollered, "Don't worry about me, I'll be fine. I'm completely indestructible!"

"Okay, Edmund!" Bartholomew gave Edmund a halfhearted thumbs up. "Oliver, take my paw and I'll blink us down to the ground. You've done it before – it will be just like when Morthram blinked us out of Oberon's ferillium mine."

Oliver nodded blankly, unable to speak. Bartholomew grabbed his paw and with a flash of light they both vanished.

Edmund, who was impervious to shaping, placed his hands across the top of his head. He was taking no chances when it came to his cherished adventurer's hat.

"I've never fallen this far before. It's rather enjoyable. Quite relaxing."

Three minutes passed and Edmund was still falling.

"Odd, at this velocity I should have reached the ground by now. We were at an altitude of one thousand feet when I opened the doorway, so it's only logical to assume we arrived in this new world at a far greater altitude than that. Odd. It's also rather perplexing why all the duplonium engines should simultaneously cease functioning. Quite an intriguing puzzle." Edmund glanced over at the *Adventurer II.* "I wonder..." His right eye turned bright blue and a thermo sensor beam shot over to the falling craft, landing directly on the outer shell of a duplonium engine. "Ah, just as I suspected, the engine is cold. That could only mean the duplonium is no longer reacting with the water, which in turn must mean the laws of physics in this world vary slightly from those of our world. Obviously, basic laws such as gravity still apply here, otherwise I wouldn't be–"

Edmund's thought was cut short as he plowed into the ground at precisely one hundred and twenty miles per hour.

* * *

Bartholomew and Oliver were sitting on top of an enormous sand dune. The roiling clouds of Edmund's doorway had dissipated, replaced with a clear blue sky and a baking hot desert sun. Oliver was holding out one of his shoes and shaking it. "Drat, all this sand is a dreadful nuisance. If there's one thing I have no time for, it's sand in my shoes."

Bartholomew shook his head. There were times when Oliver's thought processes boggled his mind. "Oliver, we're not on Earth anymore. We're in a different world now. I have no idea why Edmund brought us here, and I have no idea how we're going to get back home, or even *if* we're going to get back home. Perhaps we should think about that rather than worrying about sand in our shoes."

"An excellent sentiment, Bartholomew, but I am quite adamant about this. I will not tolerate sand in my shoes in this world or any other."

There was a tremendous "WHOOOMP!" and a massive cloud of sand and dust exploded forty feet away from them. A split second later there was a "FABOOOOMFF!" and another colossal cloud of sand billowed out past the first one.

"Great heavens, what was that??"

"I believe those two sounds have heralded the arrival of our friend Edmund and the *Adventurer II.*"

Bartholomew rose to his feet and slogged through the sand to the location of the first sand cloud, spotting a crater twelve feet long and four feet wide. With some apprehension he peered into it – apprehension which vanished the moment he saw Edmund sitting at the bottom adjusting his adventurer's hat.

"Ah, Bartholomew, there you are. I believe I know why the *Adventurer II* failed in such a spectacular fashion. Duplonium does not react with water in this world. I think we can therefore assume the laws of physics here differ slightly from those of our world."

"Are you all right? That was... a rather nasty fall you just had."

"I am quite fine, I assure you. As I have told you and Clara many times before, I am completely indestructible." Edmund rose to his feet and leaped out of the crater with a single bound, taking a quick survey of his surroundings. "It appears we have landed in a desert. Interesting. I've never seen a desert before. Do you think there will be ants here?"

"Edmund, what did you do? Why did you bring us here?"

"I merely followed the instructions given to me by my inner voice, which opened a doorway to this world. Beyond that I know as much as you do. How is Oliver?"

"He's upset because he has sand in his shoes."

"Edmund, you're all right!" Oliver hobbled across the sand, one shoe still in his paw.

"I am fine, thank you for your –" Edmund was interrupted by the screeching sound of twisting metal coming from the neighboring sand dune. Their heads spun around to see the front half of the *Adventurer II* protruding into the air, being shaken like a bunny's rattle. Their jaws dropped in unison.

"Great heavens, what is that? Something monstrous has grabbed our ship!"

"Something monstrous and very, very large has grabbed our ship."

Seconds later there was a terrible squealing of rending metal and the *Adventurer II* was yanked violently down into the sand dune, leaving nothing behind but a puffy cloud of dust. When the cloud dissipated the ship was gone. They all stared at the dune in stunned silence. Until they heard the voice behind them.

"You probably shouldn't be here. I would head for the jungle if I were you."

Their heads whipped around once again to see a four foot tall mouse wearing a dark red robe with a floppy hood and sleeves. Bartholomew blinked twice, but managed to say, "Who are you?"

The mouse responded by singing a short but exquisite melody.

The mouse's answer left Bartholomew more confused than before. "What was that?"

"That is my name. I am a Red Monk of Musinora. Our native language is one of tones, not of words. I have seen Rabbitons before. This one will carry me on its shoulders as I guide you out of the desert. Without my assistance you will perish."

"What should we call you? I'm afraid I lack the skill to sing your name properly."

The mouse studied Bartholomew's face. "Hold out your paws." Bartholomew extended both arms. "Turn them over." The mouse gazed at Bartholomew's Guild ring. "Hmmp. You may call me whatever name you are comfortable with."

"How about we call you Song, since that is how we would describe your name in our world?"

"Very well. You may carry me now, Rabbiton." Edmund gently picked up Song and set him on his shoulders. "I am Edmund, and I am pleased to meet you, Song."

"You are a Rabbiton and you have a name and wear a hat."

"Yes, thank you for noticing. This is my adventurer's hat, a cherished gift from my dear friends Bartholomew and Clara."

"You are a Rabbiton who wears a hat and has dear friends. Hmmp. Turn left and walk twenty-four feet, then stop. Walk slowly, do not create excessive vibrations."

"What was that monstrous thing that pulled our ship into the sand?"

"We do not honor them with a name. We name only those things which we hold in esteem."

"Have you ever seen one come out of the sand?"

"Turn right and walk one hundred and ten feet, then stop."

"How do you know where it is safe to walk?"

"This is not the time for talk. Later is the time for talk."

Bartholomew and Oliver silently followed behind Edmund and Song, slowly traversing the blazing hot sand dunes. Finally, Bartholomew broke the silence. "Would anyone care for a cool glass of water?" With a small flash of light three glasses of water appeared in front of him. He gave one glass to Oliver and held one up for Song, who accepted the glass without comment. If he had seen Bartholomew shape the water he made no mention of it. They marched on through the scorching desert towards an unknown destination and an unknown fate.

Chapter 14

The Island of Blue Monks

The desert seemed to go on forever. It took two full days of walking just to escape the dunes occupied by the creatures Song refused to honor with a name. The temperature dropped sharply at night and Bartholomew shaped what supplies they needed to survive the extreme environment. Song watched without expression as Bartholomew fabricated a tent, blankets, food, water and a blazing campfire. Perhaps shaping was a common practice in Song's world.

Edmund spent the chilly nights on guard duty outside the tent. He was not affected by the cold and he didn't require sleep. It was Edmund who discovered the new world had two moons, and the days were nineteen hours long. He didn't mind his time alone, and he especially liked watching the two moons as they floated across the starry night sky.

As the adventurers trekked across the desert the sand dunes gradually decreased in size until eventually the desert floor was hard and flat, with small amounts of scattered vegetation. With the deadly dunes behind them, they were able to make much better time crossing the desert.

"Look ahead, you will see the jungle." It was the morning of their sixth day in the desert, and Song was standing on Edmund's shoulders pointing into the distance. Bartholomew squinted his eyes, barely making out a thin dark line of trees. By the next afternoon they had reached the edge of the jungle.

"It is not far now. Only a half day walk to my village. You may rest there as long as you wish." They spent that night camping on the edge of the jungle, the next morning leaving the burning desert behind them.

Song was perched on Edmund's shoulders, guiding him through the dense overgrowth. Oliver was making it abundantly clear he was not very enthusiastic about the new jungle environment. "What *was* that? It sounded like something screeching. I daresay I have no interest in meeting whatever made that dreadful noise. Song, do you know what it was? I saw some tracks back there which looked rather large, but I couldn't tell if the creature who left them had claws. Are there many predators here? What about pterosaurs? Have you ever seen any pterosaurs flying about this area?"

"No pterosaurs here. Perhaps they were all eaten by far greater terrible creatures with no names."

"Good heavens, is this true? Bartholomew, is he joking?"

Edmund predictably chimed in with, "Are there any ants in the jungle?"

Bartholomew held his breath waiting for Song's answer.

"There are no ants in the jungle."

Edmund looked pleasantly surprised. "I like the jungle."

"That way." Song pointed to a barely visible trail snaking through the lush foliage.

Edmund pushed his way past the dense vines and leaves, emerging in front of an enormous blue green lake. In the center of the lake was a massive rocky island covered with several hundred stone and wooden buildings of all shapes and sizes.

Song hopped down from Edmund's shoulders and walked to the edge of the lake. He began to hum a lovely little tune. Bartholomew had never heard anything like it. It wasn't loud, but it had an eerie intensity to it.

"The boat will arrive shortly."

Sure enough, a few minutes later Edmund spied a long graceful wooden boat heading their way, propelled by four mice pulling long wooden oars. The boat scraped up onto the shore and the four red robed mice nodded mutely to Song.

Song motioned for Bartholomew to enter the craft. Edmund was the last to climb aboard. There was notable concern on the faces of the four mice, but they said nothing.

Using their oars they pushed the boat off from the shore. Though low in the water due to Edmund's massive size and weight, the boat appeared to be in no danger of capsizing. Song pointed to the island and the four mice began rowing in unison. One of them began to sing a bouncy little tune, the other three joining in. Their voices filled Bartholomew with a sense of profound joy in a way that no other song ever had. He found himself wishing they would never stop singing. Fifteen minutes later they arrived at a long wooden dock.

"Welcome to the Island of Blue Monks." Song helped them out of the boat, then led the way up a long rocky path and across a series of wooden walkways and through the narrow stone streets. They wound their way past dozens of weathered wooden buildings, many of them quite dilapidated. Song stopped when they reached a square two story wooden structure with a bright blue door. Embedded in the center of the door was a small metallic object which appeared to be made from hammered brass. Bartholomew looked at it closely. It was a single eye, the same symbol found on Bartholomew's Eleventh Ring. He did not ask Song about the eye.

"Welcome to my home, the Nirriimian Singers Guild. You are welcome to stay here as honored guests of the Guild."

Song swung the door open and was met by two smiling mice wearing robes identical to Song's.

"Welcome home, Master. I am pleased to see you have brought company. We will prepare rooms immediately for our three guests." The mice seemed quite cheerful, and could not take their eyes off Edmund.

"That will be fine. You may also prepare a lunch for all but the Rabbiton named Edmund, who wears a hat and has dear friends. He has no need of food or sleep."

After a warm bath and some newly shaped clean clothes, Oliver and Bartholomew felt quite renewed. Oliver appeared to be growing more comfortable with life in this strange new world.

"You know, this building reminds me somewhat of the Ferillium Inn. It's warm and cozy, with a pleasant, comfortable atmosphere. I do hope we can hear those four mice sing again. It was quite lovely. I can't remember when I have enjoyed a tune so much. I hope they don't kidnap us and put us to work in another dreadful ferillium mine, however." He laughed loudly at his own joke.

"Oliver, did you see the symbol on the front door?"

"Indeed I did. Do you suppose this is a Shapers Guild like the one in Penrith?"

"Song said it was the Nirriimian Singers Guild, but I don't know what that means. I would like to know who the Blue Monks are and why this island is named after them. I'd also like to know why the universe brought us here and how we're going to get home again."

Oliver nodded somberly, then brightened. "I will ask Song if there are any pastry shops on the island."

A soft knocking on the door interrupted their conversation. "Please excuse me, but Master Song, as he is called by you, requests your company at the dinner table. He has instructed me to tell you now is the time for talking."

Chapter 15

Welcome to Nirriim

"It's not very often we get a visit from two rabbits and a Rabbiton. May I ask what brought you to Nirriim?"

"Nirriim is the name of your world?"

"Yes. Our Region is called Musinora."

"I'm embarrassed to say our visit here was quite unplanned. Edmund created a spectral doorway without knowing exactly what he was doing and our flying carriage fell into your world."

Edmund interrupted Bartholomew. "What I did not know was why I was doing it. My inner voice told me to create the doorway, but I had no idea where it would take us."

Song tilted his head slightly. "Your inner voice told you?"

"Yes, it told me to create the doorway."

Song took a sip from a small wooden cup. "It was the presence of your spectral doorway which drew me to the desert. We thought it might be the Anarkkians returning. It is how their ships entered our world during the wars. I was quite relieved to see it was you and not them."

"The Anarkkians? The Elders defeated them in the Great War that ended the Age of Darkness."

"They were never defeated – they left our world of their own free will, but we never learned why. The Great War raged in many worlds, including ours. Those were dark times."

Edmund's face was grim. "I'm glad those days are gone. The Elders have changed since then and have no interest in wars, the A6 Warrior Rabbitons are a distant memory."

"Even today stories are still told of the frightful A6 Warrior Rabbitons. You have no idea why your inner voice sent you here?"

"No. But it might have something to do with ants."

Song looked curiously at Edmund. "You said ants?"

"I seem to have acquired a rather severe and irrational fear of them."

"I will give this much thought. For now, let us enjoy our dinner. Bartholomew, you seem to be a gifted shaper. How long have you been practicing your art?"

"Not very long, I'm afraid. Is shaping a common practice in your world?"

"It is not unheard of, and seems to be gaining some popularity. There are more common arts here which yield similar results. Whatever the art may be called, its goal is always the same – the manipulation of energy fields. Just as there is more than one way to throw a stone, there is more than one way to alter an energy field."

"May I ask why this is called the Island of Blue Monks?"

Song smiled. “The simple answer is this is where the Blue Monks live.”

“Who are the Blue Monks?”

“They are the thirteen Master Singers, Monks of the Blue Robe. You may think of them as Shapers whose thoughts are music and whose words are song – a novel concept perhaps, but not so strange once you become accustomed to the idea. The sound of their voices affects energy fields as readily as your mind does.”

“I would love to meet them, if that is possible.”

“It is not, I’m afraid. They are extremely reclusive and only take visitors when significant events decree it, almost always when something is negatively affecting the Infinite Chain.”

Oliver looked up from his dinner. “The Infinite Chain... didn’t Bruno Rabbit make some mention of that, Bartholomew? Is that the chain of events containing every chain of events that can occur?”

Song turned to Bartholomew, his eyes bright and sharp. “You are acquainted with Bruno Rabbit?”

“I am. He moved to the City of Mandora and left me his home in a place called Pterosaur Valley on the planet Earth.”

“Bruno Rabbit left you his house? He must think a great deal of you, Bartholomew. When Bruno Rabbit’s name is mentioned, all related events become significant. This changes everything. We must determine why Edmund’s inner voice told him to open the doorway to Nirriim. I can tell you with all certainty nothing about this was accidental. Edmund seems to be at the center of these events, so it would appear he is the one destined to meet with the Blue Monks.”

Their dinner conversation turned to more mundane

topics, including the location of several pastry shops which Oliver made plans to visit the following day. Song graciously offered one of his students as Oliver's guide. Bartholomew chose to remain at the Singers Guild to learn more about the art of manipulating energy through song. As for Edmund, he would be paying a visit to the thirteen Blue Monks, the reclusive and mysterious Master Singers of Nirriim.

Chapter 16

A Song for Edmund

Edmund gazed out his window, pondering the mice who were passing by on the street below. "There's really no difference between Rabbitons and mice other than the shape of their bodies – and of course Rabbitons don't eat or sleep like mice do. I wonder why mice sleep? I think I would like sleeping. Oliver always seems to look forward to it, and Bartholomew often tells Clara about dreams he had in the night. It sounds as though it would be both interesting and relaxing. Maybe it's similar to the feeling I had when I was falling from the *Adventurer II*."

There was a knock on Edmund's door.

"Please excuse us, Edmund, but it is time to leave."

Edmund rose up from the window seat and opened the door. Song and two red robed students stood in front of him. "Good morning, Edmund."

"Good morning, Song. I am ready to go. I am looking forward to hearing the Blue Monks sing. I have decided to analyze the sound patterns of their voices in an attempt to discover the scientific principles behind their effect on energy fields. I believe such information would greatly interest my good friend Oliver. He is a renowned scientist in our world and is quite curious about such things."

Song smiled gently. "Sometimes you may gain far more by listening to a song with your heart than by analyzing its sound patterns."

"Hmm, I hadn't thought of that. If I listen more deeply to the song, I shall better be able to analyze its effect on my neuronic synapses."

The two red robed students averted their gaze politely. Song simply nodded. "Shall we go then?"

Song and his two students led Edmund through the narrow streets and alleys to the far end of the island, a twenty-one minute walk by Edmund's calculations. "This is quite a lovely island. How long have the Blue Monks lived here?"

"A good question, Edmund. No one really knows, but perhaps thousands of years. There is much we don't know about the Master Singers. I myself have never seen them. I assure you, your visit with them today is an unparalleled honor."

"Ah, here we are." They stopped in front of a fifteen foot tall stone wall of ancient design, clearly built long before the town was created. Two massive wooden doors covered with horizontal black wrought iron bands blocked their entrance to the monastery.

Song turned to Edmund. "Edmund, you must pay close attention to what I say now. Under no circumstances must you attempt to talk to the Blue Monks, and you must avoid all eye contact with them, especially the Thirteenth Monk. He is the oldest and most powerful of all the Blue Monks. Simply stand before them, looking down at the ground in front of you. Say nothing, do nothing. The process could not be simpler. They sing, you listen. Nothing more than that. Nothing. Is this clear? There are stories of mice looking into a Blue Monk's eyes and turning to stone."

"Yes, I understand. I am a Rabbiton and I will follow your instructions to the letter."

"Very well." Song stepped over to the massive doors and grasped the heavy iron knocker with both paws. He banged it slowly three times, then walked away from the door, turning his back to the monastery. The two red robed students also turned away.

With a low groaning noise the two doors swung outward, allowing just enough room for Edmund to enter. He stepped through the doorway and the doors rumbled shut behind him.

A mouse wearing a dark red robe and hood stood before him, motioning for Edmund to follow him. They walked along a well worn stone path through an exquisite garden filled with brilliantly colored flowers. Numerous mice wearing red robes were working in the garden, pulling weeds, trimming spent blossoms, and watering. The garden was enchanting, and Edmund was sorely tempted to stop and admire its endless array of fragrant blossoms. Fortunately, he remembered Song's stern instructions and continued on.

At the end of the pathway stood a large stone building fashioned in the same manner as the outer monastery wall. There was no doubt in Edmund's mind that this was a very, very old monastery. The main building was windowless, the only point of entrance being a single blue door. In the center of the door was embedded a golden eye.

The red robed mouse motioned for Edmund to open the door and enter the monastery. Edmund nodded his thanks, lifting the heavy wrought iron latch and gently pushing the door open. With a glance behind him at the peaceful garden, he ducked down through the doorway and stepped into the monastery.

Before him stood a massive room, by his guess at least one hundred feet wide in both directions and reaching a height of over twenty-five feet. The walls and floor were all made of river stones worn flat by centuries of use. The room was absolutely silent. Edmund had never heard such silence before. The still air had an ancient smell to it, a curious mix of musty age and sweet incense. The building at first appeared to be empty, but when he looked more carefully he caught a glimpse of something moving in the front of the room. Then he noticed the row of thirteen mice wearing bright blue robes. They were all looking directly at him.

Edmund had never felt so anxious before. This wasn't like his fear of the ants, it was something else. He didn't want to make a mistake. He wanted to do everything correctly, just as Song had told him. He looked down at the floor in front of him as Song had instructed him to do. He waited patiently for the Blue Monks to start singing. He listened carefully, but heard nothing. Then he heard a shuffling, padding noise approaching him. "Oh dear, one of them is walking this way. Song will be furious with me. Perhaps I accidentally made eye contact with them." Edmund closed his eyes tightly to make absolutely certain there would be no further eye contact. He did not want to be turned to stone. The shuffling noise stopped in front of him.

"I like your adventurer's hat. That's a lovely purple feather."

Edmund said nothing, trying with all his might to close his eyes even tighter.

"You may look at me, Edmund."

Edmund peeked out between his eyelids, wanting to look but also desperately not wanting to look. A plump old mouse wearing a bright blue robe was looking up at him with an expression of great kindness and deep concern.

Edmund had never cried before, but he felt like crying now. He didn't know why, but he was suddenly filled with a terrible and profound sadness.

"You are a Rabbiton and yet you wear an adventurer's hat. Why do you wear it?"

Edmund's voice was very small. "It makes me feel like an adventurer. I have wanted to be one ever since I met Edmund the Explorer. I named myself after him when Morthram said I should choose a name for myself."

"An excellent answer, Edmund. Your friend Morthram sounds like a very wise rabbit."

"Yes, he is an excellent shaper, just like my dear friends Bartholomew and Clara. Bruno Rabbit gave Bartholomew the Eleventh Ring to wear. Oh dear – I shouldn't have said that. Bartholomew asked me not to mention it to anyone."

"Your secret is safe with me, Edmund. You are truly lucky to have such friends as these. I believe we are ready to sing for you now. You might be more comfortable if you sit on the pillows."

"I didn't see any–" The Blue Monk motioned to a large pile of soft velvet pillows which Edmund was quite certain had not been there before. He lowered himself down onto the pillows.

The Blue Monk turned, then stopped. He looked back at Edmund as though he had noticed something new. He walked back to Edmund.

“Would you mind if I sit with you? I would like to tell you a very short story before we sing.”

“Of course, if that is what you wish. It’s just that... Song told me not to make any eye contact and not to talk at all.”

The Blue Monk smiled in a way that made Edmund want to cover his mouth with his paws and giggle like a bunny. “I won’t tell Song if you won’t.” He sat down next to Edmund. “Edmund, I am the Thirteenth Monk, and I am going to tell you a story that may help you understand the true nature of the song we will sing for you. When you hear the story it may sound familiar to you, as though you have heard it before, perhaps a very long time ago when you were young, or even before then.” Edmund closed his eyes, listening to the calm, soothing voice of the Thirteenth Monk.

“There was once a bunny who lived by the ocean. Every day he would stroll along the sandy beach and pick up thoughts which had washed ashore. He would find them in shells, under rocks, and sometimes even tangled in seaweed. "Oh, this is a good one,” he would say, “we see chaos, but if we look carefully, if we look beneath the chaos, we find order and perfection." And into his bucket the thought would go. When the bunny had reached a ripe old age he gathered all the thoughts together and placed them carefully into a large silver cauldron heated by the fires of life. Using a straw broom, he stirred them thoroughly, and as he was stirring he listened carefully. Much to his surprise he heard the ocean singing a wordless song of incomparable beauty. The bunny closed his eyes and said, "Ah, it was all worth it."

The Blue Monk stood up. "We will sing for you now, Edmund. It is the ocean's wordless song of incomparable beauty. It is the song of the universe, the song of your past, the song of your future, the song of life."

Edmund's eyes were still closed when he heard the first Blue Monk sing.

Chapter 17

Into the Light

It was the single most perfect tone Edmund had ever heard. It was full, it was subtle, beautiful, transparent, round, and much more – an indescribably brilliant sound that seemed to pass through him, to become part of him, stirring long forgotten thoughts and memories. He recalled the first time he had met Oliver in the Central Information Repository. He had been surprised to see a rabbit of such diminutive stature, only half the size of the Elders. It was strange having friends. The more he thought about them and the more he cared about them, the less their physical appearance mattered, until the very sight of them was a joy to behold.

"Wait – why am I thinking these thoughts? This is quite unlike me." It was the singing, it was affecting him somehow. He would analyze the sound waves to determine exactly what they were doing so he could tell Oliver. He tried to flip open his holographic screen but realized his eyes were closed.

A second voice joined the song, melting into the first. "Oh my, that is quite lovely. It reminds me of the four mice singing in our rowboat on the way to The Island of Blue Monks. I like adventures. I wish I could meet the Tree of Eyes. It's fun to see so many new things and meet interesting mice like Song and the Blue Monks. At first I was afraid of the Thirteenth Monk, but he was so kind and seemed to truly care about me. Rabbitons aren't like that. How odd. Oh dear, I'm having those thoughts again."

The third and fourth voices joined in, forming a complex and strikingly intricate melody, the sounds flooding into the spaces between Edmund's thoughts. "How beautiful this music is. I could sit here and listen to it forever. Maybe if I adjust my auditory sensors it will be even clearer. Wait... what was I trying to do? Adjust... something..."

Another memory popped into his head. A memory from the Repository. He had read a book. The distance between electrons and neutrons is the same relative distance as the space between the stars and galaxies and planets. "I am really only empty space filled with a smattering of atoms and molecules, and those atoms and molecules are really only fields of energy. The song pours into me and fills the vast and infinite empty space between my atoms with its harmony. Did I already say that?"

Eight more Blue Monks joined in and Edmund was lost. He had left his atoms and molecules and energy fields behind and was traveling through a warm infinite darkness filled with the ocean's wordless song of incomparable beauty. He was not fearful because he was not there to be afraid. There was no past and no future, and without future there can be no fear. He was the song, he was the music, and there was nothing else.

The Thirteenth Monk joined in the song. Edmund saw a glimmer of light appear in the distance. He was drawn to it. He remembered Bartholomew telling him how he moved about when he was a thought cloud. He simply wished to be somewhere. “I want to go there, towards that sliver of light.” Edmund shot towards it, traveling faster and faster, through the song, through the infinite harmonies of the universe, through the darkness towards the brilliant fissure. He was there already, before he had started. He looked through the rift to a room below. It had a familiar feel about it. He knew he had seen it before, but it was so long ago. He tried to push through the crack, he wanted to see more, he wanted to remember. Edmund tumbled down into the emptiness below. He looked around in surprise, not certain what had just happened, or where he was. He felt a sharp slap on his back and a jolt of electricity shot through him.

“Okay, my little A2 Carrier Rabbiton, time to meet your new boss, Edmund the Explorer.”

Chapter 18

Edmund, meet Edmund

"Here you go, as promised, one A2 Carrier Rabbiton with upgraded internal dynamics and the optional Interworld Positioning System."

"Perfect. What's its max lifting capacity?"

"More than you'll ever need. Almost eight tons if it needs to. If an Anarkkian transport lands on your foot this guy will be able to lift it off."

"Hopefully it won't come to that. I keep hearing rumors about the war ending, but the fighting just seems to go on and on."

"I've heard the same rumors. We're sending out dozens of ships every day packed with thousands of A6 Warriors. You'd think they'd do the job. There's not much out there that can take the damage they dish out."

"The Anarkkians have their own version of the A6. It's brutal out there on some of the worlds. I think I'm going to send Emma to Betador. Right now it's a lot safer than Earth."

"What about Mandora? No way the Anarkkians can get in get there."

"That won't be completed for at least another year. They've barely finished the island and they're still having problems with random time fluxes. Scary."

"Betador it is then. Good luck to you both, Edmund."

"Thanks, and good luck to you too. Okay, A2, let's roll."

Edmund looked down at his new body. It was identical to the one lying back in the monastery. Had he been created as an A2 Carrier Rabbiton? He had no such memories, and yet here he was. He watched Edmund the Explorer, trying to draw forth lost memories, but there was only that vague feeling of having met him, that his face seemed familiar. It was so confusing, but the Blue Monks must have sent him here for a reason.

"Let's go, A2!"

"Yes, sir, Master Edmund."

"Good heavens, who programmed you, an A6 Warrior? Call me Edmund, and don't trail behind me like a bunny, walk alongside me. You'll be going on adventures with me, so we'd better get to be friends."

"I've never been on an adventure before, Edmund. You will teach me the correct protocols? I am programmed as an A2 Carrier, not an adventurer."

"Not to worry, A2, you'll be a seasoned veteran in no time at all. Now, let's head downstairs and we'll take the gravitator car home. You can meet Emma, the love of my life, apple of my eye, and the song in my heart. It's confusing for her to be all those things at once, I assure you. I told her I was bringing home a new

Rabbiton, which means she'll have you washing the windows and pushing a vacuumator around the house before you know it. It's not so bad, she's had me doing it for years. Ha!"

Edmund flipped back and forth between his own thoughts and the thoughts of the A2 Carrier Rabbiton. He knew he was here to observe, to witness the events of his past, but his words somehow came out of the A2's mouth. It was difficult to separate the two personalities.

He decided right off that he liked Edmund the Explorer. None of the books he'd read had mentioned how kind Edmund the Explorer was, or what a friendly laugh he had, or how he sounded when he was talking about Emma.

The gravitator car ride was thrilling, and it was wonderful to see the tunnels filled with throngs of Elders again, but there was a dark sense of urgency about them. Many wore military uniforms and walked with grim focus and determination. There was no doubt there was a war on.

"You're in luck, A2, they issued me a floater, so we don't have to walk home from the station. Hop aboard."

Edmund stepped onto the wide silver disc and grabbed one of the metal guard rails. He knew he was indestructible, but this did not seem as safe as Oliver's *Adventurer II*.

"Hold on tight."

Edmund watched nervously as Edmund the Explorer tapped on a grid of glowing circles.

"Take us home, floater."

With a soft hum the floater lifted easily off the ground. There was no rocking motion, even when racing across the open fields Edmund felt as though he was standing on solid ground. "This is quite enjoyable. I have not seen a floater before. Where do they come from?"

"They build them on sub level 4 in the Fortress. Hey, wait a minute, you're not an Anarkkian spy are you? I'd hate to have to vaporize you right after I paid good credits for you."

"I assure you I am not an Anarkkian spy, although I am not absolutely certain what a spy's function is. Logically, however, if I don't know what a spy does, the odds do not favor my being one."

"Unless you're lying to me."

"I am incapable of lying."

"How do I know that's not a lie?"

"I am unable to verify my programming parameters at this time, but if you contact your Authorized Rabbiton Service Agent they will corroborate my statement."

"Oh, dear. I can see I'm going to have to teach you about something us rabbits call jokes. A joke is a statement so absurd that it could not possibly be true, and the idea of such a ridiculous event occurring makes us laugh."

"I see, you were making one of these jokes about my being an Anarkkian spy. This is something I will remember. When I hear a joke, should I make the laughing noise, or just acknowledge that I am aware it is a joke?"

"We'll get back to that, A2. I can see it's going to take a while to whip you into shape."

"Ha ha ha ha."

"Did you just laugh?"

Yes, I was laughing at your joke. You said you were going to whip me, and I do not believe you are the sort of rabbit who would be capable of such an action, especially knowing I am quite indestructible and would not be affected by it."

"A2, I believe we're going to get along famously. Hold on, here we are. Welcome to your new home, my friend."

When he was introduced to Emma, Edmund was drawn to her immediately. She reminded him of Clara. She looked directly at him when she talked to him, and took the time to listen to what he was saying. There was a gentleness about her, as there was with Clara.

"Now A2, I know my dear husband Edmund has great plans to include you on his adventures, but someone needs to keep this house clean. Did they program you to operate a vacuumator?"

"Ha ha ha ha."

"Oh dear, he's been teaching you about jokes, hasn't he?"

It took several weeks before Edmund became accustomed to his new home. Once he had found a routine and knew what to expect each day he began to relax. He was gradually forgetting the world he lived in now was only a forgotten memory from long ago. It was a pleasant and orderly life, and he liked being around Edmund the Explorer and Emma.

All that changed one day when Edmund the Explorer returned home from an assignment.

"Emma, it's not safe here anymore. It's time for you to go to Betador. There are real signs of a possible Anarkkian invasion. They're opening doorways to this world almost as fast as our shapers can close them. We don't know how much longer until they break through."

"Absolutely not. I am staying here with you. This is where we both belong."

"I won't be here. I have to leave. They're sending me to Nirriim. There's an artifact there that must not fall into the hands of the Anarkkians. I'm taking A2 with me. I have you booked on a ship to Betador. It's a safe world. Once I get back from Nirriim I'll meet you there."

"I don't want to go. I don't want you to go. I want things to stay the way they are now."

Edmund took Emma's paw in his. "I wish with all my heart they could stay the same. The happiest years of my life have been here with you. But you have said it yourself many times, we shouldn't reject what life puts before us. There is a reason for everything, even if we don't understand it now. Emma, no matter what happens, we will find each other again." He touched his forehead to hers and whispered, "We are bound together beyond time and space, two hearts entangled in the cosmic lace."

Emma sighed deeply and put her arms around Edmund, holding him close to her. "You're such a romantic. You win. I'll pack. But when I see you again you'd better not have taught A2 any of those rude jokes you think are so funny."

Two days later Edmund the Explorer got a cloud comm from Emma saying she had arrived safely in Betador.

"Okay A2, Emma is safe and we've got ourselves some adventuring to do. We're going through the World Doors in the Swamp of Lost Things to a place called Nirriim. The Anarkkians are after an artifact there, something called a time throttle, and we have to find it before they do. But first, we have to pay a visit to a very peculiar fellow who goes by the name of Bruno Rabbit.

Chapter 19

The Cave

"Ready to go?"

Edmund nodded, picking up the enormous canvas pack and slinging it over his shoulder. "I believe I have all the items you requested. There is a mini food synthesizer, microwater purifier, three sets of clothing, medpacks, cloud comm unit, force tent, vape pistol and rifle, camofield screen, hydroboots and minifloater."

"You forgot to pack the bathtub. I might want to relax in a nice warm tub with a good book if things get too hectic."

"Ha ha ha ha!"

"A2, you are now officially a connoisseur of my fine vintage jokes. Time to head out. They're sending a scout ship to take us to Bruno Rabbit."

"He is in Pterosaur Valley?"

"Pterosaur Valley? What's that?"

Edmund panicked. He hadn't meant to say that, it just popped out. Pterosaur Valley wouldn't exist for another fifteen hundred years. "Ha ha ha ha. I was making a joke."

"Hmmm... a valiant effort my friend, but a little obscure for my refined sensibilities." He looked up at a pale blue sphere darting through the sky above them. "Here's the ship. The soldiers call them blinkers because they move so fast. Not as fast as shapers can blink, but pretty fast."

The gleaming craft landed next to them with a low humming sound, the same sound as the floater they rode from the station. "Are they powered by Cross Dimensional Energy Transfer Spheres?"

"They are. That and anti-micrograv units with force displacers. They're working on inertia deadeners but that's another twenty years away at least. Until that day comes you'll need to wear your harness."

Edmund wished Oliver was here to see this. He could almost hear him saying, "Great heavens, look at that! How astonishing!" A section of the sphere hissed down and Edmund the Explorer strode up the ramp into the ship. "Let's go A2! Time to blink!"

The pilot showed Edmund how to strap himself in with the harness. "I know you're indestructible, but we don't want a six hundred pound Rabbiton bouncing around the cabin if we have to pull any tricky maneuvers. The rest of us aren't so indestructible. Maybe one day. I hear they're working on new synthetic bodies that do all kinds of crazy things. Sounds creepy to me. I like the body I have just fine. So does my little doe." He was about to wink at Edmund, then thought the better of it. He mumbled to himself, "Them Rabbitons don't know what they're missing."

The navrabbit flipped open a holomap in front of Edmund the Explorer. "Where to, bossrab?"

Edmund the Explorer scrolled through the map,

stopping at a large mountain range with a valley cutting through it. He tapped his paw on a small area of the valley. "This'll do. We'll have to do a little climbing to get where we're going, but that's why they invented minifloaters."

"Okay rabs, strap and roll." The navrabbit tapped the map then flipped down a small green lever.

The door closed with a hiss, and seconds later the blinker shot up into the sky, stopped, then streaked south towards Bruno Rabbit's home in what one day would be known as Pterosaur Valley. As the sphere shot through the sky it darted this way and that, making Edmund feel like a leaf in a wind storm. He decided he would much rather be flying with Oliver in the *Adventurer II.*

Fourteen minutes later the ship abruptly slowed down, landing with a slight bump. "Here's where you get off. Shoot us a cloud when you need to be lifted."

"Thanks for the ride. Not sure how long we'll be. All depends."

The door hissed open and the two Edmunds stepped out into Pterosaur Valley. Moments later the blinker shot up into the sky and darted north, vanishing in a matter of seconds.

Edmund looked across the valley. He knew exactly where Bruno's house was but he couldn't tell Edmund the Explorer without having to explain how he knew its location.

"Why don't you break out the minifloater and I'll have a look."

Edmund pulled a long silver tube out of his pack and set it on the ground. He tapped the starter code into the grid and stepped back. With a soft gurgling noise the tube spread out, forming a three foot wide disc. Two black handles rose up from either side. Edmund the Explorer stepped onto the disc and took out a pair of dark glasses, tapped the side of them, then grabbed a handle with each paw. "Back in a few minutes, my friend. When I get back here I don't want to find you drinking wine with a couple of young lovelies."

"Ha ha ha ha!"

Edmund the Explorer grinned and twisted one of the grips. The floater shot several hundred feet up into the air then stopped. He adjusted his glasses, looking up and down the valley. Moments later he shot off towards the section of the valley where Bartholomew and Oliver had first spotted the pterosaurs.

"Amazing. He found the cave in seconds with those glasses. I wish I could take a pair back for Bartholomew and Oliver." He watched as Edmund the Explorer soared across the valley towards the cave entrance. He saw him slow down, drifting across the face of the mountain. A moment later he shot back across the valley and landed next to Edmund. "Hop aboard, A2. Time for your first trip on a minifloater."

Edmund cautiously stepped onto the silver disk.

"Put your hands on my shoulders and hold on tight." The floater shot up into the air and streaked off towards Bruno's house.

"Not quite so tight, Edmund. I'd like to be able to use these shoulders again sometime in the near future."

"My apologies, I was afraid I might fall off the floater. Although I am indestructible I am still wary of heights." He didn't mention it was because he had recently fallen five and one half miles from the *Adventurer II,* hitting the ground at one hundred and twenty miles per hour. The fall itself had been delightful, but the landing had been quite startling.

"Not to worry, here we are." Edmund the Explorer brought the minifloater down in front of the cave entrance. He stepped off and pointed to the tunnel. "I got a life force reading in there. Must be where Bruno lives. Not sure why he lives in a cave, but he's the rab who has what I need."

"I should like to mention there is a possibility it's not Bruno Rabbit in the cave. It could be... something else, possibly another life form. Maybe something very large with... oh, I don't know... enormous wings and claws."

Edmund the Explorer looked at Edmund with mock bewilderment.

"You know, A2, I'm starting to wonder if the rab who programmed you was drinking on the job. An enormous creature with wings and claws?"

"I... was merely suggesting the possibility that the life reading could be something other than Bruno Rabbit, and perhaps we should prepare for such a contingency."

"Well, it does makes sense when you put it like that. Hand me the vape rifle."

Edmund pulled the long glass tube out of his pack and passed it over to Edmund the Explorer.

"Follow me."

The two Edmunds moved forward into the darkened tunnel. Edmund the Explorer tapped the side of his glasses and a bright beam shot out, illuminating the cave. He placed his paw next to the vape rifle's green firing tab.

As they reached the bend in the cave, Edmund

stepped out in front of Edmund the Explorer. “I will go first since I am completely indestructible.”

“As you wish, jellyfish.”

“This is a joke, calling me a jellyfish? Should I make the laughing noise?”

“No, that was me being silly. You don’t laugh at silly, you roll your eyes and give a big sigh, just like Emma does.”

“The behavior of rabbits is quite confusing.”

“It is indeed, my friend. If you think they’re confusing now, you should try marrying one.”

Edmund thought for a moment, then rolled his eyes and gave a big sigh. He stepped around the bend and was greeted by a notable absence of pterosaurs. They moved deeper into the tunnel. Several minutes later they reached the end of the tunnel. A rabbit wearing a dark green cloak and hood was leaning up against the granite wall, arms folded. He stared at Edmund with a slightly perturbed expression.

“You’re late. Follow me.” He touched his paw to the wall and a long section of the granite began to ripple. Edmund the Explorer hesitated.

“What is that?”

“It’s called shaping.”

“I’ve seen shaping before and it doesn’t look like that.”

“You haven’t seen my shaping before. Follow me if you want the key.”

Bruno Rabbit disappeared into the rippling granite wall. Edmund the Explorer glanced over at Edmund. “Now I know why he lives alone in a cave.” He grinned, then shrugged and stepped into the wall. Edmund was three steps behind him.

Chapter 20

The Key

Bruno Rabbit's house of mystery was a good deal less mysterious than when Edmund had explored it with Bartholomew, Clara, and Oliver. There were no mysterious pterosaurs guarding it, and instead of an exquisitely decorated secret retreat with a panoramic view of Pterosaur Valley, there was only a cavernous room with a small grouping of furniture at one end. Next to the furniture was a mound of crates and boxes. Bruno hadn't created the side rooms yet, and certainly not the marvelous kitchen that kept food fresh by bending time.

The two Edmunds followed Bruno as he strode down the length of the cavern, his footsteps echoing throughout the vast granite room. Bruno took a seat in an ornately carved wooden chair and motioned for them to sit on a nearby couch.

"So you want the Seventh Key. Why?"

"We need to get into Nirriim without the Anarkkians knowing about it. We're after an artifact that cannot fall into their hands."

Bruno perked up at the word 'artifact'. "What kind of artifact?"

Edmund the Explorer hesitated.

"No key unless you tell me."

"It's a time throttle – Mintarian technology. If the Anarkkians get it they could shut our whole world down. It would be the end of Earth."

Edmund interrupted. "What's a time throttle?"

Bruno answered without looking at him. "It's one civilization's answer to an age old ethical dilemma, how do you get rid of your enemies without killing them? The answer is a time throttle. It's a three inch cube that doesn't look like much when you first see it, but it opens a doorway to the ninth dimension, which as you can well imagine is rather a poor idea. Time slows to a crawl within a fifty thousand mile radius of the cube. The depth of the time field depends on the size of the cube. The Mintarians made a few monolithic throttles to shut down entire galaxies. It's hard to fight a war when it takes you three thousand years to tie your shoe. The victims don't know it's taking that long, they don't notice any change at all, but their connection to rest of the universe has been permanently severed. They're no longer a threat to anyone outside the throttle's time field."

"So what's your answer? Do we get the key?"

Bruno appeared lost in thought, then slowly turned towards Edmund. His eyes narrowed imperceptibly. "Who are you?"

Edmund the Explorer answered for him. "It's just my A2 Carrier Rabbiton. The worst thing he does is make a few bad jokes."

Bruno's eyes didn't leave Edmund. He rose up and

walked over to him. “Have I ever met you before, or any of your friends?”

“I can honestly say I’d never even heard of you before this moment in time.” Edmund tried to smile pleasantly.

“That’s an odd way to phrase it. Why am I seeing a prehistoric pterosaur in my thoughts?”

“I’m not quite certain why that would be.”

Edmund the Explorer interrupted Bruno's confrontation with Edmund. “I need a decision. We don’t have much time. We know the Anarkkians have sent one of their best explorers after the throttle.”

Bruno turned away from Edmund. “You’ll get the key. I just have a very strange feeling about your Rabbiton, and when it comes to strange feelings I am never wrong.” He looked pointedly at Edmund. Walking over to a long wooden crate he flicked his wrist. The wood vanished, leaving a solid black rectangle 3 feet long, one foot wide, and one foot tall. On the top were twelve gold keys. Bruno reached down and picked up the seventh one. “This will open the door to Nirriim. There’s only one key for each door. Lose the key and the door is closed forever. The key is incomprehensibly complex. It operates in multiple dimensions and across time. You can’t run down to your local blacksmith and have another one made.”

“We haven’t had blacksmiths in three thousand years.”

“When it comes to this key you might as well still have them. Don’t lose the key. Am I making this clear enough?”

“Crystal clear. We’re in, we get the cube, we’re out, and you get your key back.”

Bruno gave Edmund the Explorer the gold key.

"Edmund, put this somewhere safe. You're indestructible, you should be the one carrying it."

Edmund took the key and slid it into a large flapped pocket on his pack.

Edmund the Explorer rose up from the couch. "Let's go, A2, we have a world to save." He winked at Bruno.

Bruno rolled his eyes and gave a deep sigh. "Explorers."

Edmund said nothing until they were about to leave through the rippling wall. He turned to Bruno, saying, "Do you know what would be quite lovely? If you made that entire outer wall transparent. What a nice view you'd have of the valley." He smiled again and disappeared through the granite wall.

Bruno didn't move for several long minutes. Finally he turned and looked at the outside wall, putting his paw to his chin. "Hmm, a transparent wall."

Chapter 21

The Swamp of Lost Things

Edmund the Explorer pressed a green disc, activating the cloud comm. "Blinker two nine four, we're ready to lift. One rab and one Rabbiton." He released the button and a soft blue cloud shot out of the screen and into the sky, disappearing instantly. "Next best thing to having your own shaper." Seconds later a red cloud flashed down from above and was pulled into the screen. A voice barked out of the comm.

"On our way, bossrab."

Edmund the Explorer put the cloud comm back into Edmund's pack, saying, "We're off to the Swamp of Lost Things. I guarantee the pilot's not going to like this. Blinker rabs are mighty superstitious. Oh, and don't mention anything to him about the World Doors. If he asks why we're going there just say you don't know."

"I am programmed not to lie."

"Uhh... well... this is a good lie, not a bad one."

"I am programmed not to lie, good or bad."

"Okay, how about this – it's not your lie, it's mine. You're just telling the lie for me. You're a proxy liar, not a real one. It's perfectly okay for Rabbitons to be proxy liars."

Edmund looked confused. "But... wouldn't I still be–"

"A2, if he asks you a question, don't answer him. Say nothing."

"Such an action is within my ethical behavioral programming parameters."

"You know what, I really miss the good old days when Rabbitons did whatever you told them to do."

Their conversation was brought to a halt by a rush of wind and a deep humming sound as the blinker appeared in front of them. The ramp flipped down and the pilot waved them aboard. "Let's go rabs. How was your meeting with the cave rabbit? Why's he live in a cave anyway?"

"He's a shaper, and a strange one at that. If you met him it would be very clear why he lives alone in a cave. I can tell you this though, I wouldn't want to be anywhere near him if he ever got mad."

"Always thought shapers were an odd breed. Where to now?"

"You're not gonna like this, but next stop is the Swamp of Lost Things."

"You're serious?"

"Not a joke, my friend. Break out the navmap and I'll show you the drop point. You don't need to hang around. Just blink in, drop us, and blink out. Done and done. We'll find our own way home."

"I might have to boot you out while the ship is still

moving. There's something not right about that place. Everybody knows it. It's been there forever and nothing ever changes. Rabs go in and rabs don't come out, and nobody knows what happens to them. Why in blazes are you going in there?"

"Oh, you know, time to save the world again. That's what us explorers do."

The pilot shook his head and tapped a red disc. "Strap and roll, rabs." Edmund had just finished buckling in when the ship shot into the air and flashed off towards the Swamp of Lost Things. He really wished he was in the *Adventurer II* with Oliver instead of a blinker that darted around like a mad dragonfly.

Six minutes later the ship was hovering above the putrid gurgling swamp next to a large tree covered island. The ramp flipped down, the dreadful smells of the swamp instantly filling the ship. "Holy rab feathers, what's that smell? You rabs need to bail."

The two Edmunds slid down the ramp into the swamp. Before their feet had touched the water the blinker shot up five hundred feet and vanished into the clouds.

"Well, at least he dropped us in the swamp. I was afraid he wouldn't even do that. It'll be dark soon, so let's camp on this island and we'll find the World Doors in the morning."

Edmund the Explorer showed Edmund how to set up the force tent, which turned out to be no more difficult than pushing a single tab on a small cone shaped metallic device. A twenty foot defensive sphere popped up around them, repelling rain, wind and mosquitos, and keeping the temperature inside at a comfortable level. After a less than satisfactory dinner of synthesized vegetable stew, Edmund the Explorer lay down for the night. "See you in the morning, A2. Tomorrow the adventure begins. We go through the seventh World Door. First thing on our agenda is a visit to the Blue Monks of Nirriim."

"What?" Edmund's eyes opened wide. If he had a heart it would have been pounding. This was the last thing he had expected to hear.

"We're paying a visit to the Blue Monks of Nirriim. They live on an island in an ancient monastery, and if anyone knows where the artifact is, it's the Blue Monks."

Edmund stared at Edmund the Explorer blankly. Visiting the Blue Monks fifteen hundred years before his first visit sounded like a very bad idea. "Oh, Blue Monks. Yes, that sounds interesting."

"Good night, A2."

"I think I'll explore the swamp while you're sleeping. Maybe I can find the World Doors."

"Good luck. Don't get lost."

"Ha ha ha ha. I have the optional Interworld Positioning System. It is impossible for me to get lost."

Right before he dozed off Edmund the Explorer mumbled, "I think I've created a joke monster."

Edmund exited the force tent, listening closely to the sounds of the swamp. He heard only the faint buzzing of mosquitos and an occasional distant splash made by some slippery scaled inhabitant of the swamp. He tried to remember where Bartholomew had told him the World Doors were. He knew it was near a larger island, and the blinker pilot said the swamp never changed. It was an odd place, and the swamp did feel strangely detached from the rest of the world. Edmund stepped into the foul muck and watched as bubbles gurgled to the surface of the dark water. “This is rather an unpleasant smell. I can see why Bartholomew was not very fond of this place.”

He decided to circle the island and look for any sign of the World Doors. He had no expectations of running into the Skeezle Brothers, as they wouldn’t build their den of thievery for another fifteen hundred years. He sloshed his way around the perimeter of the island while adjusting his scanning sensors for the widest band of frequencies, both light and sound. He could see lifeforms now, and watched as several violet glowing eel shaped creatures swam past him, and the occasional bird flashed by overhead. Insects showed up as tiny specks of light. It reminded him of the bubbles in some of the fizzy drinks Oliver made for special occasions. He looked up at the stars. “So many stars. I wonder if I will ever visit those worlds? Oliver says they’re too far away, but books in the Central Information Repository discussed at great length the varied life forms on those worlds, and I heard Edmund the Explorer say he had sent Emma to one of them.”

Edmund sat down on a small sandy beach and found himself gazing at individual stars, wondering if that was where Emma was. He hoped he would see her again. There was something about her that deeply affected him. Perhaps it was the way she treated him – not just like a Rabbiton, but like a friend, the same way Bartholomew and Oliver and Clara treated him. He gave a long sigh. “Even the power of my synthetic neuronic brain can’t help me understand why I am so different from the other Rabbitons. Sometimes I envy them. They never question who they are, they just perform the task they have been programmed for."

He walked back onto the island, having decided to cross directly through the dense thickets to the other side. As he fought his way past the brush and vines he stirred up a myriad of flying insects and found himself swimming in a sea of tiny glowing lights. "They look like stars, each one with a little life of its own. Maybe that's what I am, one little star of life in the universe." When he emerged on the other side of the island he saw a shimmering blue figure looking directly at him.

Chapter 22

The Blue Spectre

Edmund was not afraid. He was indestructible, and whatever else this might be, it was not an ant. The blue figure did not look away. Edmund adjusted his sensors, trying to determine the nature of the creature. It was tall, almost ten feet tall, and was the general shape of a rabbit, but its body was never quite in focus. He couldn't tell if the creature was solid or made of light. Parts of it were momentarily sharp and clear, then faded from sight or became a strange translucent glowing blur. The result was an eerie shimmering effect, giving the creature an unnatural spectral feel, as though it had floated out of some ethereal realm. Edmund walked towards the figure. The shimmering rabbit creature did not back away, but kept its eyes locked on Edmund. When he got closer Edmund could see the blue spectre was floating several inches above the swamp.

Edmund heard a voice in his head. "You must face the transforming fires of life." He didn't know what to think. What did that even mean, 'the transforming fires of life'?

He heard the voice in his head again. "It means you will be transformed by your earthly struggles, by facing your deepest fears. That is the purpose this world serves. In this case you are not the shaper, you are the one being shaped."

"Are you my inner voice?"

"I am not. Edmund, you are going to suffer a terrible loss along your journey, but if you are steadfast you will come to find a deep and eternal joy. I hope we shall meet again, old friend. Nothing would please me more." The shimmering blue creature vanished in a small blink of light, leaving Edmund alone in the foul smelling morass known as the Swamp of Lost Things.

Old friend? Who was this creature? "I have no desire to suffer a terrible loss, and I don't like the sound of those fires of life." Edmund suddenly remembered the story told to him by the Blue Monk. The bunny who lived by the ocean had placed all his thoughts into a silver pot *heated by the fires of life*. This had to be more than a coincidence. He remembered Bartholomew saying all events were connected by hidden strings beneath the fabric of the world.

Even knowing this, there was nothing he could do but wait. He walked around the island back to the force tent where Edmund the Explorer was sleeping. "I think I would like sleeping. At least for a while I wouldn't have to worry about the fires of life." It popped into his mind that this was all a memory, that he was reliving something he had experienced before. Had he already been through these fires of life? It was confusing. He realized he had no answers, and so for the rest of the night he watched the stars until they faded away to a blue morning sky.

"Good morning, A2. I trust you had a pleasant night tromping around this ghastly swamp?"

Edmund was unsure how to respond, but was not capable of lying. "I spent a lot of time watching the stars move across the night sky and I walked around in the swamp but could find no sign of the World Doors."

"Finding the World Doors isn't like finding a ten credit copper on the street. You won't find them without these." He reached into an inner pocket, pulling out a silver case. Flipping it open he pulled out a pair of dark glasses. "These are called World Glasses, my friend. It is only when you look through these that the World Doors make themselves known."

Edmund nodded. Bartholomew had shown him such glasses several times in the past. "How will we know where to look?"

"We're close. It won't take us long. This isn't my first trip through the Doors. I have been to seven of the twelve worlds, and for two of them, one visit was one visit too many. I can tell you from experience that life picks some very terrifying forms to inhabit. I nearly lost my life to a few of them. But enough about that, it's time to move out." He grinned to Edmund, mimicking the blinker pilot's raspy voice, "Strap and roll, rabs!"

"Ha ha ha ha." Edmund packed up their camping gear and slung the pack over his shoulder. Edmund the Explorer donned the World Glasses and surveyed the swamp. "Nothing that way. Let's head around to the other side of the island." They stepped into the murky waters of the swamp and made their way around the shoreline of the island. Edmund the Explorer's gaze slowly traversed the swamp. "Ha! I think we might have something." He gave the glasses to Edmund.

"Look through these and magnify your vision."

Edmund held the World Glasses over his eyes and looked in the direction Edmund the Explorer was pointing. He saw a barely visible dark rectangle in the distance and dialed his vision to twelve hundred percent for a closer look. It was just as Bartholomew had described it to him – a single wooden door with a brass door knob floating above the surface of the water. "I see it. It's about two miles away."

"Let's break out the minifloater. No point slogging through this creepy swamp if we don't have to."

Five minutes later they were zipping along above the dark stagnant waters, Edmund standing behind Edmund the Explorer, trying not to grip his shoulders too hard. Within a few minutes they had arrived at the World Doors. They hopped off the floater and Edmund converted it back to tube form, returning it to his pack.

"How do the World Glasses work?"

"Good question. It's a combination of seeing into another dimension plus seeing a wavelength of light which is normally invisible to us. Hey, why don't you look with your spectrum analysis beam dialed as wide as possible? You might be able to pick up a glimmer of the doors."

Edmund adjusted his vision and once again could see all the lifeforms plus oddly colored rays of energy and light streaming down from above. He could make out the very faint shape of a door.

"I see the World Door. It's a pale green color and almost transparent. I would have missed it if I wasn't looking for it."

"See if you can touch it and open it."

Edmund walked closer to the door and reached for

the knob. It felt solid. Gripping it tightly he twisted it and the door sprung open.

"I'll be darned, it worked. Good for you, A2."

Edmund peered into the Hallway which lay behind the opened door. "There are thirteen doors inside."

"Yes. There used to be only twelve but we added the door at the far end. It will open to the Isle of Mandora once it's complete. The door to Mandora is closed for now because of the time flux issues. We lost a few engineers to a random flux. They're still alive, but we have no idea when they're alive. I'm not a big fan of the time traveling business. Too easy to get lost and never find your way home."

Edmund nodded, hoping he would be able to make his way back to the Island of Blue Monks.

Edmund the Explorer stepped up from the swamp into the hallway of doors. "Well, give me the key and we'll give it a whirl. If the seventh door doesn't open we're in trouble."

Edmund stepped into the hallway and removed the key from his pack, passing it over to Edmund the Explorer.

"Thanks. Here goes nothing. Okay, six doors on this side, so that means the last door on the right side of the hallway is door number seven." He walked down the hallway and stood in front of the seventh door. "Watch this."

As he moved the key closer to the door a keyhole appeared under the doorknob. When he pulled the key away the keyhole vanished. "So far so good." Edmund the Explorer put the gold key in the keyhole and turned it. There was a clicking noise and a soft melody echoed through the hallway. "No one has ever figured out the purpose or meaning of the song. Each of the twelve doors has its own song."

The tune reminded Edmund of the ocean's wordless song of incomparable beauty, but he said nothing. It would be impossible for him to explain it without telling the story of the Blue Monks.

Edmund the Explorer twisted the knob and pushed the door open. Brilliant sunlight flooded the hallway. "Welcome to Nirriim, A2."

Chapter 23

Creekers

The two Edmunds stepped through the seventh door into Nirriim. Edmund was greeted by a familiar landscape. They were standing in the desert, well past the sand dunes where Song's unnamed terrifying creatures lived – the ones who had dragged the *Adventurer II* down into the sand. At least they wouldn't need to sneak past them again. Edmund wondered if Edmund the Explorer was aware of the dunes' deadly inhabitants. "Have you ever been here before? Are there any dangerous creatures we must avoid?"

"Well, I wouldn't take a stroll across those sand dunes behind us unless you want to spend the rest of your existence trapped inside a Nirriimian sand worm. Fortunately we don't have to cross the dunes to get to the Blue Monks."

"What is a Nirriimian sand worm?"

"It's big, it's a worm, it lives in the sand, and you don't ever want to meet one. More than one explorer has lost their life to them. They're ancient, and as far as

I know there's nothing else like them on Nirriim. It's possible to get safely through the dunes but you need a special kind of vision to avoid them. It's a vision that doesn't involve your eyes. I've seen the Red Monks do it. I tried once with a neutronic botscanner, but it didn't work. I just avoid them altogether now."

"Oh. You said something about Red Monks?"

"Yes, they're a fairly common sect of Nirriimian monk. The Blue Monks are different. There are only thirteen of them. Let's get that minifloater going. We have a lot of territory to cover before we reach the monastery."

Edmund pulled the floater tube out of the pack and set it on the ground, tapping the start code into the grid. Moments later they stood on the gleaming silver disc.

Edmund the Explorer grabbed the two black handles. "Well, A2, if you're not going to say it, I will. "Strap and roll, rabs!"

Edmund grinned. He liked the jokes Edmund the Explorer made and he liked having him for a friend.

Edmund the Explorer twisted one of the handles and the minifloater rose into the air with a deep hum. He tapped the side of his glasses and looked across the desert. "Hey, wait a minute, why am I doing all the work? I paid good credits for your Interworld Positioning System upgrade. How about you search for a big lake with an island in the center, one with a big stone building sitting on it."

A translucent screen appeared in front of Edmund. He tapped several buttons and swiped across a large map. "Lake, island, stone building." The map blurred, then a beautiful three dimensional image came sharply into focus. Edmund recognized it as the Island of the

Blue Monks. "That way." He pointed to a dark area scarcely visible across the hazy desert.

"Well, that made the extra twenty-thousand credits all worth it." He laughed and twisted the right handle. The minifloater hummed loudly and sped off across the flat desert, a thick plume of pale yellow dust trailing behind it. As Edmund felt the warm breeze rushing past him and the occasional bug splat against his ears, he wished he could be an adventurer just like Edmund the Explorer. The light of realization flashed in his eyes. This was the moment! This very moment was why he had always wanted to become an explorer! It was why the book he had read about Edmund the Explorer had such a powerful impact on him. This moment was the forgotten memory that had driven him to adventuring, driven him to befriend Oliver and Bartholomew and Clara. His thoughts soared. What about other lost memories? What about this terrible loss the shimmering blue figure had told him about? And what about the ants? Why was he so afraid of ants? He felt a chill inside him. He didn't want to think about this. "I hate ants."

"What did you say?"

"I hate ants."

"I hate spiders, and if you saw the spiders I've seen you'd hate them too. Hey, what's that dark cloud up ahead? Magnify and tell me what you see."

Edmund looked towards the gray swirling cloud and zoomed in on it. It was a mass of flying creatures, but they were moving so quickly it was hard to tell what they were. He froze the image, enlarged it and examined it closely.

"They look something like birds, but much bigger,

faster, and with very large talons, razor sharp feathers, and three red eyes. There are thousands of them heading towards us at approximately ninety-seven miles per hour."

"Creekers! That's the worst thing I've heard since my old adventuring friend Jonathan the Explorer said, 'This isn't rope, it's a spider web!' You should have seen the look on Jonathan's face. I've never seen fur turn white like that before."

"What should we do?"

"Get the force tent out and turn it on. Push the red tab. Do it now!"

Edmund pulled the metallic cone from his pack and pushed the red tab. A transparent defensive sphere popped up around them.

"We have to put her down right now – hold on tight, A2!" Edmund the Explorer twisted both handles sharply. The minifloater shuddered violently and dropped to the desert floor. A split second later they plowed head on into the cloud of creekers. The two Edmunds flew off the minifloater, spinning wildly inside the sphere as they careened across the hard-packed desert floor. The minifloater veered away and shot up into the sky, disappearing in seconds. Dozens of dazed creekers were sprawled across the sand, shrieking and blinking their glowing red eyes. Thousands more viciously attacked the sphere, clawing and stabbing and spraying it with a noxious blue mist.

"Are you all right? Wake up! Are you hurt?"

Edmund the Explorer cracked his eyes open and moaned. "Did we get hit by a battle cruiser?" He looked through the blue tinted defensive sphere at the mass of black razor feathers, talons, and dagger beaks. "I hate creekers almost as much as spiders. That blue venom they spray used to dissolve defensive spheres, but the new emergency force fields put an end to that. Three cheers for new tech. They'll attack for a while then leave. Where's the minifloater?"

"It flew off on its own. Can we get it back?"

"Not without a shaper. We're going to have to hoof it the rest of the way to the Blue Monks. Hey, how about you be a nice Rabbiton and carry me?"

"Ha ha ha ha!"

"I'll say it again, A2, I miss the old Rabbitons. They never laughed at me and they didn't cost half what you did." He grinned, putting his paw on Edmund's shoulder. "Welcome to the world of adventuring, my friend. You know what, crashing a minifloater and being attacked by ten thousand creekers always makes me hungry. Why don't you break out the food synthesizer and whip up a big salad. You can watch me eat. It'll be fun."

Edmund rolled his eyes and gave a big sigh.

Chapter 24

The Thirteenth Monk

With a furious flurry of black wings the creekers were gone. Edmund the Explorer watched as the swirling black cloud of deadly flying beasts faded away across the windswept desert. "Right on time. We can shut down the force tent and move out. Another four or five hours of traveling and we'll have to camp for the night. The last thing I want to do is run into a flock of creekers in the dark."

Edmund switched off the force tent, securing it in his pack while Edmund the Explorer scouted the area for any sign of the minifloater. Finding nothing, they headed off on foot towards the Island of the Blue Monks.

Edmund enjoyed walking with Edmund the Explorer and listening to stories of the strange worlds he had visited and the rare artifacts he had brought home with him. Edmund had read many books about other worlds, but it was different listening to someone who had really been there and seen the often bizarre and terrifying inhabitants up close. As Edmund knew first hand, it was one thing to read about creekers, but quite another to be swarmed by ten thousand of them, each one filled with a burning desire to turn him into an afternoon snack.

At times Edmund the Explorer had traveled alone, but more often he had been accompanied by his old adventuring friend Jonathan the Explorer. Jonathan's reputation as an explorer was on a par with Edmund's and the two got along famously, although Jonathan did do his best to annoy Edmund by claiming 'Jonathan the Explorer' was destined to be a household word, while 'Edmund the Explorer' would wind up as a small footnote in a dusty history book. Edmund the Explorer also took on missions for the military, something which had been occurring more frequently as the war increased in ferocity.

The tales of adventure were marvelous, but Edmund also enjoyed the stories about Emma. He wasn't sure why, but for some reason it calmed him and took his mind off ants and the terrible loss he was supposed to suffer. He liked the way Edmund the Explorer was transformed when he talked about Emma. Edmund found himself wishing he had someone like Emma waiting for him back at the Fortress of Elders.

The days and nights rolled easily by, with no sign of creekers or any other terrifying predators. One morning as the desert haze cleared away, a dark line of jungle foliage appeared in the distance. The following day they exchanged the blistering heat of the desert for the sweltering damp of a lush rainforest. Edmund grinned to himself, remembering how worried Oliver had been about the odd array of shrieks and squawks coming from the trees. It made him feel better knowing someone as brilliant as Oliver was scared by the noisy jungle denizens, but it unfortunately did nothing to diminish his own fear of ants.

Edmund the Explorer tapped the side of his glasses and scanned the wall of vines and branches. "Through here. It's been used as a path before. I can follow the old heat trails. It should take us about five days to reach the Blue Monks. If they don't know anything about the time throttle, I'm not sure what I'll do. We'll cross that bridge when we come to it. There isn't much the Blue Monks don't know. I should warn you though, they are mighty hard to fathom. I've been there more than a few times and when I'm around them I always feel like a dim little bunny who can't tie his shoes yet. Their understanding of the universe is beyond me, but I do know this world is a far better place with them in it. In the end, all I really need to do is bring back the time throttle."

The two Edmunds pushed on through the dense vegetation, often resorting to the vaporizer pistol to blast through the thick vines. They fought their way through the tangled foliage for almost three days, running into several large snakes and a massive hive of deadly spinner bees. Edmund the Explorer was held hostage by the bees in the force tent for over three hours as he waited for them to lose interest in him.

Edmund passed the time by climbing one of the taller trees to get a better view of the jungle. As he was peering out through the forest canopy he saw several unfamiliar skyships zipping across the horizon. He zoomed in on them and froze the image, running it through his IPS data banks. The ships were identified as an older Anarkkian scout ship and a small but heavily armed Anarkkian attack vessel. Edmund the Explorer was less than enthused when Edmund told him about the ships.

"Low profile from now on, my friend. No force tent, no vape guns, no food synthesizer – nothing the Anarkkians can pick up with their scanners." He removed a small, gray cube from a flapped pocket and pressed several tabs on it. "This will hide my heat signature. I'll look like a small monkey – something I'm sure Emma would find quite amusing."

"Ha ha ha ha. Wait, that was a joke?"

"It was both a joke and not a joke, and your laugh was a very appropriate response. I suppose it's time for us to move out and find the Blue Monks. We do have to save the world after all."

Edmund wasn't quite certain how to respond, so he just nodded. Sometimes it was hard to distinguish between a joke and not a joke.

After another day of struggling through the dense thickets they reached the end of the jungle, emerging to the sight of an enormous blue green lake. In the center of the lake was a great rocky island. Edmund recognized it as the Island of the Blue Monks, but there was no town to be seen, only the stone monastery and the immense wall surrounding it.

"There it is, my friend. Welcome to the Island of the Blue Monks."

"How do we get to the island?"

"That will not be a problem." Edmund the Explorer reached into a pocket and pulled out a small gold tube about three inches long. "The monks gave this to me.

It's my name." He put the device to his lips and gently blew into it.

A soft melody floated out that filled Edmund with a deep sense of joy. For a brief moment he saw Emma's face in front of him. The tune echoed across the lake.

"It won't take them long." Edmund the Explorer pointed towards the island. A long graceful craft had already appeared in the water and was heading towards them, rowed by four mice wearing dark red robes and hoods. "Okay, it's probably best if you don't say anything. Let me do the talking. You never know what to expect from these monks."

With a gentle scraping sound the boat slid up onto the sandy shore. The four mice raised their oars but said nothing.

Edmund the Explorer motioned for Edmund to enter the craft, then climbed in after him. The mice put their oars back in the water and pushed off from the shore. Then they stopped. One of them turned to Edmund and nodded. "Hello, Edmund. It's good to see you." A chill ran through him. They knew who he was. How could they possibly know, and how could he explain this to Edmund the Explorer?

Edmund smiled politely at the mouse. "Hello, it's very nice to meet you." He leaned over to Edmund the Explorer and whispered, "They must think I am you."

"As I said, they are hard to fathom."

The mice began rowing again, and ten minutes later the two Edmunds were standing on the dock. Edmund the Explorer made no mention of the Red Monk's unexpected greeting as they followed the four mice along the wooden boardwalk and up the rocky path to the island. They strolled across the island towards the monastery, Edmund surveying the area curiously. There were no houses or streets, only the walled monastery. They waited outside the massive wooden gates as one of the robed mice raised the heavy iron door knocker and let it fall against the door three times. With a creaking groan the two mammoth doors opened wide enough for them to pass through, then rumbled shut behind them.

Nothing had changed inside the monastery walls. Red robed mice tended the flowers, weeding and clipping, taking no notice of the visitors. The two Edmunds trailed behind the red robed mouse down the stone path and through the exquisite garden to the main door of the monastery. It was the same blue door, with the inlaid golden eye in the center. The Red Monk mouse raised the iron latch and swung the door open, motioning for them to enter. Edmund the Explorer looked over at Edmund with a grin.

"You break anything, you pay for it." He entered the monastery with Edmund close behind.

It took several moments for their eyes to become accustomed to the dark. The room was the same now as it would be fifteen hundred years in the future.

Edmund the Explorer whispered, "It takes a minute till you see them."

Edmund waited, finally seeing a slight movement at the front of the room, then the familiar thirteen blue robed mice, all looking at him.

Edmund the Explorer did not look away from the Blue Monks, but he did remain silent. The Thirteenth Monk stepped out of the line and walked towards them. Edmund's eyes widened. It was the same monk who had sent him here.

The Thirteenth Monk slowly padded his way across the smooth stone floor until he stood only six feet from them. He looked at Edmund and smiled with his eyes, a smile of recognition, a smile that said he knew him for who he truly was. Edmund heard the Thirteenth Monk's voice in his head. "Did Edmund the Explorer happen to mention he saved the monastery and all the Blue Monks from a ghastly fate? I suspect he did not. Perhaps one day he will tell you that story. There is far greater depth to Edmund the Explorer than is readily apparent. You must learn what you can from him during your time together." The Thirteenth Monk turned to Edmund the Explorer.

"Hello, Edmund. We are in your debt as always. I hope dear Emma is doing well. How may I be of service to you?"

Edmund had never seen Edmund the Explorer display such humility. This was a very different Edmund the Explorer from the one he had come to know.

"I thank you sincerely for seeing us, and I deeply apologize for interrupting your peaceful day. I would not have come if it was not a matter of great importance."

"I understand. I am happy to do whatever I can to put an end to this terrible war."

"There is a Mintarian artifact I must retrieve before the Anarkkians find it. They will use it to sever our world's connection to the universe."

"The time throttle. I am aware of it."

"Do you know where it is?"

The Blue Monk nodded. "I do. Past the Timere Forest, halfway up the Mountain of Klaatu lies a disabled Anarkkian scout ship. Sitting next to the ship is an Anarkkian warrior. She will be heavily armed, but alone. She has possession of the time throttle. She does not know you are coming, and yet she waits patiently for you."

Edmund the Explorer looked confused. "She has the time throttle but hasn't activated it? Why is she waiting for me?"

The Thirteenth Monk looked at Edmund the Explorer for many long moments before speaking. "Edmund, who fights wars?"

Edmund the Explorer blinked. "Armies do. Countries do."

"No. Wars are not fought by armies, they are fought by individuals, each one blessed with the gift of free will. Remember this when you meet the Anarkkian warrior. She is a single being filled with the same universal life force as you. Listen to your inner voice, listen to the ocean's wordless song of incomparable beauty, and only then should you act."

"Thank you. I will do as you say, but I fear my actions will depend on what the Anarkkian warrior does."

"No. Your actions will depend on what you choose to do."

Edmund the Explorer looked down at his feet. "You're right, of course. It's difficult to remember these things in the heat of war."

"Or in the fires of life." He turned, smiling at Edmund, then stepped closer to him. He was only two feet away when he began to sing. It was the most beautiful song Edmund had ever heard. It was the ocean's wordless song of incomparable beauty. When the song was done the Thirteenth Monk said, "Remember this well." Edmund was filled with the terrible sadness again, but had no idea why. He could do nothing more than nod his head to the Thirteenth Monk.

The Thirteenth Monk turned and slowly padded back to the other side of the room, returning to his place in line. Edmund kept his eyes on the monks, but after a full minute he realized they had already vanished.

"We should go. We have to get the time throttle."

Edmund the Explorer turned and walked towards the door.

An hour later they were on the jungle shore watching the four mice rowing back to the island.

"Next stop, the Timere Forest."

Edmund's IPS holomap blinked up in front of him and he swiped across it. "The Timere forest is twenty-one miles to the west."

"Don't forget the Anarkkians must not become aware of our presence. I know you're indestructible, but the Anarkkian scout ships can knock out an A6 Warrior Rabbiton with a single neuro beam, and I'm sorry to say it, but your armor is nothing compared to an A6. So, no vape guns, no force tent, and only use IPS when absolutely necessary."

It took them three full days of battling the jungle before finally arriving at the magnificent Timere Forest. Edmund had never seen such trees before. He gazed up at them in wonder. "These trees must be eight hundred feet tall. Their trunks are enormous."

"They're many thousands of years old. Who knows what lives up in the canopy."

Edmund pointed northwest. "This way to the

Mountain of Klaatu." He took a step forward.

Edmund the Explorer grabbed Edmund's arm. "Hold on there, my friend. We can't just go tromping into the Timere Forest. This is where the ants live."

Chapter 25

The Timere Forest

Edmund's vision blurred, his world went dark. He blindly stumbled into a gigantic tree trunk, grasping it with both hands so he wouldn't fall. He leaned against the rough bark, his vision gradually returning.

"A2, what's wrong?"

Edmund gave a low groan. "Ants. I didn't know there would be ants here."

"Not just ants. Huge ants. Twenty feet long and over four thousand pounds. Their mandibles can crush a scout ship. I've seen it happen. I've seen a battle between the red ants and the black ones. There were hundreds of them slaughtering each other. It was one of the most horrific things I've ever witnessed."

With an odd whispery moan, Edmund the Rabbiton slithered down the side of the tree into a tangled pile of gleaming silver on the forest floor.

Five minutes later he woke up, Edmund the Explorer shaking his arm. "A2, wake up. It's okay, I've been through the Timere Forest before. I know how to avoid the ants. We'll be okay. Don't forget, you're indestructible. These ants can't hurt you. You could take one out with a single punch to it's head. They have a weak spot right under their tongue."

Edmund sat up with a groan, his thoughts traveling back to the Swamp of Lost Things and his meeting with the Blue Spectre.

"You must face the transforming fires of life... it means you will be transformed by your earthly struggles, transformed by directly facing your deepest fears."

This was what he was talking about. Ants. Everything had been leading him to this moment. The signs were clear now. The fear of ants, the doorway to Nirriim, the Blue Monks sending him here to relive this memory, and the story told to him by the Thirteenth Monk. He looked up at Edmund the Explorer, who was returning his gaze with a look of deep concern. It was almost the same look the Thirteenth Monk had given him. Edmund the Explorer was his first true friend, and Edmund would do anything to help him. They had to retrieve the time throttle, and to accomplish that Edmund must face the ants. Of his own free will he must walk directly into the fires of life.

"Sorry, I don't know what happened. I was just surprised when you told me about the ants. I'll be fine."

"It's not as bad as it sounds, A2. Ants feel vibrations in the ground through their legs, and they smell with their antennae. If we walk slowly and quietly we won't create strong enough vibrations for them to pick up, and you're a Rabbiton so they can't smell you. As for me, I have a clever little device called a scent magnet, made precisely for a situation like this." He pulled out a small sphere on a chain that hung from his neck. "Scent is nothing more than molecules floating through the air that ants smell with their antennae. The scent magnet attracts all the scent molecules within a ten foot radius of me, so I have no scent for the ants to smell. We'll be fine. Worst case, you punch him in the face and we'll both run home like scared little bunnies."

"Ha ha ha ha."

"That's more like it. Time to head out, my old friend. We'll be fine, I promise."

The two Edmunds stepped quietly into the Timere Forest. Edmund was feeling better. In some ways not knowing why he was afraid of ants was worse than actually facing the ants. He also realized he was reliving the memory that lay behind his fear of ants. He had survived this once before, even if he couldn't remember it, and he would survive it again.

"We can talk, as long as we whisper. Our voices are vibrations of the air, but I'm not certain if ants can sense that."

The two Edmunds strolled silently along the forest floor, and as the minutes and hours rolled by there was no sign of the ants. Edmund's fear diminished enough that he found himself marveling at the beauty of the majestic trees. He looked up, the sight of them almost dizzying. He wondered what it would feel like to be so high up, then laughed. He had been that high many times in the *Adventurer II.* On his arrival to Nirriim he had fallen from an altitude of almost five miles. Maybe Edmund the Explorer was right, these ants couldn't hurt him no matter how big they were. They were just ants and he was a Rabbiton, and not just an ordinary Rabbiton, but one with upgraded internal dynamics.

"Shhhh. Hear that rumbling noise? Get down

between these trees and don't move. I think we're on an ant trail." The Edmunds ducked out of sight in the dense brush between two gigantic trunks.

"They can't fit between these trees. We're safe here."

The rumbling noise grew louder, gradually turning into an intense pounding. Edmund peered out, spotting a thick dust cloud moving towards them along the trail.

The ants were remarkably fast. Edmund's jaw dropped at the sight of them as they thundered past, the ground shaking for hundreds of yards around them. They were black ants, at least eight feet tall and twenty feet long, racing along the trail in single file. Their passage stirred up thick clouds of dust and debris, safely concealing the two Edmunds. Edmund saw one of the ants carrying something in its mandibles, but the ant was traveling too fast for him to identify it, and truth be told, he didn't really want to know what it was. It struck him that the ants were almost too big to be afraid of. It was like being scared of the sky or the earth. He also realized he didn't have to fight them, he could simply hide where they couldn't go.

Finally the last ant had passed. Edmund the Explorer whispered,"You did great, A2. I'm proud of you. Now you know what it feels like to be an ant in our world. Just find a good hiding place and wait till it's safe to come out. Ready to go?"

Edmund was feeling much braver. "Strap and roll, rabs."

Edmund the Explorer put his paw over his mouth to keep from laughing. "You might just be the funniest adventuring partner I've ever had, A2. There's something about you, my friend. I can't put my paw on it, but you are one of a kind. It was my lucky day when I plunked down those three credits and brought you home."

"Ha ha ha ha! Three credits for a Rabbiton with upgraded internal dynamics and the optional Interworld Positioning System!" Edmund laughed at Edmund the Explorer's joke, but he also beamed with delight at being called an adventuring partner. He could hear the wind rushing through the branches high overhead. It was a sound he hadn't heard before, it was almost a melody, almost the ocean's wordless song of incomparable beauty. Maybe the trees had their own song.

"Let's head out, partner."

The two Edmunds stepped back onto the trail heading northwest. Neither of them was in a very talkative mood, but Edmund could tell Edmund the Explorer enjoyed the forest as much as he did. A day later they found themselves passing a group of the gigantic trees that appeared to be growing in a huge circle. The trees were too close together for the ants to pass through.

"This looks like a safe place for us to spend the night. Looks like a natural defense barrier against the ants."

Edmund slipped between two of the huge trunks and into the dense foliage beyond. He could hear Edmund the Explorer trailing behind him. Edmund pushed forward through the thick stand of trees and underbrush out into a broad clearing. In the center of the clearing lay a small lake, and standing on the edge of the lake was a single tree. It was not exceptionally large, but it was covered with eyes. Edmund froze like a silver statue in the middle of winter. He could not move. "Good heavens, it's the Tree of Eyes."

Edmund the Explorer broke through the thicket into the clearing.

"What in blazes is that? Are those eyes?"

Edmund couldn't lie and he couldn't reveal what he knew. What he didn't know was how the Tree of Eyes could be in this world and in his world. "I think I heard it talking." Edmund wondered how Edmund the Explorer would deal with the Tree's immature pranks.

Edmund the Explorer gave a dubious look but said, "Well, I've seen stranger things than a talking tree." He walked towards the Tree, but stopped short when the Tree began to speak.

"We are pleased to meet you, Edmund the Explorer. We have a mutual friend in Bruno Rabbit."

Edmund's eyes widened. "You know Bruno Rabbit?"

"When we were young we knew our creator as the Great Tree. When our depth of understanding had grown, he revealed to us his true name and the purpose of our creation. Using the Eleventh Ring, Bruno Rabbit created us from his own life force. The twelve worlds accessible through the World Doors all exist within the same physical space, each in a parallel dimension and invisible to the others. We are one tree which exists simultaneously in all twelve worlds, but the natural ebb and flow of time has caused us to age at a different rate in each world. We are far older and wiser in Nirriim than we are on Earth."

"Why would Bruno create a tree covered with eyes?"

"We were created to experience the joy of our own

self-awareness. It was Bruno Rabbit's intention that we never experience loneliness, so he created us as many. As we grew older we came to realize we were many eyes, but we were one Tree. Being many was the illusion, being one was the reality hidden beneath this illusion, the order beneath the chaos."

"You remind me of some friends of mine called the Blue Monks."

"We are familiar with the Blue Monks. We have exchanged thought clouds with them for over thirteen hundred years."

"You're a shaper?"

There was a flash of light behind the two Edmunds. A complete campsite had blinked into existence, including a large tent, cooking facilities, and all manner of fresh foods and beverages.

"We are. Our skills mirror those of our creator. Please help yourself to whatever food you would like. There is also a feather bed waiting for you inside the tent."

"Any chance you could teach Emma how to do that? It would sure help our grocery bill." Edmund the Explorer grinned, stepping towards the heavily laden table.

The Tree of Eyes shifted its gaze to Edmund.

"You are the A2 Carrier Rabbiton purchased by Edmund the Explorer?"

"I am." Edmund felt uncomfortable being the focus of a thousand eyes.

"Please approach us. We would speak with you."

Edmund stepped nearer to the Tree.

"Closer, please." Edmund drew closer still. The Tree's leaves brushed against his silver metallic skin.

A dozen leafy tendrils unraveled from within the Tree and wrapped themselves around Edmund. The moment they touched him his fear vanished. He knew the Tree of Eyes would never hurt him. When the vines had ceased moving he heard the Tree's voice in his head. There were many voices, all harmonizing as one.

"Edmund, the Thirteenth Monk has told us who you are and why you must relive this memory. We drew you and Edmund the Explorer to us with our thought clouds. Listen carefully to the two things we shall tell you. First, when you are in need of help, you must come to us. Do you understand this?"

"Yes. Why would I need help?"

"We cannot tell you this. You must experience the fires of life without any knowledge of the outcome. All we can tell you is a very complex and difficult transition is occurring."

In me or in Edmund the Explorer?"

"It doesn't matter. We are many, but one. All living creatures are many, but one. What happens to one happens to all. You may have heard this before, perhaps from your dear friends Bartholomew and Clara. Secondly, you must be aware of your actions and the effect they have on others. A single act of kindness can ripple across your world with a life of its own, across the fabric of space and time until it has altered beyond recognition the world you know. Treat all living creatures with kindness and respect. You must remind Edmund the Explorer of this when the time comes."

The tendrils unraveled, withdrawing back into the tree. "In the morning you and Edmund the Explorer must leave for the Mountain of Klaatu. There is not much time left. The Anarkkian warrior is growing impatient."

Edmund looked at the Tree curiously. "Why is the universe interested in anything I do? I am only a Rabbiton."

"Have faith in the perfection of all things, Edmund the Rabbiton. We promise you the day will come when you clearly understand the purpose you have served."

Chapter 26

Neilana

"Creekers, I feel like a new rabbit after a night in that big feather bed. I think I found my new favorite campsite. Ready to go meet an Anarkkian warrior?"

Edmund noticed Edmund the Explorer had a vape pistol strapped to his hip and the vaporizer rifle slung over his shoulder.

"Why are you carrying those weapons?"

"There's a war going on, in case you hadn't heard. The Thirteenth Monk said the Anarrkian would be well armed. I know the Blue Monks mean well, but sometimes a good vape gun is a great negotiating tool."

"We should not be unnecessarily hasty in the choices we make."

"You're not turning into a Blue Monk, are you?" Edmund grinned. "All right, I promise you I won't go in with my guns blazing. We'll see what the Anarkkian has to say, though I suspect her heavy particle projector will do most of the talking."

"Thank you."

After bidding farewell to the Tree of Eyes, the two

Edmunds slipped through the circle of trees, first peering up and down the ant trail. Edmund the Explorer put his ear to the ground and listened. "Nothing. Let's head out."

They traveled for another day and a half without running into any ants, although Edmund did spot some in the distance from the crest of a large hill. He could also see the Mountain of Klaatu.

"The Forest ends in a half mile or so. You did it, Edmund. You made it through the land of ants in one piece. You're a brave one to face your fears like that. I'm not sure I would be able to make it through the land of spiders, if there was such a place."

Edmund smiled, but his thoughts were now on the Anarkkian warrior and the uncertainty of what their meeting would bring.

A few miles after exiting the forest, Edmund the Explorer found a small cave where they could spend the night before heading up the mountain.

"It's not a feather bed, but I guess it will have to do."

Edmund grinned. "I will sit at the cave entrance and keep a watchful eye out for gigantic venomous spiders. Sleep well. Ha ha ha ha."

Edmund the Explorer groaned. "You're starting to sound like me. That's even scarier than spiders. See you in the morning, my friend."

The rising sun found Edmund the Explorer standing at the base of the mountain, his paw tapping the side of his glasses. He moved his gaze across the mountain.

"Got it. I found the ship's signature, and there's definitely a life form next to it. The Anarkkian is still there." He took the vape rifle off his shoulder, then saw the look Edmund gave him. "Okay, fine." He slung the rifle back on his shoulder and they headed up the rugged mountain trail.

"It's not the steepest mountain I've ever seen, that's for sure. Did I ever tell you about the time I had to climb a four thousand foot vertical rock face while being chased by deadly poisonous snow spiders?"

Edmund grinned. He suspected there was a certain amount of embellishment in the tales told by Edmund the Explorer. He didn't mind though, that's what made the stories interesting. "Great heavens, did you say *deadly poisonous snow spiders*??"

"Why do I suspect your unbounded amazement is not altogether sincere?"

"Ha ha ha ha!"

After three hours of climbing the rugged mountainside, Edmund the Explorer held up his paw for Edmund to remain still, then pointed over the tops of the trees. Edmund could see a section of the disabled Anarkkian scout ship gleaming in the afternoon sun. Edmund the Explorer signaled for Edmund to circle around to the left of the ship and he would take the right. Edmund nodded, creeping forward through the trees, staying as low as he could.

Edmund the Explorer moved stealthily around towards the right side of the ship, carefully avoiding any dry twigs or branches that might give him away. Several times he was forced to climb paw over paw up steep rock faces. He grinned as he was climbing, "Thank goodness there's no deadly poisonous snow spiders chasing me."

Almost an hour later he was peering at the Anarkkian ship through a dense grouping of trees. It didn't look damaged, and it certainly hadn't crashed.

Maybe there had been a mechanical failure. The sight of the ship sparked a thought. "If the Anarkkian would be good enough to let us borrow her ship, we could use it to get back to the World Doors. Or even if she doesn't let us." He put his paw on the vape pistol hanging from his hip. "I guess we'll find out soon enough."

A voice called out from near the ship. "You do know I've been watching you for the last hour with a botscanner, right? Your climbing skills are most impressive, by the way. "

Edmund the Explorer cursed. Sometimes the new technologies took all the fun out of being an explorer. He hollered back to the Anarkkian, trying to sound as much as possible like an A6 Warrior. "We have you surrounded. You may as well hand over the time throttle right now."

"Well, since I'm completely surrounded by a furry explorer and his little A2 Carrier Rabbiton I suppose I have no choice but to surrender. Oh, wait, I just remembered – I have a Model 14A Heavy Particle Beam Projector. Correct me if I'm wrong, but I believe it is quite capable of turning both of you into space dust."

Edmund the Explorer gave a deep sigh. In his heart of hearts he knew he wasn't much of a warrior. What he liked was exploring new lands and worlds and learning about the inhabitants. After many years he'd come to realize all lifeforms had far more similarities than differences. He also knew the Blue Monk was right – kindness resolved conflicts far more easily and quickly than a vape gun battle. "What happened to your ship?"

"Power core is gone. They don't put spare CDETS

in the scout ships."

Edmund the Explorer knew what a CDETS was – a Cross Dimensional Energy Transfer Sphere. They were a source of unlimited power transferred from the tenth dimension. At least until they ceased functioning and were transformed into an astronomically expensive boat anchor. "That's tough. Why haven't your scaly little pals come to rescue you?"

"I'm afraid I'm not very popular among my fellow warriors. I don't seem to get the same giddy pleasure they do from killing the enemy."

These words struck a chord deep within Edmund the Explorer. He thought carefully. What would the Thirteenth Monk say if he were here? He grinned. The Blue Monk wouldn't be hiding behind the trees. By now he'd be sitting next to the Anarkkian looking at family photos and swapping vapormail addresses and bread recipes.

"How about we put down our weapons for a bit and have a chat. We can always kill each other later if we want to."

"Sure, why not. But just so you know, there's a very good chance I'll dust you with the beamer the instant you step out from behind those trees."

Edmund the Rabbiton burst out through the foliage on the left side of the ship. He glared at the Anarkkian, who was half sitting and half lying on a flat rock next to the crippled ship. "I would advise against that, or you'll have me to contend with! I might remind you I am indestructible."

"Hey explorer, you never explained to your Rabbiton what jokes are?"

Edmund the Explorer put his paw over his mouth to

keep from laughing. This was getting ridiculous. He hollered out to Edmund. “She made a joke A2. She’s not really going to dust me.”

“Ha ha ha ha.”

“I’m impressed, explorer. I could never get my Beeter to laugh out loud like that. I’m not sure who programs them, but I hope I never meet them.”

Edmund the Explorer put down his vape guns and walked out through the trees. He stepped into the open and spotted the Anarkkian warrior hunched over on the large flat rock. “Are you hurt?”

“I had a bit of a fall about a week ago. One broken arm, one broken leg, and no medpacks. Half the time the Warrior Narkks steal them from the ships and sell them. Never have quite understood the logic behind that.”

“You have the time throttle?”

“You don’t waste time. Yes, I have it.”

“Where’d you find it?”

“In a cave up the mountain, along with the remains of an old Mintarian scouting party. Not sure what got them but it wasn’t pretty. Why do you want it? You going to shut down Anarkkia? I can’t let that happen, you know. You’ll have to kill me to get it.”

“Relax. Nobody is killing anybody. They only sent me here so it wouldn’t be used against us. That’s all. If you want we can vaporize it right here and now.”

“Now there’s a good solid plan. I guess you were busy exploring some creepy cave during that class on Mintarian technology. Try to vape it and Nirriim will be frozen in time for the next trillion years or so. You don’t think the Mintarians thought of something as simple as that? The only real problem is I have no idea how to destroy it. If I did know, we wouldn't be having this conversation."

"Mintarians were a little before my time. I don't know much about them."

"You wouldn't want to meet one. They've got some terrifying teeth on them. The ones in the cave look like they got marinated for ten years in ugly sauce."

Edmund the Explorer burst out laughing. "Good one. I suppose now would be a bad time to mention those two lovely green tusks of yours."

"I'd rather have tusks and scales than walk around looking like a fluffed up Quintarian furball."

"You know what? I'm starting to like you. My name is Edmund the Explorer. What do they call you?"

"That depends. I'm Neilana to my friends. I won't mention what the other ones call me. I wouldn't want you to faint or anything."

"I do appreciate your restraint. So, Neilana, what are we going to do about all this?"

"Well, do you have any medpacks?"

"A2, how many medpacks do we have?"

Edmund approached, reaching into a side pocket on his pack. "We have two."

"That'll do it." Edmund the Explorer took the two medpacks from Edmund and stepped over to Neilana. "Where's it hurt?"

"The arm and leg that look most like a pretzel."

Edmund the Explorer unwrapped the medpacks and held the first one next to Neilana's broken leg. He pressed the blue tab and a two foot sphere of brilliant green light surrounded the leg. He used the second pack on Neilana's broken arm. "Never have quite understood how these things work."

"Shapers invented them. They figured out how to confine shaper energy inside a carrier tube. Break the tube and it heals about anything."

"Live and learn I always say."

Five minutes later Neilana rose up, gently putting pressure on her leg. "Just like new. Okay, you want to hand me my beamer so I can dust you both and get out of here?"

"Ha ha ha ha."

"You had a good teacher, Rabbiton. Maybe if they programmed our Beeters to laugh, the war would be over by now. I haven't missed the fighting, I can tell you that. It's been quite enjoyable sitting here listening to the wind blow through the trees for the past month – before I fell, anyway. Sometimes I could almost hear a melody, a kind of song."

An odd feeling rippled through Edmund. "Perhaps the trees have their own song, just as the ocean does."

Neilana looked surprised. "How do you know about that? You're a Rabbiton."

Edmund told his first lie, realizing that perhaps Edmund the Explorer had been right about good lies and bad lies. "The Tree of Eyes told me about it. It sang the song for me, and now I hear it when I listen. The song is everywhere."

Neilana looked questioningly at Edmund the Explorer, who shrugged. "Hey, I was asleep in a big feather bed when all that happened."

Neilana studied Edmund the Rabbiton. "You're right about the trees having their own song. I've heard the song since I was young, but I quickly learned never to talk about it. The Narkkers laughed at me the first time I told them I could hear it. I never mentioned it again.

The ocean, the trees, the sky, the earth... they all have their own song, and when you hear them together it's..." Neilana didn't finish her sentence. "I guess there are no words to describe it. Let's just say if the Anarkkians could hear it, this war would be over in about five minutes."

Edmund the Rabbiton said, "Perhaps if you returned to Anarkkia you could teach others to hear the song. You never know what might happen."

Neilana stared at Edmund. "What *are* you?"

"I am an A2 Carrier Rabbiton with the upgraded internal dynamics package and the optional Interworld Positioning System."

"Uh huh. I think you may have a few extra crystals they didn't tell you about, my friend." Neilana turned to Edmund the Explorer. "I don't suppose you have a CDETS in your back pocket?"

"I had a sack of them but I traded it for a keg of magic ale."

Edmund the Rabbiton spoke up. "I have one."

Neilana turned towards Edmund. "What do you mean you have one?"

"I am powered by a CDETS."

Edmund the Explorer broke in. "A2, you can't do that. If you take out your CDETS you would... stop working. You would die."

"You are incorrect. The internal dynamics upgrade includes an auxiliary power source which will keep me going for almost three months. We will be back to Earth long before then and you can install a new CDETS."

"A CDETS costs almost forty-thousand credits, A2. Emma and I can't afford something like that."

Neilana pulled out a small cloth sack. She tossed it over to Edmund the Explorer. “This should cover it.”

Edmund the Explorer eyed the small bag. It was made of green velvet and was decorated with the image of an arrow piercing a gold spiral. “What is it?”

“Nirriimian white crystals. I found them on one of the Mintarians.”

Edmund the Explorer opened the sack and peered into it. “This will buy ten CDETS.”

“It’s only credits.” Neilana studied Edmund the Explorer. “You may as well take this while you’re at it.” She opened her hand, revealing a gleaming blue iridescent metallic cube. “It’s called a Mintarian time throttle.”

Edmund the Explorer took the time throttle from Neilana. “A2, are you sure you want to give up your CDETS? You don’t have to.”

“I want to do it. It is the right thing to do.”

“Okay, if you’re sure. Neilana, let’s go fix your ship.”

* * *

Sunrise found the two Edmunds and Neilana standing next to a fully operational scout ship. “What will you do when you get back to Anarkkia?”

“I will go into hiding. I have friends I can stay with outside the city. They are more open to the songs there. I will teach them how to listen. No words can express how grateful I am to both of you. You should know our meeting was not accidental. The trees whispered this to me long before you arrived.”

“Well, it seemed like a better idea than killing each

other. Be safe then. I'll spend half the white crystals on Nirriimian brew and the rest on a new floater for Emma. After that maybe I'll get around to buying a CDETS for A2, but only if I can find an old beater in a junk shop."

"Ha ha ha ha!"

Neilana smiled at Edmund the Rabbiton. "I'm still not sure what you are, my friend, but you are far more than you seem to be. I am forever in your debt." Neilana turned and climbed into the ship. "Better move back. I'd hate to accidentally turn you into a mound of charcoal."

With a wave, the two Edmunds walked away, disappearing into the trees. "She'll be home before we are." Moments later a brilliant flash lit up the mountainside. Neilana was on her way back to Anarkkia.

"All's well that ends well, I guess. We got the time throttle and I didn't have to wipe out half the Anarkkian army doing it. I'm thinking we should make our way back to the Tree of Eyes then head back to the World Doors. I could sure use another night in that feather bed. You haven't managed to lose the Seventh Key have you? I'd hate to have to tell Bruno Rabbit you were the one who lost it."

"I have the key safely in my pack. I check daily to make certain it is still there."

"Good. Go ahead and pop this in with it and we're good to go." He tossed the time throttle to Edmund, who strapped it securely inside the pocket with the Seventh Key.

As they strolled down the mountain path towards the Timere Forest, Edmund the Explorer clapped his paw on Edmund's shoulder. "I hate to admit it, but we did a good thing today, A2. Emma will be proud of us, and that makes me happy. Speaking of Emma, did I ever tell you about the time my ship crashed on Deailderon? Spiders the size of scout ships. It was terrifying. The only weapon I had was a small pocket knife that Emma gave me for my..."

Edmund the Rabbiton was happier than he had ever been. There was nowhere else in the universe he would rather be right now. He heard the trees and the ocean singing, their exquisite harmonies whirling and soaring through the clear mountain air.

Chapter 27

The Fires of Life

Hiking down the mountain was much faster than hiking up the mountain. In less than a day the two Edmunds had reached the edge of the Timere Forest. "Are you ready to face the ants again?"

"I'm ready. I am amazed by their size and strength, but I seem to have lost some of my irrational fear."

"Good. I'm in the same boat as you when it comes to spiders. I don't like them, but I've almost conquered my fear of them. Let's head back to the Tree of Eyes. At this rate it should take about a day and a half to get there. Tread lightly, my friend, and don't forget to whisper."

The forest was beautiful, narrow beams of sunlight angling down through the cathedral of trees, covering the forest floor with a soft flickering light.

"I can't wait to see Emma. There's something special between us, in case you hadn't noticed. I feel as though I've known her forever. She always says no matter what happens we'll find each other again, and I believe her. We're all so much more than a bunch of furry rabbits scurrying about looking for food. When I look into Emma's eyes I see a reflection of what we truly are."

Edmund the Rabbiton nodded. "The Tree of Eyes said we live on after... you know. I wonder if I will? I know I'm a Rabbiton, a machine, but I feel more than that."

"You will live on, my friend. I know it. You're different from any Rabbiton I've ever met. Put a little fur on you and you're one of us."

"Hmmm. Perhaps I should think about buying a fur coat. Ha ha ha ha."

Edmund the Explorer never saw the ant that grabbed him. He saw its mandibles whip around his chest, and was turning his head to look when his world went black.

Edmund the Rabbiton was gazing up at the glorious sunlight filtering through the trees when he heard Edmund the Explorer's terrible gasp. He turned and saw the ant. With a roar that echoed through the forest, Edmund leaped towards the ant. He grabbed one of its mandibles, and with every ounce of strength he could muster, slammed his fist into the ant's head below its tongue. The four thousand pound ant dropped to the forest floor with a dull, earthshaking thud. Edmund pried apart its mandibles, freeing Edmund the Explorer. His pack fell to the ground as he picked him up, cradling him in his arms. He was still breathing, but just barely. There was a thundering crash and the sound of trees snapping and splitting. More ants were emerging from the side of the trail. Edmund ran. Faster and faster he raced down the forest trail, holding Edmund the Explorer as gently as he could.

They had used both their medpacks to heal Neilana. Edmund's mind was racing. The Tree of Eyes had warned him about this, telling him to return to the Tree if he needed help. The Tree was a powerful shaper and could heal Edmund the Explorer, but he had to get there before...

Edmund ran and ran and ran, never slowing down until he reached the circle of trees. He had been running for over five hours. For the first time in his life he felt tired, his legs and arms shaky. He carried Edmund the Explorer through the trees into the clearing. The Tree of Eyes was waiting for him.

"Quickly, bring him here, close to us." Edmund ran to the Tree and held out Edmund the Explorer. Hundreds of tendrils shot out from the Tree and wrapped around him until he disappeared inside a leafy cocoon. "We will do what we can to heal him, but it is not as simple as that. We have stopped time within the cocoon. He must remain here with us. He is not dead, but he is not alive."

Edmund the Rabbiton was feeling dizzy and wasn't sure how much longer he could remain standing. He had never experienced this before and didn't know what to expect. This would be the first time he had ever died.

The Tree of Eyes spoke to him in a gentle soothing voice, like a mother to its bunny. "You told Edmund the Explorer your secondary power supply would last for three months when you knew it would only last for several days at the most. You used up all your reserve power running here."

"We had to get Neilana back to Anarkkia. I knew it was the right thing to do, but I also knew Edmund the Explorer wouldn't let me give up my CDETS if I told him the truth." He stopped, his thoughts muddled and confused. He couldn't remember why he was here. What was this tree with so many eyes, all looking at him? He tried to pick out a single pair of eyes to focus on but couldn't seem to do it.

Dozens and dozens of tendrils reached out and wrapped around him. It was a comforting feeling, like lying in a soft bed, or what he thought that would be like. He had never slept before, but imagined this is what it must feel like to drift off to sleep. He heard a quiet voice in his head, but the meaning of the words was unclear to him.

"You have made a great sacrifice, Edmund the Rabbiton, and it was not made in vain. Neilana's teachings bring an end to the Anarkkian wars. It takes almost four years, but as more and more Anarkkians hear the Songs of Life, they rise up and bring to a close this terrible chapter in the life of Anarkkia. Never again will Anarkkians wage war. Edmund, it is time for you to sleep now. We have shaped you a new CDETS, but you have wounds which lie beyond this physical world. This is not the end of your life, only the end of this short chapter, and you still have much to accomplish. These are dark moments for you, but in time you will awaken to a great happiness."

Edmund the Rabbiton was drifting, then soaring through an inky infinite blackness. He was in the Void, the space between all worlds, on his way back to the Blue Monks. The words of the Tree of Eyes were still in his thoughts when he saw a familiar sliver of light in the distance.

He willed himself towards the light, watching it grow larger as he approached it. Then he was next to it, looking down into it, gazing at a silver Rabbiton sitting on a pile of soft velvet pillows. Edmund tumbled into the blazing light.

Once again he was sitting on the pillows in the monastery. Standing in front of him was the Thirteenth Monk, his face a curious mix of deep sorrow and infinite joy.

Wave after wave of memories rolled through Edmund, filling him with an unbearable sense of loss. With a dreadful wail he rolled forward, wrapping both arms around his head. He would never again see Edmund the Explorer and never again see Emma. His cries echoed through the empty stone building.

"Edmund, come with me. It will be all right, but you must come with me into the garden." The sound of these words drew Edmund out of the darkness for a brief moment, long enough for him to look up at the Thirteenth Monk.

"You are in shock, Edmund. You need to stand up and follow me into the garden."

Edmund rose to his feet, his legs wobbly. The Thirteenth Monk hummed two short notes and the blue door swung open, brilliant sunlight flooding into the darkened monastery. They walked into the garden of the Blue Monks, stepping across a smooth stone path to a nearby bench. The Thirteenth Monk motioned for Edmund to sit next to him.

He took Edmund's hand between his paws. "It will be all right. What you just experienced took place almost fifteen hundred years ago. Edmund the Explorer and Emma have moved on to other places, other times. The death of our physical body is not the end of us, Edmund. Edmund the Explorer and Emma will find each other again. It can be no other way. Do you remember what Edmund the Explorer said to Emma?"

Edmund shook his head.

"We are bound together beyond time and space, two hearts entangled in the cosmic lace." They will be drawn together again, just as a dropped marble must fall to the earth. This is a law of the universe as immutable as the laws of physical motion. Your dear friends Edmund the Explorer and Emma will be together again, and in time you will see both of them."

There was something enormously comforting about the Thirteenth Monk. It wasn't simply his words, but it was the way he said them, the way he empowered them with an overwhelming sense of hope.

Edmund looked at the Thirteenth Monk. "I miss them both so terribly much. Edmund the Explorer was my first true friend, and showed such kindness to me. It is not something I can ever forget."

"I would expect nothing less from you, Edmund. His friendship will remain a part of you always. Edmund, remember also you have your dear friends Bartholomew and Oliver waiting for you in this world. For them only a short time has passed since you left. It is very important that you tell them what happened here. The chain of events which began back then is not over. I cannot tell you more, but together the three of you must find the Seventh Key and return it to Bartholomew's house in Pterosaur Valley. Edmund, you can be proud of yourself and proud of Edmund the Explorer. The sacrifices you made so long ago saved countless millions of lives, and brought new hope to the Anarkkians."

Edmund nodded, his eyes on the magnificent garden

surrounding them. There was still great beauty in the world. The monks were still clipping and weeding and planting and watering. The sun was still in the heavens, sending its warm rays of energy to this very garden where he sat. The Thirteenth Monk was right about Edmund the Explorer and Emma finding each other again. Emma had known this all along. He let go of the Thirteenth Monk's paws. "I will tell Bartholomew and Oliver everything."

"You must tell them about the sacrifice you made."

"I will tell them."

"It's time for you to go now, Edmund, but I will see you again, under far happier circumstances than these."

Chapter 28

The Traveling Eye

Song was waiting outside the monastery walls when Edmund emerged through the massive wooden doors. His eyes revealed an intense curiosity, but he did not question Edmund about his time with the Blue Monks. This was Edmund's concern and no one else's.

Edmund told him everything. "The Blue Monks sang for me and I relived a long forgotten memory. I was a friend of Edmund the Explorer, an Elder who lived fifteen hundred years ago. I was with him when he died, killed by a gigantic ant in the Timere Forest. My fear of ants was the result of that terrible experience." It was hard for him to say Edmund the Explorer had died. He wondered who had told Emma that Edmund would not be coming home.

"Edmund, I don't wish to intrude into your personal affairs, but there must be more to this than resolving your fear of ants. The Blue Monks would not have seen you for that reason alone."

"You're right, there is more. I have to find a lost World Key. I was carrying it when the ants attacked.

The Seventh Key and a Mintarian time throttle were both in a pack I dropped as we made our escape."

"Ah, a World Key is indeed something the universe would be interested in. That could affect the Infinite Chain. You never went back to look for it?"

"I don't know if I did or not. I returned here and anything I did after that is lost to me. I have no idea what happened to the pack or its contents. I do know three more ants emerged from the forest before I left. It's possible they took the pack."

"Hmm. I will need to consult several of my brother monks who possess greater knowledge of the Timere Forest ants. Unfortunately, I know almost nothing about them. Bartholomew and Oliver might have some ideas also."

An hour later Edmund and Song arrived at the Nirriimian Singers Guild. They found their way to the Guild Library and into several comfortable chairs, chatting about the Blue Monks until Bartholomew and Oliver returned. Oliver was carrying two green boxes containing Nirriimian pastries. Bartholomew greeted Edmund, asking, "How was your visit with the Blue Monks? What happened?"

Hours later Bartholomew was leaning forward in his chair with a stunned expression. "You and Edmund the Explorer were responsible for bringing an end to the Anarkkian war?"

"We were one link in a chain. Neilana was the one who brought the Life Song teachings to the Anarrkians."

"And Edmund the Explorer was your first friend in this world."

"He was. The Thirteenth Monk said one day I will

see both Edmund the Explorer and Emma again."

"I believe you will see them too, Edmund." Bartholomew looked over at Oliver, who was nibbling quietly on a Nirriimian pastry.

Oliver stopped, looking like a bunny caught with his paw in the snack jar. "Oh, yes, of course, most certainly you will see them again. Would anyone care for a pastry? They are different, but still quite delicious."

"Perhaps later, Oliver." Bartholomew turned back to Edmund. "Do you have any idea where the World Key might be?"

"I suppose it's possible the ants took the pack back to their colony."

Bartholomew frowned. "Fifteen hundred years ago – I don't know if it's even possible to track down one key after all that time. I wish Clara was here. She has a sense for finding lost things. Song, do you have any thoughts? Are there any Red Monks who are adept at finding lost things?"

Song thought for a moment. "There is one. He lives in a small house on the southern side of the island. He is a recluse and seldom leaves his house. Well, that's not entirely accurate – he often leaves his house, but not in physical form."

Bartholomew looked confused. "How is that possible? If his body is in cloud form for more than two seconds he cannot convert back to his original physical form."

Song nodded his agreement. "Quite true, but in this case he doesn't convert his body to cloud form. He is able to move his center of consciousness to any point in the universe he wishes, a skill he calls the Traveling Eye. He also possesses a powerful inner voice which will often describe to him the location of a missing object."

"Then that is where we will go. Tomorrow morning we will visit your gifted friend."

Bartholomew had a restless night filled with anxious dreams. He woke up the next morning filled with a vague feeling of dread, but had no idea the source of the feeling. After breakfast they headed off to the reclusive monk's house on the southern shore of the island. Song pointed out some of the landmarks as they walked, including the first house built outside the monastery nearly six hundred years ago. After a half hour they arrived at a humble wooden home built into the rocky island shoreline. The house was painted red, the same color as the robes worn by the Red Monks. Song rapped several times on the front door, then sang a lengthy and beautiful melody. "I told him the Thirteenth Monk has sent visitors who are trying to locate a significant lost object, and we would be most grateful for any help he could give us."

The front door opened a crack and a red robed mouse peered out. He gave a quick smile when he saw Song, then withdrew back into the house, closing the door quickly behind him after everyone had entered. One by one he carefully studied the faces of his guests, remaining silent until he had finished this somewhat quirky examination. He turned to Song. "They are looking for a lost key?"

Song nodded. "Yes, it is a World Key and was lost fifteen hundred years ago in the Timere Forest by Edmund the Rabbiton and Edmund the Explorer."

The reclusive monk turned to Edmund. "You may call me Ennzarr. I have read about Edmund the

Explorer and his near mythical adventures. You are fortunate to count yourself among his friends. Not many rabbits know this, but it has been told that Edmund the Explorer and his A2 Carrier Rabbiton helped bring an end to the Anarkkian wars."

Edmund's face softened. "He was my first true friend."

Ennzarr put his paw on Edmund's arm. "I will help you find your lost World Key. It is a great honor to help a friend of Edmund the Explorer." Ennzarr took a seat in a high backed maroon chair. He closed his eyes and his head began to nod. Fifteen minutes later Oliver looked over to Bartholomew with raised eyebrows and whispered, "Should we wake him?"

Song gave Oliver a gentle look of disapproval, whispering, "He is not sleeping. He is practicing the Traveling Eye and speaking with his inner voice. He can roam the world while his physical body remains here."

Another half hour passed and Ennzarr still had not opened his eyes. Bartholomew's head was nodding, and even Song was looking droopy eyed.

Ennzarr awoke with a start. He sprang to his feet, stepping in front of Edmund. "For the Infinite Chain to remain balanced, many essential events must occur. I will repeat to you the direction given to me by my inner voice. You must go to a tavern known as the Paw and Dagger, located in the lower dock district on the southern shore of this island, and there seek assistance." Ennzarr padded across the floor, standing in front of Bartholomew, staring pointedly at his Eleventh Ring.

"The Eleventh Ring is new to you?"

"I have worn it for a little over a year."

"That explains why you do not practice the art of the Traveling Eye."

"I had not heard of it until yesterday."

"It is one of the powers granted by your Eleventh Ring, and one of the reasons you have been brought here. It is time for you to learn this art."

Ennzarr waved both paws towards the front door. "Everyone except Bartholomew must leave now. We will be finished in less than one hour."

Bartholomew soon stood alone in front of Ennzarr.

"Bartholomew, please face the wall, standing five paces away from it."

When Bartholomew was in position Ennzarr continued. "With your eyes closed, imagine you are standing only inches from the wall. See in your mind every scratch, every indentation, every speck of dust on the white plaster. Visualize the wall clearly in your mind. It will be quite simple for you to do this. If you did not wear the Eleventh Ring it could take a lifetime for you to learn the Traveling Eye. Now, when the wall becomes real to you, lean forward slightly and touch it with your nose for three seconds. Then turn around quickly and look back at your physical body standing five paces behind you with its eyes closed."

Bartholomew examined the wall closely in his mind until he could see every detail. He had practiced this visualization skill many times before on the Isle of Mandora with Clara's Thought. He turned around suddenly and saw himself standing on the other side of the room with his eyes closed. He felt dizzy and disoriented. "I can see myself. I feel sick. I think I'm going to throw up."

"It will pass. I will join you now, appearing as a

silver shadow."

Bartholomew looked around but didn't see Ennzarr. He did notice his new body was a barely visible liquid silver cloud. He was a center of awareness floating in the room. Finally he saw Ennzarr, or something vaguely resembling Ennzarr. A silvery flowing shadow sailed over to him. The more he focused on the shadow, the more it took on Ennzarr's appearance. He heard Ennzarr's voice in his thoughts. "Bartholomew, take my paw."

He reached out for Ennzarr's paw and they drifted through the outer wall of the house, floating up into a clear blue sky. Bartholomew's feeling of nausea vanished. This was far more enjoyable than he had imagined it would be. He could see Edmund, Oliver, and Song standing outside Ennzarr's house. "You may stay in this state as long as you wish, as long as your physical body remains undisturbed. If someone touches your physical body you will instantly return to it, no matter how far away you are. Move your center of consciousness by using your will. Practice flying for a few minutes."

Bartholomew grinned at Ennzarr, or at least he thought he was grinning. He didn't know if his silver essence was capable of making facial expressions. He shot down towards the sparkling surface of the lake and flashed across it as fast as he could go. Almost instantly he arrived on the other side of the lake. Ennzarr was there next to him. "Your movement is not limited by worldly laws of motion when you are in the Traveling Eye. You are only limited by your thoughts. Fly down to the bottom of the lake, then come back and tell me what you saw."

"I won't drown?"

"Your physical body back in the house is breathing normally. You are only awareness here, nothing more. Go to the bottom of the lake now."

Bartholomew shot down into the lake. The water did not slow him down, he passed through it as though it wasn't there. As he was flying across the bottom of the lake he spotted a padlocked metal chest chained to a massive boulder. Was this what Ennzarr wanted him to see? What could be inside the box? How could he unlock it? With shaping? He laughed at his own foolish question – as pure consciousness, he could simply enter the box. He zipped over to the huge chest and poked his head into it. The box was empty except for a sheet of parchment paper with writing on it. Seconds later he was soaring above the lake next to Ennzarr.

"You saw something down there?"

"I did. A metal chest, padlocked and chained to a boulder."

"And did you see the sacks of Nirriimian white crystals inside it?"

"The box held only a piece of paper with a single word written on it."

"Excellent. You have found the greatest treasure of all, placed there by the Blue Monks nearly five thousand years ago. You are a quick study. Now, fly down through the earth beneath the lake and tell me what you see."

In a flash Bartholomew shot through the lake, deep into the layers of rock and soil beneath it. As he flashed through the earth he spotted several dense veins of Nirriimian white crystals. Whoever harvested these would be wealthy beyond compare. He willed himself back to Ennzarr and was instantly there.

"I saw a king's ransom in white crystals down there."

"And what will you do with this knowledge?"

"I will do nothing. The crystals are only physical objects, no different from a pebble or a leaf."

"I see now why Bruno Rabbit selected you to wear the Eleventh Ring. We are done. When you wish to return to your physical body you have only to envision it in your mind."

Bartholomew had scarcely started to visualize his physical body when he found himself back in Ennzarr's house. He opened his eyes and saw a smiling Ennzarr across the room. "Welcome to the world of the Traveling Eye, my friend."

Bartholomew's body was shaking slightly from the experience, but this soon passed. "That was astonishing. To be free of this physical form is amazing. I have never experienced anything quite so liberating."

Ennzarr gave a studied look. "It is liberating to be free of your body, Bartholomew, but it is also miraculous to smell an apple pie baking in the oven, to feel the warmth of the sun on your back as you stroll through an ancient forest, or to hear the sound of chirping birds outside your window. There is a deep purpose in all things and in all forms, and we are meant to be shaped by both our forms and our experiences."

"I will remember your words. Thank you for everything you have taught me, Ennzarr."

"You are welcome to visit whenever you wish, Bartholomew. I wish you luck in your quest to recover the lost World Key."

Bartholomew turned and headed towards the door.

Ennzarr spoke softly. "Wait. There is something else."

Bartholomew turned back towards him.

Ennzarr's face was grim. "I had been uncertain whether or not I should tell you this, whether or not it was my place to do so. I have made my decision. I will tell you that you must find the Seventh Key soon and you must return it to Bruno Rabbit's old home. If you do not find the Queen's Treasure Chamber and retrieve the key, Edmund the Rabbiton will be lost to you. I can only tell you that he will cease to exist. I'm sorry."

"But, I don't understand. Is this something to do with the change he is going through?"

"Yes. It has everything to do with that. I can tell you no more. Find the key, take it back to Bruno Rabbit's house. You should go now." Ennzarr motioned him towards the door.

Bartholomew stared blankly at him for a moment, then turned and exited through the blue door to find Song, Oliver and Edmund waiting for him. A chill passed through him when he looked at Edmund. "We should get back to the Singers Guild. Tomorrow we pay a visit to the Paw and Dagger Tavern."

Chapter 29

Thunder and Lightning

Edmund stared out his window at the starry Nirriimian sky. He liked the two moons, especially the yellow one. It was peaceful sitting by himself, alone with his thoughts. He found himself humming a lovely melody, but had no idea where he had heard it before, or why he was humming it. This was something new. Perhaps it was from listening to the Blue Monks sing. Thinking about the Blue Monks rekindled his memories of Edmund the Explorer. "I miss him almost every day. I wish I knew who told Emma what happened to him." Edmund didn't really want to think about that, but he couldn't control his thoughts the way he used to. They seemed to jump all over, going to places he didn't want them to go, like a wild monkey leaping from branch to branch.

"I suppose it could have been Bruno Rabbit who told Emma. He could have talked to–" It hit Edmund like a blast of light from Zoran the Emerald Shaper's paw. "I can ask the Tree of Eyes! Why in the world didn't I think of this before? The Tree of Eyes will still be there, and it can tell me what happened to Edmund the Explorer, and possibly what happened to Emma."

Edmund felt a deep pang of sorrow when he said Emma's name. It was hard to separate the two of them, hard to imagine them apart. Edmund the Explorer had said it himself – he was linked to Emma outside of space and time.

Edmund was pulled from his thoughts by a flickering blue light coming from behind him. When he turned around he saw the Blue Spectre, the apparition which had confronted him in the Swamp of Lost Things fifteen hundred years ago. Whatever this creature was, it was still alive.

The Blue Spectre no longer held any fear for Edmund. There was a kindness about the figure which was clear to him now. Edmund asked, "Are you a ghost?"

Edmund couldn't tell if the figure had smiled, but he thought it might have. "No, Edmund, I'm not a ghost. I live in the world just as you do. I am a friend you do not remember, and I am here to help you. You must seek out the Queen's Treasure Chamber. This is where you will find the lost Seventh Key. You will be tested again, once again walking of your own free will into the fires of life. Do what you know to be right."

Edmund's insides twisted into a painful knot. The last time he met the Blue Spectre it had warned him of a terrible loss, which turned out to be the death of Edmund the Explorer. Now it was telling him he would once again be walking into the fires of life. "Where is this treasure chamber? Why must I be tested again?"

The Blue Spectre vanished before the words were out of Edmund's mouth.

In the morning Edmund told Bartholomew and Oliver about the Blue Spectre and it's cryptic message regarding the Queen's Treasure Chamber.

"What queen could it be talking about? There are no kings and queens in Nirriim. Could it be back on Earth? Perhaps Grymmore?"

It was Oliver who solved the riddle. "Great heavens, there *are* queens on Nirriim! Ant colonies have a queen, and the ants of the Timere Forest would be no exception. The Blue Spectre must be referring to the ant queen's treasure chamber."

"Oliver, you are brilliant. It has to be the ants – they must have taken Edmund's pack back to their nest. Now we know what we are looking for."

Oliver covered his mouth with his paw. "Oh dear, I just had a rather unnerving thought – if the ants are twenty feet long, how big will their queen be?"

Edmund felt cold fear creeping up his arms like a thousand tiny marching ants.

Bartholomew took one look at Edmund and changed the subject. "Let's have breakfast and then we'll head out to the Paw and Dagger Tavern."

Edmund's fear diminished over breakfast as they discussed their impending visit to the Paw and Dagger, but now he had a new concern. "Song told me we need to be wary of the Paw and Dagger Tavern. It's frequented by ruffians, treasure hunters, and vicious bandits. I'll keep my eyes open for troublemakers, but you and Oliver need to be careful just the same."

"We'll be fine, Edmund. I'll just blink a defense sphere up if there's any danger."

"Of course, but if things go bad, I'll be there." Edmund smacked his two fists together.

Bartholomew didn't know what to think about Edmund's comment – it was unlike him to say such things. The pace of Edmund's worrisome transformation seemed to be increasing. "I'm not expecting trouble, Edmund. We're simply seeking out a treasure hunter who can help us find the Queen's Treasure Chamber. The Seventh Key certainly could be in the Timere Forest, but you never know. Ants that big could have tunnels extending out hundreds of miles. A seasoned treasure hunter will know more about these things than we do."

They left their room and walked downstairs to the dining hall where Song was waiting for them.

"Ah, good morning, everyone. You're just in time for breakfast. I trust you all slept well?"

After listening to a few lively stories from Song about the shady goings on at the Paw and Dagger Tavern, Bartholomew, Oliver, and Edmund made their way through the streets and alleys toward the southern end of the island, then on to the dock district. Song had been quite correct about this being a rough part of town. Edmund was getting more than his share of surly stares, but his imposing presence also kept the ruffians at bay. Nobody wanted to tangle with a Rabbiton, especially in a world where they still told tales of the ancient A6 Warrior Rabbitons.

Following Song's directions they arrived at the Paw and Dagger in less than a half hour. It was a dilapidated two story structure protruding out over the lake, supported by heavy wood pilings. The sign hanging out in front was gray, weathered, and barely readable.

THE PAW & DAGGER TAVERN

Walk In and Crawl Out

Oliver frowned. "Good heavens, Bartholomew, do you really think we should go in there? This establishment looks disreputable at best, and completely treacherous at worst."

Edmund snorted. "Just the way I like 'em." He swung the door open and strode into the tavern.

Oliver looked as though he might come unraveled. "'*Just the way I like 'em??*' Bartholomew, what has come over Edmund? Why is he behaving this way? Is he looking for trouble?"

Bartholomew shook his head. "I have no answer. Maybe reliving his memories of the ants changed him somehow. Nothing seems to scare him anymore. I hate to say it, but he does seem to be looking for a fight. I guess we'd better make certain he doesn't cause any trouble. Stay close behind me. I'll pop up a sphere of defense if anything goes wrong."

Bartholomew swung the door open and they stepped into the tavern, their noses instantly assaulted by the pungent odors of stale smoke and week old ale. As his eyes grew accustomed to the dim light, Bartholomew saw at least twenty patrons in the tavern. Most were sitting at tables with pints of ale in front of them, some sat at the bar, and a few were lying unconscious on the floor. Song was right, this was a tough looking group of individuals, a ragged mix of rabbits, muroidians and mice. Bandoleers seemed to be the accoutrement of choice, most holding daggers or throwing knives. A few had glass vaporizer pistols strapped to their belts, and several carried the ancient but still deadly bender bows.

The tavern was eerily quiet, with only a few low whispers. Every patron there was staring at Edmund, who was leaning back against the bar facing the tables. Some of the customers had their paws resting nervously on their weapons. Edmund's presence was making them very uncomfortable.

Bartholomew decided he'd better take control of the situation. "The Rabbiton is with us. We're not looking for trouble, we're looking to hire a treasure hunter."

Seconds later the tavern was once again filled with the sound of a dozen conversations and the clinking of ale mugs. No treasure hunters came forward so they found an empty table and sat down. The bartender shuffled over to them, drying his hands with a ratty gray towel. "What'll it be, rabs?"

Oliver slowly tapped his chin, trying to decide. "Hmm... I believe I shall have a small glass of Orvieto Pinot Grigio and an éclair, if they are freshly baked."

The bartender's face could have been carved from stone. "You got two choices. Ale or ale."

"Ah, very well then, I shall have a tall glass of ale. I trust your glasses are clean?"

"When you're drunk enough it don't matter."

Bartholomew spoke up. "Ale for me too. You know any treasure hunters looking for work?"

"Ehh. Most of these derelict furballs would rather sit and drink than earn a few honest credits. I got two mice who might be lookin'. I'll send them over. Watch yourself though, they don't come any tougher than these two." The bartender shuffled back towards the bar.

Edmund had been watching Bartholomew talk to the

bartender and strolled across the room to their table. "Any luck with a treasure hunter?"

Bartholomew nodded. "He's sending a couple of hunters over now. He said they're tough."

Edmund gave a snort. "We'll see about that."

Oliver gave Edmund a worrisome look. "Great heavens, Edmund, what a strange thing to say. Please don't cause any trouble."

Edmund looked sincerely perplexed. "Why would I start any trouble?"

Oliver shook his head. "I apologize, Edmund, I'm not sure why I said that." He glanced over to Bartholomew, who was studying Edmund's face closely.

"These must be the treasure hunters." Oliver pointed to two mice heading across the tavern towards them. The bartender hadn't been joking, this was a pair of tough looking hunters. Each had two bandoleers forming an X across their chest, both filled with an assortment of gleaming daggers and knives. The mouse on the left was carrying a wicked looking two-bladed axe, while the mouse on the right had a battered old sword in a worn leather sheath strapped to his back. Their hats were pulled down low, almost covering their eyes. Both of them had vicious scowls on their faces.

Oliver whispered, "I don't like the looks of them. Perhaps we should leave now."

Bartholomew gave a reassuring smile. "I'm wearing the Eleventh Ring, Oliver. That puts the odds in our favor, no matter what happens."

The two mice approached the table. The axe-wielding mouse looked them over slowly, then growled, "Who's in charge here?"

Bartholomew replied. "I guess that would be me. You're the treasure hunters?"

The mouse snorted. "Good guess. You must be the smart one, cause it sure ain't him." He nodded towards Oliver. The mouse turned his head and spat disgustingly onto the floor. The second mouse gave an unpleasant laugh.

Oliver gulped, his eyes darting over to Edmund.

Bartholomew saw a green thought cloud float out of the second mouse's ear and drew it to him. He blinked twice, rubbing his paw quickly back and forth across his mouth. "Umm... what do they call you?"

"I'm Lightning..."

Without missing a beat the second mouse added, "...and I'm Thunder."

This was followed by a strained silence, broken a moment later by Oliver. "Why do they call you Lightning? Is that what your parents named you?"

The scowl on Lightning's face grew more pronounced. "They call me that because I move like lightning."

Oliver nodded, the light of understanding in his eyes. "Ah, so you're a shaper then. You have the ability to blink instantly from place to place?"

Lightning stared coldly Oliver. "Did I say I was a shaper?? I said I move like lightning. It's an expression. You know, to move like lightning? Get it?"

"So you're saying you don't have shaping skills, but in general you move a great deal faster than ordinary mice do?"

Lightning's temper boiled over. "Holy creekers, are you even dimmer than you look?? Do you need to have a talk with the blade of my axe??"

Bartholomew stepped in to rescue Oliver from the rapidly escalating confrontation. "I'm pleased to meet you, Lightning. My name is Bartholomew. We're looking for a couple of experienced treasure hunters."

Oliver was oblivious, turning to the second mouse. "Why do they call you Thunder? It seems beyond simple chance that two treasure hunters named Thunder and Lightning would meet and become partners. Do all Nirriimian treasure hunters have weather related names?"

Thunder glared at Oliver, his lip curling with unmasked derision. "They call me Thunder because my fists MAKE THE SOUND OF THUNDER WHEN THEY RAIN DOWN DESTRUCTION ON MY ENEMIES!" He pounded his fists on the table, his face contorted with anger.

"That's extraordinary. Did you know thunder is caused by lightning? The intensity of the heat from the lightning expands the air so rapidly it creates explosive shock waves, resulting in the sound we know as thunder." Oliver looked as though he expected Thunder to find this a rather fascinating bit of knowledge.

Thunder looked helplessly over to Bartholomew. "Creekers, what's wrong with your friend? Our names are Thunder and Lightning and we are rough and tumble treasure hunters. There's no need to make this so complicated."

Lightning growled, "Perhaps this will help you understand my name!" His arm shot up and a gleaming dagger appeared in it. There was a silver blur and the dagger stood quivering in the wooden table top. A cold smile played across his face. He twirled his long whiskers with one paw.

Edmund nonchalantly plucked the dagger out of the table with two fingers and held it in front of Bartholomew. Bartholomew flicked his wrist and the dagger vanished in a blink of light. He flicked his wrist again and the dagger shot down from the ceiling, burying itself to the hilt in the table top only inches from Thunder's paw.

Lightning looked at the dagger, then at Edmund and Bartholomew, then back at the dagger. He held up one paw, a frozen smile on his face. "Excuse us for one moment, please." Thunder and Lightning walked out of earshot, glancing back at Edmund and Bartholomew. Thunder was whispering to Lightning in a highly animated fashion. Lightning held up both paws, making a vehement reply, obviously upset by whatever Thunder had whispered. Their conversation continued on for several minutes, replete with waving paws, stomping feet, and the occasional shouted insult, but finally they returned to the table. Lightning smiled pleasantly, his eyes on the silver dagger protruding from the table top.

"Perhaps we should begin again. We may look a little tougher than we really are. The problem is no one will hire us if they think we can't handle danger."

Bartholomew nodded, doing his best not to smile. He had seen through their facade the moment he drew Lightning's thought to him. "It's a pleasure to meet you both, and we would like to hire you. We are not looking for hardened warriors or murderous bandits, we are looking for treasure hunters – mice who can think clearly and unravel a trail of clues which will lead us to a lost object of great importance. I believe you are exactly who we are looking for."

Thunder and Lightning gave each other gleeful

grins. “When do we start?” Lightning set the oversized axe down on the floor. “Whew, that thing is a *lot* heavier than it looks. My name is Klanndirr, and this is Binndirr, but you should call us Thunder and Lightning. We grew up together and always wanted to be treasure hunters. We made up our own names.”

Oliver nodded stiffly. His feathers were still ruffled by Lightning’s comment about him looking dim. “Bartholomew and I are old friends also. May I ask what experience you have in the field of treasure hunting?”

“This will be our first job.”

Chapter 30

The Map

After finishing their ale the group exited the Paw and Dagger, heading back to the Singers Guild to discuss their plans. Edmund struck up a conversation with Thunder and Lightning, eventually telling them he had met the Blue Monks.

Lightning was enthralled with Edmund's tale. "I can't believe the Blue Monks sang for you – the Master Singers of Nirriim! Creekers, weren't you afraid? I heard you burn to ashes if they even look at your eyes. And your friend Bartholomew is a shaper– that's amazing! My mom's cousin knew a shaper who could stick a dagger through his arm and it didn't hurt him. Can you imagine? A dagger right through his arm! Hey, what are you guys looking for anyway?"

After listening to Thunder and Lightning for a few minutes, Oliver lost all hope the two mice would be of any help to them. He leaned over to Bartholomew and whispered, "I hope you're not paying them very much." He chuckled at his own joke.

Bartholomew just smiled. "Oliver, you should know

by now things are seldom what they seem to be. I have a good feeling about them."

Edmund answered Lightning's question. "We're looking for something called the Queen's Treasure Chamber."

Lightning took a step back. "What now? You're looking for what??"

"The Queen's Treasure Chamber."

Thunder let out a raspy, "Holy creekers, the Queen's Treasure Chamber?"

Lightning began laughing wildly, pounding Thunder on the arm. "I told you! I told you! Didn't I tell you?"

Thunder nodded. "Holy creekers, you were right. You did tell me."

Lightning turned to Bartholomew. "We have to go. We'll see you tomorrow at the Singers Guild." He grabbed Thunder by the arm. "Hurry up! Let's go!" The two of them took off down the cobblestone street, laughing and yelling until they disappeared around a corner.

Oliver was the first to speak. "Great heavens, what in the world was that about? Are they dim? Are you sure it's safe to be around those two? To be quite honest, they seem a little unstable."

Bartholomew shrugged. "They're just young, that's all. I have a strong feeling by tomorrow afternoon we'll be very glad we met them. They were certainly excited about something."

During dinner that evening Bartholomew recounted to Song the details of their visit to the Paw and Dagger. Song had spoken with his inner voice earlier in the day, asking about the Seventh Key, but had received no information of any practical value. "Why do you think

Edmund needs to find the key? Is it possible the key's return will trigger an event?"

Bartholomew answered. "I don't think so. The keys have been together for thousands of years and nothing has happened. More than likely returning the Seventh Key will affect some event far in the future. Look at how much Edmund has influenced our lives, fifteen hundred years after he was created. Perhaps a thousand years from now some adventuring rabbit will desperately need the Seventh Key, just the way Edmund the Explorer needed it to retrieve the time throttle. We simply have no way of knowing why the key must be returned. There could be a hundred separate reasons, each one important in its own way."

Early the following morning there was a furious pounding at the front door of the Guild. A rather vexed Song hurried from the dining room to answer it. "What ever happened to patience?"

Two rough looking mice stood at the entryway wearing crossed bandoleers and daggers, their hats pulled down low. "We are here to see Bartholomew Rabbit regarding an extremely urgent matter of the utmost importance."

"Ah, you must be Thunder and Lightning."

"You've heard of us??" Lightning grinned with delight.

"Indeed so. Bartholomew has told us... all about you. Do come in. Have you had breakfast yet?"

Thunder shook his head. "No time for breakfast. We have to talk to Bartholomew, Edmund, and Oliver immediately. This is urgent business. Urgent."

Song nodded. "Of course, you must see them immediately. Wait here and I will inform Bartholomew of your arrival."

Before Bartholomew was halfway down the hallway, Lightning dashed towards him hollering, "Look! Look at this!" He held up a tattered piece of cloth in front of Bartholomew."

Bartholomew looked at it carefully. "May I?"

Lightning handed him the cloth.

Bartholomew showed it to Oliver and Edmund.

Oliver said, "Good heavens, is that what I think it is?"

Bartholomew nodded. "It's old, and it's only a portion of a map, but it's clear as day right here – it says 'Queen's Treasure Chamber'. I'm not quite sure what these other words are. This one looks like 'unes', whatever that means."

Oliver pointed to the map. "I don't like the looks of that one. It says '*All Beware the Wyrme of Deth*'."

Bartholomew turned to Lightning. "Where did you get this?"

"It's been passed down through our family for generations, but nobody knows how old it really is. My grandpa and I tried to decipher it, but none of it made sense except the Queen's Treasure Chamber."

It was Edmund who solved the mystery. "I know where that is. We've already been there."

Oliver looked dubious. "I would most certainly recall having met a creature named the Wyrme of Deth."

Edmund continued. "We never saw the Wyrme of Deth, but we did see what it did to the *Adventurer II* in the sand dunes. The word 'unes' only lacks the letter 'd' to make it 'dunes'. The Queen's Treasure Chamber is located beneath the sand dunes where our ship crashed."

Oliver's eyes grew wide. "That monstrous creature was the Wyrme of Deth? We cannot face a beast like that. It's not even remotely possible. That dreadful monstrosity would swallow us in an instant! Look what it did to our ship – shook it like a pterosaur shaking a–" He was about to say 'mouse' but remembered who their hosts were. "My point is, it sadly appears we must return home without the Seventh Key."

Edmund shook his head. "No. We have no choice, we have to recover the key and the time throttle. Even if we wanted to go back, we still need the Seventh Key to open the World Door. I have no idea how to open a spectral doorway leading back to Earth. We will have to find a way to defeat the Wyrme of Deth, even if–."

Lightning cut Edmund off. "What key? What's a time throttle? You know where the Queen's Treasure Chamber is?"

Bartholomew answered, "We know more or less where it is. This drawing of trees on your map represents the Timere Forest. If we had traveled directly north rather than west after we crashed we would have entered the forest. It's a good thing we didn't because I doubt we would have survived the ants."

Edmund spoke up. "We have to face the ants again. I must visit the Tree of Eyes to learn the fate of Edmund the Explorer. Maybe the Tree will also know what happened to the Seventh Key and the time throttle."

Bartholomew was remembering Ennzarr's words. If they didn't return the Seventh Key to Pterosaur Valley the change Edmund was going through would somehow destroy him. He would cease to exist. Bartholomew put his paw on Edmund's arm. "Edmund, you're right.

We have no choice in the matter. We have to find the Seventh Key. There are some things that must be done, just as we had to defeat Zoran the Emerald Shaper."

Thunder and Lightning looked completely baffled by the ongoing conversation. Oliver was looking ill.

Bartholomew handed the map back to Lightning. "Come to the library and I will explain everything to both of you. Then you can decide whether or not to join us on this quest. Don't make your decision lightly. There is a real possibility one or more of us will not return. We have no idea how to defeat the Wyrme of Deth. We don't even know what the Wyrme of Deth is."

Edmund's eyes were burning bright. "And the ants. We can't forget the ants." He smacked his fists together.

Chapter 31

Return to the Timere Forest

One day later, a pair of long wooden boats pushed off from the Island of the Blue Monks. Thunder and Lighting had enthusiastically joined the quest, undeterred by Oliver's terrifying tales of the Wyrme of Deth. The Red Monks dropped them off on the northern shore of the lake and bid their farewells. One of the monks presented Edmund with a small golden whistle. "Should you visit us again, blow this whistle and a boat will appear to carry you across the lake. A friend of Edmund the Explorer is always welcome here." Edmund thanked the monk and the five adventurers set off into the jungle towards the Timere Forest.

As they fought their way through the tangled undergrowth, Thunder and Lightning kept up a steady stream of stories about their life on the Island of Blue Monks. It turned out that Thunder had been adopted by Lightning's family after they found him wandering in the jungle as a mouseling, and Thunder and Lightning had essentially grown up as brothers. When they were of an age to leave their home they rented a small shack on the island and found employment which soon proved to be less than fulfilling. They had dreams of becoming treasure hunters – dreams spurred on by Lightning's grandpa and the mysterious map passed down through their family. Their initial attempt at being treasure hunters had proven to be remarkably unsuccessful, despite their recovery of a few small artifacts in the area. They eventually took work doing chores for the owner of the Paw and Dagger Tavern, hoping this would lead to a spot on a real treasure hunt. After six long months of waiting, they finally got their wish. It hadn't hurt that the other treasure hunters were all too drunk to care who got the job.

Thunder and Lightning were drawn to Edmund, more than likely because he was different from anything they had ever seen. "What are you going to do to the ants when you find them, Edmund? Are you going to clobber the Wyrme with your fists or let Bartholomew vaporize it with shaping? How strong are you? Could you lift me and Thunder and Oliver all at once? How come you're so tall?"

Surprisingly, Edmund enjoyed the attention and began telling them stories of his adventures with Edmund the Explorer, plus many of the tales Edmund the Explorer had told him. "Escaping the creekers was *nothing* compared to the time Edmund the Explorer had to climb an icy four thousand foot vertical rock face while being chased by *deadly poisonous snow spiders.*"

Bartholomew was glad to see Edmund laughing again. Thunder and Lightning were just what he needed to help him recover from the loss of Edmund the

Explorer. Bartholomew wished Clara was here to see this. She would appreciate the appearance of Thunder and Lightning as a gift bestowed upon Edmund by the universe. Cavern had said it many times before. "The most valuable gifts in life often arrive in very strange packages."

Despite the presence of Thunder and Lightning, Edmund's mood began to darken as they drew closer to the Timere Forest. His stories about Edmund the Explorer grew shorter and then came to an end. He stopped laughing. Bartholomew suspected his terrible fear of the ants was returning, but when he reminded Edmund he could shape a defensive sphere to protect them, Edmund had only nodded absently. His mood worsened after they entered the forest. He became distant, hardly speaking. Perhaps the sight of the towering trees was bringing back the painful memories of his first visit, memories of what had happened to Edmund the Explorer.

One full day passed with no sign of the ants, then another. Everyone except Edmund began to relax, including Oliver. "You know, it has been fifteen hundred years since... since you were here before, Edmund. It's quite possible the ant colony died off, or moved on to another location. A queen ant doesn't live forever, and the new queen will often fly great distances to start her own colony. It's also very possible these gigantic ants were an anomaly, the last of their kind, and died off due to their great size, just as the pterosaurs did."

Lightning cried out, "I see an ant!"

Edmund's head whipped around. Bartholomew shot up a defensive sphere around them. "Where??"

Embarrassed by the unexpected stir his comment had made, Lightning pointed to the ground. "Uh... right here, next to my foot?"

Edmund saw the tiny black ant meandering past Lightning's foot. He stared at it, his fists rapidly clenching and unclenching. Something about this harmless little creature triggered a dreadful rage in Edmund, a rage that spiraled with every step the ant took. Ants. It was the ants who had filled him with his blinding helpless fear, it was the ants who had crushed Edmund the Explorer and ripped him from Emma's world, and it was the ants who had stolen the Seventh Key. He saw once again the cold and expressionless face of the giant ant as it squeezed the life from Edmund the Explorer. Something inside Edmund twisted and snapped. He knew what to do now. He would kill all the ants. He would smash them and hammer them and pound them to dust. Edmund stomped his foot as hard as he could on the ground. Let them come. He would kill them all. He would obliterate each and every one of them. Before he could stomp his foot again, however, he heard a voice coming from deep inside him.

"Edmund, what matters in this world is intention. Just as Rabbitons were programmed by the Elders, the ants were programmed by nature.When they attacked Edmund the Explorer there were no evil intentions, they were simply doing what they had been programmed to do. They were surviving. It is hard for you to see clearly now, but your choice to walk of your own free will through these terrible fires of life will eventually bring you a great happiness."

Edmund weaved slightly, then fell to his knees and,

like a sinking ship, rolled over onto the sunlit forest floor.

"Something happened to Edmund!" Lightning's eyes were wide with fear. Bartholomew and Oliver dashed over and knelt down next to him.

"Edmund? Are you all right? What happened?"

Edmund slowly sat up, a dazed look on his face. "I don't know. I wanted to kill the ants. I wanted to kill them all, but it wasn't their fault. A voice said it wasn't their fault."

Bartholomew stared at Edmund. "What voice? Who told you that?"

Edmund shook his head. "I don't know. It seemed like something the Thirteenth Monk would say but it wasn't his voice."

Bartholomew put his paw on Edmund's shoulder. "Are you okay? We need to keep moving."

Edmund rose to his feet. "I believe I am fine. I am no longer angry at the ants. Perhaps it was my inner voice, although it was not the same voice which told me to open the spectral door to Nirriim. It's all quite confusing. On my return to the Fortress I shall have the A9s check my programming crystals for any possible corruption."

Conversation was subdued for the rest of the day, but gradually picked up as their journey progressed. Edmund's mood seemed to be improving rapidly, something Bartholomew attributed to the loss of his anger towards the ants. He would make a joke now and then, especially with Thunder and Lightning, and was telling Edmund the Explorer stories again. This may have made him feel as though Edmund the Explorer was once again walking alongside him.

The giant ants never came, and the trek through the forest became far more enjoyable without the constant fear of being attacked. They could walk and talk normally now. Despite Edmund's curious incident with the unknown voice, Thunder and Lightning were as exuberant as ever, dashing here and there, often climbing the smaller trees just because they could. On one occasion Bartholomew shaped a two hundred foot rope ladder from the one of the great trees, but as it turned out Thunder and Lightning were not especially fond of heights. After they had climbed twenty feet they decided they'd had enough, returning to the safety of the forest floor.

Edmund did not tease them about it. He simply said, "That's why they invented minifloaters." Then he had to explain what minifloaters were and tell a few hair-raising stories about his experiences with them, usually involving a chase and some hideous flying beast with razor sharp teeth.

On the morning of the sixth day Edmund spotted the circle of trees surrounding the clearing where the Tree of Eyes grew. He held up his hand for the party to stop. "The Tree of Eyes is in here. Bartholomew, this is not the Tree you know. Fifteen hundred years ago this tree was far older and wiser than the Tree of Eyes in our world. I have no idea what it will be like today." Edmund slipped between the massive trunks, pushing his way through the brush and foliage and into the clearing, followed closely behind by Bartholomew, Oliver, Thunder, and Lightning.

Chapter 32

Edmund the Explorer Goes Home

Edmund walked towards the Tree of Eyes. A thousand eyes turned towards him. Thunder and Lightning murmured to each other. “Holy creekers! It has eyes all over it!” The truth was they couldn’t wait to get back and tell their friends about this extraordinary creature.

Edmund was having a very different reaction. He was remembering the sight of Edmund the Explorer wrapped in a leafy cocoon. The anger that had flared so brightly inside him was gone now, and all that was left was a deep sadness. He missed Edmund the Explorer and Emma.

The Tree was the first to speak. A long tendril reached out and wrapped itself around Edmund’s arm. “Hello, Edmund. We are pleased to see you after all these years. We see you are healing nicely from the events which occurred during your last visit. We also see you wish to know the final fate of your friend Edmund the Explorer."

"Yes, I would like to know what became of him, if he has moved on to another world beyond this one."

"We have come to understand the nature of time and are able to move about within this river at will. We can tell you what happened, or if you would prefer, we can show you. You will see Edmund the Explorer and others you may know, but you will be unable to communicate with them."

Edmund looked back at Bartholomew. "What do you think I should do?"

The Tree of Eyes looked at Bartholomew and Oliver. "We are pleased to see you also, Bartholomew and Oliver. We have fond memories of your visits when we were very young. We understand how foolish we must have appeared back then, but that is the nature of creatures born into this world. We have grown in awareness since those distant times. We remember teaching you how to read thought clouds, Bartholomew. We also clearly remember the look on Oliver's face the first time he heard us speak." One of the eyes giggled.

Oliver bristled slightly, but then laughed, remembering how astonished he had been. "My word, when I think about that it makes me realize how much I too have changed since then, and all the astonishing things I have seen and learned."

Bartholomew answered Edmund's question. "I would let the Tree show you what happened. It will seem real to you then."

Edmund nodded and said to the Tree, "Please show

me what happened to Edmund the Explorer, and what happened to me."

"Very well." The Tree's branches rustled in an invisible wind and everything around it blurred, returning sharply into focus moments later. Edmund looked down at his hands but saw nothing. He was only awareness floating in empty space. It reminded him of his journey through the Void.

Edmund saw a gleaming Rabbiton lying on the ground by the Tree of Eyes. He recognized it as his own A2 body. It was partially wrapped in the Tree's green tendrils, but they were quickly unraveling. He heard the familiar hum of a blinker and looked up.

Like a great dragonfly, the blinker hovered overhead. A pale green beam of light shot down, scanning back and forth over Edmund's old body. The beam disappeared and the blinker darted down next to the Tree, setting down silently on the ground. The ramp flipped down and a pilot emerged from the craft. He strode quickly over to the A2 body, kneeling down next to it, opening a small panel on its chest. A transparent holoscreen popped into the air above the A2 and the pilot swiped through several pages.

"It lost power for a while. That's why its memory is fried. It's going to need a total refurb. Other than that it's fine." The pilot stood up and pulled a silver cylinder out of a side pocket. He was about to flip it on when he noticed the Tree of Eyes for the first time.

"Holy Narkks, that's one weird lookin' tree. Looks almost like it has eyes. This world gives me the creeps. Load the A2 and let's get the blink out of here. I can't wait to get back to Earth. Keep your eyes open for Anarkkian attack ships – I don't want to get dusted in some loopy world like this. I'm guessing a neuro beam got this A2. Who knows what it was doing way out here."

The pilot pressed a small tab on the metallic cylinder and a shimmering gray light hit the A2. The Rabbiton vibrated, rising several feet into the air. He used the cylinder to maneuver the floating A2 through the blinker door. Edmund heard the words, "Strap and roll, rabs." The ramp snapped shut and the blinker zipped straight up several hundred feet, held for a moment, then shot forward, disappearing into a large bank of clouds.

The world blurred once again, then returned to normal. There was a brilliant flash of light and a rabbit appeared next to the Tree of Eyes. Edmund drew his breath in sharply. He would recognize the long green cloak anywhere. It was Bruno Rabbit, and Bruno's expression was grim. "How is he?"

The Tree of Eyes replied, "We will show you." The center of the Tree began to rustle, a long leafy cocoon emerging. The cocoon was connected to the tree by hundreds of green tendrils, some almost a half inch in diameter. The Tree gently lowered the cocoon until it came to rest on the grass. The tendrils unraveled, withdrawing back inside the tree. Lying in front of Bruno Rabbit was the body of Edmund the Explorer. His eyes were closed, his body still.

Bruno asked, "Is he alive?"

"He is not alive, but neither is he dead. We have stopped the passage of time around him."

Bruno looked down at Edmund the Explorer. "I liked him. He was different from most of the explorers I've known. He cared more about rabbits than he did about treasure. What happened to the A2 he had with him?"

"A blinker scout picked it up and took it back to Earth."

"You did everything you could?"

"We did. The key was nowhere to be found, nor was the time throttle."

Bruno gave a sigh. "He did the best he could. He prevented the Anarkkians from using the throttle and he sent Neilana back home. Edmund the Explorer will be one of Earth's great unsung heros, which is probably how he would have wanted it. I will do what I can for him."

Bruno kneeled down next to Edmund the Explorer and cupped his paws together, a small gray swirling sphere appearing above them. Edmund recognized it immediately. It was a spectral doorway like the one he'd created to enter Nirriim. The familiar flashes of lightning appeared within the stormy sphere as it grew in size. When it had grown to almost four feet in diameter, Bruno took Edmund the Explorer's paw and they vanished through the doorway. With a single clap of thunder the doorway was gone. Bruno Rabbit had taken Edmund the Explorer back to Earth.

The clearing around the Tree blurred briefly. Edmund looked down and saw he had his body again. He turned around, gazing at his four friends.

Oliver said, "Bruno brought him home, Edmund. He brought Edmund the Explorer home."

Lightning blurted out, "Was that you lying on the ground, Edmund? What happened to you after the flying ball took you away?"

Edmund shrugged. "I don't know. The next thing I

remember was my first day in the Central Information Repository. It wasn't until I read a book about Edmund the Explorer that I had any recollection of having met him. I had forgotten everything about our adventures together, and everything about Emma."

They decided to rest for a day at the Tree of Eyes. Bartholomew shaped several large tents and all the usual creature comforts. Oliver kept busy preparing meals and baking his delightful pastries. Thunder and Lightning told him his éclairs were the best they'd ever had, but Oliver still wasn't completely satisfied with them. "They're good, but they're not of the same calibre as Madame Beffy's éclairs. Try as I might, I can't seem to duplicate a certain flavor in hers. It's quite maddening. Perhaps the next time I visit I will get down on my knees and beg her to tell me the secret ingredient." He laughed loudly, imagining himself begging for her recipe.

It took Edmund a day to process what the Tree of Eyes had shown him. He knew how he'd gotten back to Earth, and he knew Bruno had taken Edmund the Explorer home. But where did he take him? And what had happened to him after he got there? Was he frozen in time forever?

Bartholomew took several long walks alone in the Timere Forest. He wished Clara was there with him to see the magnificent trees. She would love them. Maybe when this was over he would use the Seventh Key and surprise her with a trip to the Timere Forest. It would also be fun for Clara to become acquainted with the older and wiser Tree of Eyes. He gave a rueful smile. It was always a little embarrassing to think back on the days before he had found his Great Gem, back when he had been a silly and self-absorbed rabbit. He remembered his confrontation with the rabid wolf on his first adventuring trip. He had heard the wolf growling and thought it was his own stomach growling, telling him it was time for lunch. It seemed like a lifetime ago. Anything before Clara seemed like a lifetime ago.

Now he was a seasoned adventurer and wore the Eleventh Ring, a ring few shapers even knew existed. He thought about the new skill Ennzarr had taught him. The Traveling Eye skill was mind-boggling – he could travel anywhere in the universe instantly, flying through matter as though it wasn't even there. An idea popped into his head, but he wasn't certain if it came from the Cavern of Silence or his own mind. These two centers of awareness seemed to be slowly merging into one.

His new idea was quite simple. Once they reached the sand dunes he would use the Traveling Eye to explore the ant tunnels, uncovering what secrets he could regarding the queen ant and the mysterious Wyrme of Deth. He might even be able to locate the Queen's Treasure Chamber. This would keep everyone safe for a while, but eventually someone would have to go down into the Queen's Treasure Chamber to retrieve the Seventh Key and the time throttle. Whoever did that would have to face the Wyrme of Deth. This was a creature who had pulled a thirty foot long flying carriage beneath the sand in a few seconds. They didn't even know what the beast looked like. He recalled his confrontation with the evil and powerful Zoran the Emerald Shaper. At the time it had seemed an unsurmountable obstacle, but he had emerged victorious. Hopefully this adventure would end as well as that one had. It had to end well. Edmund's life depended on it. A wave of fear rolled through Bartholomew.

Thunder and Lightning kept themselves busy writing in their new journals. Bartholomew had shaped each of them a leather bound journal and a gold pen and pencil set. They were having great fun writing and sketching everything they had seen on the trip. They were also learning from Edmund the art of embellishing their tales of adventure. One of the drawings Bartholomew saw was of Lightning riding on the back of a gigantic ant. Besides his own stories, Lightning was also recording the tales he heard from Edmund about Edmund the Explorer. In the evenings Lightning would read them aloud to Edmund, making certain he had not missed anything. Thunder and Lightning told Edmund they hoped they would see even half the things Edmund the Explorer had seen during his lifetime.

Chapter 33

Lightning's Lesson

"Let's move out." Bartholomew swung his pack onto his shoulder, grinning at the party of adventurers. "I think we might need a duplonium wagon to carry us all. What do you think, Oliver?"

Oliver laughed loudly. "A duplonium powered steam locomotive might be more suitable for this crowd. If I remember correctly the duplonium wagon was rather confining, especially when we were hiding under the crates from the pterosaurs."

After saying their farewells to the Tree of Eyes they headed back out into the Timere Forest. Edmund flicked on a transparent screen in front of him and swiped through the pages until he found a map of the area. They would walk north for five days, then head directly east for another three days until they reached the sand dunes.

Bartholomew pointed to a small yellow area on Edmund's map. "According to Lightning's map, the Queen's Treasure Chamber should be about here. We arrived through the doorway almost fifty miles away from the Chamber. This Wyrme creature covers a lot of territory, and there could be more than one of them. They must have tunnels running for hundreds of miles beneath the sand dunes."

Oliver's ears perked up at the mention of the Wyrme of Deth. "What do you suppose it is? A creature that large would have to consume an enormous amount of food simply to survive. What would it eat? I didn't see any large creatures in the desert. Rather strange. I suppose there could be other creatures living beneath the sand we aren't aware of. Oh dear, I wish I hadn't thought of that. The Wyrme is frightening enough by itself."

Lighting snorted. "Relax, Oliver. Bartholomew and Edmund can handle the Wyrme, no problem. Edmund can just punch the big dimmer in the nose and Bartholomew can shape it into pieces, and then you can cook it up into a big juicy worm stew."

Thunder made a gagging noise. "Urrrghhhh. Worm stew! Creekers! I just ate!"

Edmund smiled as he listened to Thunder and Lighting. It reminded him of Edmund the Explorer's joking before an especially risky undertaking. Underneath his humor, however, lay a realistic appreciation for the dangers involved. Edmund the Explorer had not been one to underestimate an adversary. Edmund didn't think Thunder and Lightning were capable of such forethought yet. He would have to keep a watchful eye on them to make certain they didn't do anything foolish and hurt themselves.

The walk through the forest was an enjoyable time for the adventurers. Thunder and Lightning dashed around, scouring the edge of the trail for lost treasure.

"Oliver! Are these Nirriimian white crystals?"

"Those are quartz crystals. They're more transparent than the white crystals. Keep looking though. Many times you'll find white crystals near deposits of quartz."

Oliver found the local flora and fauna to be most intriguing, making sketches of the various plants and animals he spotted along the way. Nirriim was a strange world, in many ways quite different from Earth. There were times when Oliver was uncertain whether a certain life form was plant or animal. On more than one occasion they ran into what appeared to be a sunlit patch of lovely purple wildflowers, only to have them make squeaking noises and run off into the forest.

"You know, Bartholomew, I remember when I thought I knew all there was to know about the world of science. It's quite astonishing how little we really do know. I could study the life in this one forest for ten lifetimes, and this is one forest on one planet in a universe filled with more planets than there are grains of sand on the beach. I have spent most of my life studying science, but there are moments when I feel like a bunny who can barely count his toes."

Bartholomew smiled. "Only the very wisest rabbits know they don't really know anything."

Their days in the forest rolled on as they headed north. Bartholomew shaped tents and food for them in the evenings, although Oliver always insisted on preparing the meals. On the morning of the sixth day they reached the northern edge of the forest and turned east.

Early that afternoon Thunder and Lightning were cavorting about at the edge of the forest trail when Lightning spotted a large vine covered mound between two magnificent trees, each with a trunk at least fifty feet across. "I'm king of the hill!" Lightning clambered up the side of the mound and stood on top waving his arms at Thunder. "I'm king of the hill, knock me off if you dare!"

Thunder grabbed what looked like an overly ripe tomato from a large leafy plant and hurled it at Lightning, who danced wildly out of the way, in the process slipping on a patch of wet leaves. As he careened down the side of the mound he grabbed a pawful of vines to slow his descent, landing safely on the ground. Thunder stopped laughing and looked at the mound with a puzzled expression.

"What *is* that?"

Everyone looked. Beneath the dense covering of vines that Lightning had pulled away lay a gleaming blue metallic surface.

Bartholomew shot up a defensive sphere around everyone as a precaution. He had no idea what was inside the mound. "Everyone stand still!"

They waited for several minutes, and when nothing happened Bartholomew dropped the defensive sphere. He moved closer to the mound, motioning for everyone to stay where they were. A wide green beam shot out from his paw and scanned the mound. "There's no life inside it." A second beam then appeared, this one bright orange. He held the beam above the mound, then slowly moved it downward. The dense vines and branches covering the mound vanished instantly when the beam touched them. The object had been revealed.

Edmund let out a gasp. "It's a blinker! It's a blinker just like the one I flew in with Edmund the Explorer!" He strode over to the front of the blinker and put his hand on the smooth cool surface. A distant look appeared in his eyes. "I never thought I'd touch one of these again."

Oliver said, "Are you sure you should touch it? It must be hundreds of years old. It's power source could be very unstable."

Edmund shrugged, saying, "Everyone move back. I'm going to open the hatch." He tapped four nearly invisible tabs on the front of the craft. With a slight whirring noise the hatch flipped down. Edmund peered inside. "It's empty. Whoever was flying it must have survived the crash." He entered the blinker, studying the control panels. There were still a few small lights flashing on one side of the main panel. He tapped a triangular red tab but nothing happened. "The main power core is gone. They must have taken it with them. It won't fly without it." He glanced around the cabin but found nothing of any interest. The crew had stripped the craft of any usable technology.

Thunder and Lightning were peering into the blinker. "Can we look? Is there any treasure in there?"

Edmund hesitated, then said, "You can look. Don't touch anything. The power core is gone but there are still plenty of ways to hurt yourself in there."

Edmund stepped out of the craft as Thunder and Lightning dashed into it.

"Holy creekers, this is amazing!"

Edmund stepped over to Oliver and Bartholomew. "This makes real all my memories of flying with Edmund the Explorer. There really were blinkers, and I really did fly in them. I don't know why I can't seem to let go of this. I still miss Edmund the Explorer and Emma. I remember the first time Emma said–"

"Treasure!! We found treasure! Look at this, Edmund! This has to be worth at least a million credits!" Lightning came bounding out of the ship waving a transparent glass tube four inches in diameter and three feet long. "We're rich!"

Before anyone could even blink Edmund had leaped over to Lightning and ripped the glass tube from his paws. Edmund roared, "WHAT ARE YOU DOING? Are you trying to kill someone? What is wrong with you??"

Lightning shrunk away from Edmund, a terrified look on his face. "I... I just thought it was..."

Thunder stood in the doorway of the ship gaping at Edmund.

Bartholomew thought Lightning was going to burst into tears. He knew beneath all the bravado Lightning was not much more than a mouseling wearing a treasure hunter's costume. Edmund's behavior was startling, another symptom of his mysterious transition. When they had first met him there was an air of bunnylike innocence about him, but that had changed. Bartholomew wasn't altogether sure he liked this change. He was even more determined than ever now to find the Seventh Key.

Edmund lowered the glass tube. The only sound was the birds chirping in the forest canopy high overhead. "I'm sorry I scared you, Lightning, but I had to stop you. You could have killed any one of us, including yourself or Thunder."

"But I was just..."

"It's called a vape gun. They used them during the Anarkkian wars. Vape is short for vaporizing. It vaporizes matter." Edmund raised the glass tube to his shoulder, aiming it at one of the trees. He pressed the green tab at the base of the gun. There was a brief hum and an eight inch wide hole appeared in the tree, a hole that traveled deep into the trunk. "That could have been one of us if you had accidentally pushed the firing tab."

Lightning stared at the tree, then down at his feet. Edmund's face softened. "Everyone makes mistakes, Lightning. No one was hurt and next time you'll be careful. The Elders had technology far beyond anything you can imagine. There's a lot of it even I don't understand. If you're going to be a treasure hunter you have to know about the treasures you're hunting and the creatures you may encounter. I will teach you and Thunder as much as I know about the Elders' technology and about some of the beasts who inhabit the other worlds."

Lightning didn't say anything for several moments. Finally he looked up and said, "I'm sorry, Edmund. I won't do anything dumb again."

Edmund placed his hand gently on Lightning's shoulder. "We all do foolish things. Learning is never easy, and believe me, I've learned plenty of things the hard way."

The next morning Bartholomew covered the blinker with shaped leaves and vines so it would not be disturbed. Oliver wanted to have it brought back to the Fortress to study its technology. Edmund knew a little about their function, but not nearly enough for Oliver to fabricate one. Oliver already had plans to integrate the ship's technology into his next generation of flying carriages.

Chapter 34

The Beast from Below

"Strap and roll, rabs – and you too, treasure hunters!" Edmund slung the vape gun onto his shoulder and turned east, followed by Bartholomew, Oliver, Lightning, and Thunder. In three days they would arrive at the sand dunes.

As they trekked eastward through the forest the trees diminished in size while the distance between them increased. The adventurers' conversations were not as animated as they had been. They were, each in their own way, thinking about their inevitable confrontation with the Wyrme of Deth. They knew there was a realistic possibility that one or more of them would not survive the encounter.

Bartholomew revealed his plan as they strolled along through the forest. "Once we arrive at the dunes we'll set up camp on the desert's edge, well out of the Wyrme of Deth's reach. When we're settled in I'll use the Traveling Eye to explore the tunnels beneath the desert, hopefully locating the Queen's Treasure Chamber. It's unclear to me why the ants roamed the Timere Forest, and yet their queen's treasure chamber is located deep in the desert. I also don't know what role the Wyrme of Deth plays, whether it was friend or foe to the ants. But, as I always say, if we knew what was going to happen, it wouldn't be an adventure."

Edmund nodded, then gave a laugh. "You know, all this talk about sand dunes reminds me of the time I was trapped beneath the Quintarian Red Desert by a gigantic sand spider. I was wrapped inside a silk cocoon, being dragged through a pitch dark tunnel by two ferocious..."

Bartholomew was getting an uncomfortable feeling about Edmund's story. He was telling an Edmund the Explorer story as though it was his own adventure, as though he was the one who had experienced it.

Bartholomew wished Clara was there with him. "Clara could make sense of it. She can feel why rabbits do the things they do, even without reading their thoughts. She always tells me rabbits do everything for a reason. If a rabbit's behavior seems irrational, it's only because we don't understand the hidden logic that drives the behavior. What could Edmund gain from telling these stories? "Maybe he's taking on Edmund the Explorer's personality as a way of holding on to him, a way of keeping him alive. All I know is I don't want Edmund trying to be Edmund the Explorer. I like Edmund just the way he is. Or... the way he was." Bartholomew watched as Lightning scribbled madly in his journal, trying to get every word of Edmund's story. Nobody else questioned why Edmund was telling the story as though it was his own.

Three days later they crested a steep hill and

Lightning shouted out, "Desert! I see the desert! Creekers, it's a whopper!"

Bartholomew stepped to the top of the hill and scanned the horizon. Lightning was right, it was huge. An endless sea of sand dunes stretching out as far as he could see – and all of it possibly inhabited by deadly life forms. Bartholomew also knew they might have more than one Nirriimian sand worm to contend with. The universe never creates only one of any creature, and that rule certainly applied to the Wyrme of Deth. Bartholomew gave a long sigh. This was a painfully familiar feeling. He had felt it the day he faced Zoran the Emerald Shaper in the Fortress of Elders. The odds were stacked heavily against him and the clock was ticking. "What have I gotten myself into this time?" He turned around and looked at Oliver, who had a remarkably grave expression on his face.

"Bartholomew, how many Wyrmes of Deth do you think there are? I do know exceptionally large creatures will often stake out their own vast hunting area, and can be quite territorial about it. It is possible there might only be one Wyrme of Deth in this area. It's all quite nerve-racking, I must say. You saw how the Wyrme demolished the *Adventurer II* in a matter of seconds. All we have is the one vaporizing gun, and I doubt that is enough to stop something as monstrous as the Wyrme of Deth. Oh dear, I simply have no idea what to do. I'm afraid all my scientific knowledge will not be of much help to us here."

Bartholomew put on a positive face. "We'll think of something, my old friend. We always do. You seem to forget I can shape whatever we need to defeat the Wyrme. I can shape ten vape rifles if we need them. In the meantime, how about I shape us a couple of comfortable chairs and a bottle of fine Orvieto Pinot Grigio?"

"Ah, now that is an excellent plan, Bartholomew. One or two éclairs to accompany the pinot would also be quite lovely." Oliver rubbed his paws together in anticipation.

An hour later Oliver's mood had improved considerably. Bartholomew set down his empty glass and said, "I'll shape our camp on top of this hill. We'll be perfectly safe here. Tomorrow morning I'll use the Traveling Eye and see what I can find. Things may not be as bleak as they seem now."

Bartholomew cleared a wide area on the crest of the hill and shaped tents, cots, blankets, and a well equipped cooking area. As he worked he kept a wary eye on the desert for movement, but saw none. If the Wyrme of Deth was out there it wasn't showing itself.

The five adventurers sat around a blazing campfire that evening eating another of Oliver's memorable meals. Bartholomew had shaped all manner of fresh fruits and vegetables, and of course Oliver baked the bread and pastries from scratch. "Not to diminish your skills, Bartholomew, but I still argue that shaped bread and pastries are no match for those made the good old fashioned way. There's really nothing in the world like the smell of baking bread."

Their conversation continued late into the evening with no mention of the Wyrme of Deth. When Thunder and Lightning began a boisterous competition to determine who could count the most stars in one minute, Bartholomew retreated to his tent where he shaped several earplugs and a glass of white wine before retiring.

Even with the wine and earplugs Bartholomew woke in the middle of the night. He lay on his back staring at the ceiling for several minutes before calling on the Cavern of Silence.

"Cavern, will we survive our confrontation with the Wyrme of Deth?"

"You know I can't answer that, Bartholomew. I would only tell you that things are not always as they seem to be. This is a complex and delicate web of events you are entangled in. A great many future events are dependent on the outcome of this adventure, many of them having to do with Thunder and Lightning. They are young now, but they will not always be, and their influence will come to affect the entire world of Nirriim. You only have to do what you know is right, no matter how impossible it may seem. Perhaps a pleasant stroll in the moonlight might help you to think more clearly."

"A stroll in the moonlight?" There was no response from Cavern.

With a sigh, Bartholomew rose from his cot, threw on his clothes and stepped out into the cool night air. Cavern had been right, the two moons were quite spectacular, their shimmering light reflecting off the rolling dunes. The desert was beautiful, mesmerizing. He stood transfixed, his thoughts gradually turning to Clara, and how much he wished she was there with him.

He was jarred from his reverie by a startling movement in the desert. The creature rose up out of the dunes only a hundred yards from him like some gargantuan behemoth roaring up from the ocean depths.

It was a magnificent monstrosity, several hundred feet long and at least forty or fifty feet in diameter. It hung for a brief moment above the sand, brilliant gold beams of pulsing light shooting out from its eyes, its tail leaving behind it a glowing violet fog. It was gone as quickly as it had appeared, vanishing beneath the dunes, leaving the sands untouched in its wake. Bartholomew could scarcely breathe. This was the most terrifying creature he had ever laid eyes on. The sheer mass of the creature was overwhelming, the power it possessed was staggering. They could not defeat a creature of this magnitude. Why had Cavern shown him this? Certainly not to help him think. The desert was still again, reflecting only the distant light of the two moons drifting across the night sky.

Bartholomew remained motionless for many minutes after the Wyrme of Deth was gone. He had no idea how to defeat this creature and find the lost Seventh Key. He trudged back towards his tent, head down, lost in his dark thoughts. A terrible thought flashed through his mind. If something happened to him, if the Wyrme killed him, who would tell Clara? How would she know? Bartholomew felt sick inside. He didn't see the glimmering silver figure hidden in the trees scant yards away from him. Edmund the Rabbiton had also been witness to the Wyrme of Deth's terrifying display.

Chapter 35

City Beneath the Sand

Bartholomew was the first to rise the next morning. He shaped a small breakfast, got dressed, then sat on his cot, legs crossed, paws resting gently on his knees. He closed his eyes and took three slow deep breaths, just as Ennzarr had taught him, visualizing himself on the opposite side of the tent, facing the wall. Once he could see the tent wall clearly in his mind, he turned around quickly and opened his eyes. He saw himself sitting on the bed, eyes still closed, paws still resting on his knees. He drifted over to his body, looking curiously at his own face. It was odd, his face was so familiar and yet it didn't feel like him, it was like looking at the face of a stranger. As he circled around himself he realized Clara had always been right. His true self was not his physical body, but was this electric awareness he was currently experiencing, this invisible part of him that was now floating above his cot watching his own body. His thoughts began to go deeper, but he stopped himself.

"We are here to find the Seventh Key." He shot through the tent wall down to the edge of the desert. The sun was rising, the low morning light giving the dunes a surreal magical glow. "There must be ant tunnels here that lead to the Queen's Treasure Chamber." Bartholomew zipped down beneath the sand, flying through it like a bird through the sky. It was an astonishing feeling to pass through physical matter, and hard for him to get used to. He found himself flinching each time he sped through one of the massive boulders buried deep beneath the sand, waiting for the impact that never came. The sand was translucent, almost transparent, allowing him to see into the distance, as if he were swimming beneath a clear ocean. The earth surrounding him was illuminated by a new and unfamiliar form of light. It was not possible for sunlight to be here, yet he could clearly see. He had no explanation for this.

He flew on beneath the desert sands seeking out the ant tunnels, but in the end he found none. He had a growing doubt the ants had ever lived beneath the dunes, and yet Lightning's map showed the Queen's Treasure Chamber clearly located deep in the desert.

Bartholomew swept straight up out of the sand, catapulting across the sky towards the Timere Forest. He was there instantly, high above the forest near the area where Edmund the Explorer had been killed by the ants. He could see the clearing where the Tree of Eyes stood. A split second later he was under the forest floor, darting through the dense roots of the magnificent old trees. He stopped instantly, finding himself in a dark tunnel. Moments later he could see, the tunnel lit by the strange new ethereal light. The tunnels were circular, about ten or twelve feet in diameter and seemed to be the proper size for the giant ants. He spotted partial remains – mandibles, legs, antennae. The tunnels had most certainly belonged to the ants.

Following the tunnels eastward towards the desert, he crisscrossed beneath the forest floor to make certain he didn't miss anything, specifically the Queen's Treasure Chamber. It was possible Lightning's map was incorrect, or the landscape had changed over the last thousand years, desert and forest shifting positions. As he drew closer to the desert, the tunnels began to circle back around the way they came. After nearly an hour of exploring this borderland, Bartholomew was forced to conclude the ants never lived beneath the desert. Whatever the Queen's Treasure Chamber was, it did not belong to the ants.

"The mystery has deepened. If the ants didn't take Edmund the Explorer's pack, then who did? And how did it find its way to this mysterious Queen's Treasure Chamber in a world where there are no kings or queens?

Bartholomew zipped up out of the forest floor and into the blue sky above. He looked down at the vast desert sprawling out before him. Somewhere out there was the Seventh Key. Once again he sped down beneath the desert sands, flying at ever increasing speeds. His powers of perception were growing stronger, objects which he passed at blurring speeds could be examined as if he were standing still. His mind was unencumbered now by the limits of his physical brain. It was astonishing, and he realized how truly little he understood about the nature of the universe and his own existence.

In a fraction of a second Bartholomew's speed went from blurringly fast to full stop. He was deep under the desert sands in a colossal cavern. He remembered when he and Oliver had been held captive in King Oberon's ferillium mine. Oliver was astonished by the size of the mine when he first saw it, at least a mile across in both directions and well over five hundred feet tall. The cavern he was seeing now made the ferillium mine look paltry by comparison. This cavern contained the remains of a sprawling and lifeless ancient city.

Bartholomew was dumbstruck. How was it possible for a city of this magnitude to be hidden beneath the desert? This was a metropolis far larger than any in Lapinor or Grymmore, possibly larger than any on Earth. As he gazed at it the city grew brighter and brighter, filled with the new ethereal light. It was then he realized it was not the light around him which was changing, but it was his ability to perceive light that was changing. Just as his physical eyes adjusted to the dark and let more light in, his awareness was somehow adjusting for the lack of light. This process was well beyond his understanding and beyond anything Oliver had ever discussed.

He floated down to the streets below, which now appeared as bright as a summer day. There were hundreds of buildings, many three and four times as tall as the tallest buildings in Lapinor. There was an organic look to them, none were sharp and square and structured, but they were curved and irregular, almost as if they had grown where they stood. He had never seen anything like this.

He was sweeping down one of the wide main streets when he saw the corpse. More accurately, it was a skeleton. It had walked on two legs and appeared to be eight or nine feet tall, its spine extending out into a tail which was long enough to drag on the ground. Its arms were quite short, but equipped with vicious looking claws. The skull reminded Bartholomew of a snake's head, its teeth were the stuff of nightmares. The upper and lower jaw had two rows of long curved yellow teeth, the front row much longer than the back row. Nothing would have been able to escape from its bite. There were a few scraps of rotting cloth and some metal objects lying near the creature, remnants of clothing it had once worn. Bartholomew looked at one of objects, which appeared to be a gold button. He had discovered that when he was using the Traveling Eye he could look at an object from a great distance and see even the tiniest detail. He had no idea how this was possible, but it was vastly different from his normal vision. He zoomed his vision in on the small round button lying next to the skeleton. In the center was the image of a spiral with an arrow piercing it. This meant nothing to him, but from past experience he suspected it would hold great significance later on. Whatever the creature was, it had been there for many hundreds of years.

Bartholomew soared above the buildings for a better view of the cityscape. At the far end of the cavern he spotted a singular building which stood out from all the rest. It was magnificent, fluid and organic, covered with complex and detailed architectural forms. Bartholomew was in front of it instantly. The entrance to the building was through three sets of ornately carved doors created from an unknown gleaming metallic substance. The central set of doors was far taller and more elaborate than the others. Bartholomew zipped through the massive doors into the building.

Dozens of skeletons were scattered about the foyer, all similar to the one he had seen on the street, clumped together in groups of two or three. Something very bad had happened here, more than likely the event which caused the demise of the city. This was not like the city beneath the Fortress of Elders, with its gravitator trains and food synthesizers and Rabbitons. This was different, strangely alien. It was as though the buildings had grown to their final shapes, but were composed of a metallic substance. Bartholomew had no idea how this could be done, but it didn't feel like shaping.

He flitted through the building from room to room, finding more and more remains of the snake creatures. Reaching a formidable set of ornate red doors, he sailed through them into a lavishly decorated room with forty foot tall ceilings. This was the central room of the largest building in the city, undoubtedly where the leaders worked and lived. He studied the front area of the room, not yet fully grasping the significance of what he was seeing.

There were two intricately carved, rather grandiose white marble chairs on a raised platform facing outward towards the main floor. Behind the huge chairs was a colossal set of golden doors. There could be no doubt about it – he was looking at a throne room. "And who sits on thrones? Kings and queens sit on thrones. If there was a queen, more than likely there is a Queen's Treasure Chamber."

Those last three words were echoing in his thoughts when something grabbed his shoulder from behind. Before he realized he didn't have a shoulder to grab, he was back in his tent sitting on the cot. Lightning was shaking him, trying to rouse him from the Traveling Eye.

"Bartholomew! Wake up! Edmund is gone – we can't find him anywhere, and Oliver found footprints leading out to the sand dunes. He thinks the Wyrme of Deth got Edmund!"

Chapter 36

In the Belly of the Beast

Edmund was leaning back against a tree contemplating the two Nirriimian moons as they drifted across a clear night sky. "They travel a good deal faster than the Earth's moon. I wonder if that's why the–" He stopped, his ears perking up at the sound of rustling tent flaps. Peering around the tree he spotted Bartholomew, who was now also gazing up at the luminous moons. Edmund did not call out to Bartholomew. Clara had told him sometimes rabbits needed to be alone with their thoughts, and this looked like one of those times.

He wondered what Bartholomew was thinking about. Perhaps he was attempting to quantify the relationship between the varying elliptical orbits of the two Nirriimian moons. Probably not – Oliver would be the one to do that. Bartholomew was more likely thinking about Clara. Edmund thought, "It must be nice to have someone who misses you when you're gone and is excited to see you when you return. I did like it when Clara and Bartholomew and Oliver said they had missed me. Other Rabbitons don't care about that sort of thing, but to me it meant a lot. I know I'm different from the other Rabbitons. I suppose it could be something as simple as a programming error." It was at that moment the Wyrme of Deth made its dramatic appearance, leaping out of the desert sand and plunging back into the depths again.

Edmund found it fascinating, and was especially intrigued by the golden and violet lights emanating from the beast. "Perhaps it's some sort of natural organic illumination. There are a number of books in the Central Information Repository mentioning creatures who live deep beneath the ocean that possess such bioluminescent abilities. It could also be a means of communication between Wyrmes."

Another outcome of witnessing the Wyrme of Deth's startling appearance was Edmund now realized Bartholomew could not defeat it. It was simply impossible. He watched as Bartholomew trudged back to his tent. It was clear to Edmund what he must do. "I can't let anything happen to Bartholomew. I can't lose another friend and I can't take him away from Clara, not after everything they've been through. I couldn't prevent Edmund the Explorer's death, but I can prevent Bartholomew's. As much as I would like to be him, I know I am not Edmund the Explorer. I am Edmund the Rabbiton, and I am the one who must defeat the Wyrme of Deth. I owe it to Edmund the Explorer and to dear Emma."

Edmund walked to the edge of the desert and knelt in the sand. As the two moons made their way across the sky he formulated what he thought to be a suitable plan, given what little he knew about the Wyrme of Deth. He strode back to his tent, emerging several minutes later with the vape gun slung over his shoulder. He adjusted his cherished adventurer's hat as he walked down to the desert's edge, wondering if Edmund the Explorer was watching him from some distant realm. He imagined what Edmund the Explorer would say right about now. "Strap and roll, rabs! We'll be having worm stew for dinner tonight!"

Edmund stepped out onto the sand, moving tentatively at first, then breaking into a run. When he was several hundred yards out he halted at the top of a dune, pausing to take in the stark beauty of the desert. The moonlight surprised him with its almost magical quality, the sand around him sparkling like the glimmering stars above.

Edmund thought of the Blue Spectre. "This must be what he meant. This is where I walk of my own free will into the fires of life." Edmund leaped high into the air, landing with a resounding thud, just as he had done when he tried to attract the giant ants. This time, however, he was not driven by blind anger and fear and revenge, but by love. He had no special desire to kill the Wyrme of Deth, but he would do whatever it took to protect his friends. If somehow the Wyrme bested him, it would be all right. He had died once before and survived it well enough.

At first he couldn't tell if the ground was trembling or if his legs were. He didn't feel exceptionally anxious, so he reasoned it must be the ground. He was right. The tremors grew strong enough that Edmund could see the grains of sand around him shifting slightly. Then came the deep rumbling noise, so low that it was something he felt more than heard. Then the earth opened up with a stupendous shattering roar and a blinding golden light. He was tossed about like a moth in a tornado, vaguely aware of metal scraping against metal, his arms and legs flailing wildly as they smashed into the sharp and tearing insides of the gargantuan beast. Then there was silence. Edmund the Rabbiton had been swallowed by the Wyrme of Deth.

Inside the Wyrme it was pitch black, the heavy darkness reminding Edmund of the Void. He was disoriented, but after a brief assessment realized he had suffered no damage. When he tried to stand up, however, he found he could not. In fact, he was unable to move his legs, which was worrisome. He flicked on his ear lights, illuminating the inside of the Wyrme.

"Great heavens, this is most astonishing! I wish Oliver could see this." Much to his surprise, Edmund had discovered that the Wyrme of Deth was not a living creature, but was a machine, a monstrously large vehicle of unknown purpose. The interior of the Wyrme was made of a pale blue alloy unfamiliar to Edmund. The reason for his current state of immobility was now quite clear. When he had been pulled into the Wyrme, he was sucked into a massively powerful destructive device filled with row upon row of piston driven crusher blocks and vicious whirling blades. Fortunately for Edmund he was indestructible and his legs had jammed the deadly device. No matter how hard he pulled, however, he could not free himself. He lay back for a moment, hanging upside down while studying the interior of the Wyrme.

"Where is it?" He spotted the vape gun lying on the floor six feet away from him. By rotating his torso and stretching out with one arm he was able to pinch the strap between two fingers and pull the gun to him. Twisting upwards, he aimed the vape gun at the section of the machine gripping his legs and pressed the green tab. The gun hummed and a six inch hole appeared in the blades. He fired five more times, falling to the floor after the final shot. He was free. The machine screeched back to life, filling the craft with the sound of pounding crusher blocks and whirling blades. Edmund spied the machine's control panel on the opposite wall and a single vape shot permanently silenced the monstrous device.

The Wyrme was on the move again and Edmund struggled to maintain his balance as it swept along beneath the sand. He snaked his way through the immobilized crusher machine towards the stern of the craft. "What *is* this machine? The engineering is quite extraordinary, but I am unclear as to what function the Wyrme serves. It's certainly not for transportation purposes, not with those deadly shredding blades."

As he moved further back into the ship he was startled by a shatteringly loud noise and spun around to locate the source of the sound. He saw the wide aperture in the bow closing. A huge chunk of what appeared to be copper ore was smashed up against the front of the now lifeless shredding machine.

Edmund had solved the mystery. "It's a mining vehicle! A self-contained autonomous mining vehicle. This is amazing." He was fascinated by the mechanics of it. "Why does the piece of ore enter the machine but the sand does not? And how can the machine move at such great speeds through the dense sand? When I observed it leaping out of the desert I saw no obvious means of propulsion, and for a craft that moves so quickly it's extremely quiet."

Edmund made his way to the stern of the ship to confirm his suspicions that the craft would be filled with all manner of pulverized ore.

He found the walls and floor of the craft were not smooth, but were covered with long stiff fibrous hairs. When he dropped a handful of crushed ore on them the hairs moved in concert, carrying the rock to the rear of the craft. "Ah, this is how the craft conveys the ore. Fascinating."

He studied the various types of ore for several minutes, then turned back towards the bow. If he found the main control panel for the ship it might be possible for him to drive the Wyrme back to their camp. By now Bartholomew would have discovered his absence and might be out searching for him.

Snaking his way through the banks of shredder blades and crusher blocks, Bartholomew returned to the front of the craft. He examined the machinery and various panels, finally spotting a metal ladder on the starboard bow wall near the ore intake aperture. The ladder led to a small control room at the top of the Wyrme. In the room were two oversized metal chairs bolted to the deck in front of a wide curved panel covered with colored tabs, gauges, slider controls, and two silver control sticks. Edmund pulled one stick back but the ship did not respond. "Hmm, I will need to switch the craft over from autonomous to manual control."

Through trial and error, Edmund learned how to control the Wyrme. When he pulled back on one stick the ship rose up, and when he pushed the stick forward it went down. The second control stick turned the craft left and right. Basic operation of the Wyrme turned out to be surprisingly simple, similar in many ways to flying a blinker. He still had no idea why the sand didn't come in through the aperture at the front of the craft.

When Edmund took the Wyrme up to the surface, a wide metal panel above the control board slid down, revealing a row of five portholes, each about two feet in diameter. The Nirriimian moons were still in the sky, now just above the horizon.

Edmund flicked on his translucent screen, swiping through pages until he found the Nirriimian maps he needed, quickly locating the four telltale blinking orange dots. The dots were Bartholomew, Oliver, Lightning, and Thunder. They were almost forty miles away at the edge of the desert.

Edmund adjusted his adventurer's hat and swung the Wyrme around, aiming it towards the four dots. He flipped open one of the portholes, letting the cool fresh air rush in. He knew Edmund the Explorer would have been proud of him for what he'd just done, maybe even slapped him on the back and said, "Not bad for a Rabbiton, A2!"

Chapter 37

Worm Guts

"Where *is* Edmund? What are we going to do?" Lightning was terribly upset, and Thunder looked close to tears. Edmund was the first real hero they had ever had.

Bartholomew did his best to sound optimistic. "We'll find him. His tracks lead out into the desert for a few hundred yards, then stop. It's very likely he survived his confrontation with the Wyrme of Deth. Don't forget Edmund is indestructible."

Lightning nodded. "Nothing can hurt Edmund. But suppose the Wyrme ate him? How could he escape from the inside of a giant worm?" Lightning gave Thunder a horrified look. "What will he do if he's stuck inside a monster worm like that? Maybe he'll cut his way out! Wait – he took the vape gun, so maybe he'll blast a hole in the worm's guts and climb out!"

"Ewww... he'll be all covered with slimy worm guts. Suppose he gets back and tries to hug us and he's all covered in worm guts? Would you still hug him?"

Lightning hesitated. "Well, of course I'd hug him.

But probably really carefully so I wouldn't get the worm guts on me."

"Well, suppose he's totally covered with mounds of slimy wet worm guts and he wants to give you a huge bear hug. Would you–"

"STOP TALKING ABOUT WORM GUTS, PLEASE!" Oliver had heard enough. "Good heavens, we need to find Edmund, not have a discussion regarding the nature of worm entrails. Bartholomew, what about the Traveling Eye? Can you locate him using that?"

"Probably, though there is a rather archaic shaping skill which creates a trail of vapor leading to–"

"What's that light?" Lightning jumped behind Bartholomew, pointing into the desert at a tiny bobbing golden light in the distance.

Bartholomew shook his head. "I can't tell, but it's heading this way, whatever it is."

Bartholomew heard Cavern's voice in his head. "I think you're going to like this part."

"What do you mean, I'm going to like this part?"

Lightning looked up at Bartholomew. "Were you talking to me?"

Thunder was now hiding behind Lightning. "Who is he talking to?"

"I'm not talking to anyone, I was just thinking out loud." Bartholomew heard the Cavern of Silence laugh, and without thinking replied, "What are you laughing about?"

Thunder whispered to Lighting. "Nobody is laughing. Is Bartholomew going crazy?"

Oliver hollered out, "It's getting closer! The light is stupendously bright!"

The four adventurers scurried back from the edge of the desert until they were halfway up the hill. The brilliant light was careening across the desert sands directly towards them.

Thunder hollered, “I can see it! It’s gigantic! I think it’s the Wyrme of Deth!”

Lightning shrieked, “Bartholomew, is it going to get us??”

Bartholomew flicked his wrist and a defensive sphere popped up around them. “We’re safe inside the sphere. I think.”

The Wyrme of Deth began to slow down. They could see clearly now how incredibly massive the beast was.

“It’s slowing down! What’s it doing?”

Oliver answered, “I don’t know. Is that light coming from its eyes? How is that possible?”

Finally the Wyrme came to a grinding halt at the edge of the desert. The piercing golden beams of light from its eyes blinked off. There was absolute silence.

Lightning tapped Bartholomew on the shoulder and whispered. “What should we do?”

“Just wait, and we’ll see what happens. We’re safe inside the sphere.”

With a soft whirring noise two immense semicircular doors at the front of the Worm of Deth slid apart, revealing a figure silhouetted in the opening.

“Who *is* that?”

The figure picked up a gleaming cylindrical object and slung it over his shoulder.

“WHO WANTS A BIG BOWL OF WORM STEW FOR DINNER???”

Thunder and Lightning screeched wildly, dashing

out from behind Bartholomew and tearing down the hill towards Edmund.

"EDMUND! You're back!! You did it!! YOU DID IT!!"

Thunder screeched to a halt. "Wait, is he covered with worm guts?"

Lightning gave an incredulous look. "It's not a real worm, worms don't have sliding doors on the front of them. Everyone knows that."

"Well, it could be like a crunchy worm shell on the outside and then all squishy worm guts on the inside."

"If it had a shell it wouldn't be a worm. Worms don't have shells!"

Oliver and Bartholomew swept past Thunder and Lightning, who were still arguing about worm guts.

Edmund threw his arms around Oliver and Bartholomew. "It was a machine all along! And quite an amazing one. It's an autonomous mining vehicle, though I'm still unclear how it propels itself through the sand."

Oliver broke away from Edmund. "Autonomous? How does it gather the ore? You have no idea what moves it?"

"I'll show you the controls and perhaps you can figure it out. I was able to switch off the autonomous function and learned how to control it manually."

"This is quite remarkable, Edmund. How did you ever gain entrance to this behemoth?"

Oliver and Edmund disappeared inside the Wyrme of Deth, leaving Bartholomew standing alone on the sand. Behind him, Thunder and Lightning were still arguing over whether Edmund would be covered with gooshy worm guts.

Bartholomew plunked himself down on the sand and eyed the massive Wyrme of Deth. A monstrous weight had been lifted from his shoulders. He would live another day. “Clara is not going to believe this. I’m not even sure I believe it. The Wyrme of Deth has been defeated.” With a flick of his wrist, a glass of white wine appeared in his paw. Moments later the glass was empty and Bartholomew was more relaxed than he’d been a few minutes earlier.

Edmund showed Oliver the control room and the inner workings of the ship, including the long fibrous hairs, then they took a stroll around the outside of the Wyrme. “Look here, Edmund, the external surface of the ship is covered with the same stiff fibrous hairs. That must be how the Wyrme moves. It’s rather similar to how a rowboat moves, but instead of two oars there are hundreds of thousands of these fibrous hairs. Quite ingenious, although I believe this is based on one of nature’s more elegant designs. Quite a number of insects use a similar method to propel themselves through their environment.”

Edmund ran his hand across the bow of the ship. “What about the sand? Why doesn’t it come rushing in through the opening at the front of the Wyrme?”

“Very curious. It looks as though these circular discs are the source of the brilliant golden light. Their function may be more complex than simply a source of illumination. We should get Bartholomew’s expert opinion, but it appears the sand is blinked from the front of the craft to the rear of the craft as it travels through the desert. The ship creates its own never-ending tunnel beneath the sand, then propels itself through that tunnel using the fibrous hairs. Quite amazing technology, but I am at a loss as to who may have created it."

"Edmund the Explorer called it a Nirriimian sand worm and thought it was very old, a thousand years or more. He didn't know where it came from."

"Quite incredible. I wonder if it would be possible to fabricate a similar craft on a smaller scale, something suitable for a small party of adventurers. This system is far more advanced than the diggers used in King Oberon's ferillium mine. Hmmm... perhaps we could combine–"

Bartholomew strolled up behind them, sipping his second glass of white wine. "Did I happen to mention I found the Queen's Treasure Chamber?"

Chapter 38

Edmund Loses Control

There was no end to Oliver's questions about Bartholomew's lost city. "But who on earth – or should I say, who on *Nirriim* created this city beneath the desert?"

"I have no idea who built it. There were any number of symbols carved onto the building facades, but I assumed they were there to identify the individual buildings. The letterforms used were unknown to me, although I did find one rather peculiar symbol on a gold button lying next to a skeleton – a spiral pierced by an arrow."

Oliver shook his head. "I'm afraid that's not one I'm familiar with."

"I've seen that before." Edmund was sitting on the sand cleaning the vape gun. "I remember it quite well. When Edmund the Explorer and I were helping Neilana the Anarkkian, she gave us a small velvet sack of Nirriimian white crystals. Painted on the bag was the same image of a spiral being pierced by an arrow. She said she had taken the crystals from the remains of a Mintarian in the cave where she found the time throttle. She also mentioned they had frightful teeth similar to the skeletons you described in the city. I believe the inhabitants of your lost city were Mintarians."

Bartholomew looked perplexed. "Who are the Mintarians? I've never heard of them."

"I only know they were the ones who constructed the time throttle. Neilana did not seem very enamored with them. She said they were a rather oppressive civilization known for their ruthless plundering of other worlds."

Bartholomew rubbed his paw against his chin. "If the Mintarians did build the Wyrme of Deth, then they have my thanks, for they have opened a doorway to the lost city. Edmund, if you're willing to captain the Wyrme, I can guide us there."

"It would be an honor, Bartholomew. If you don't mind, I should like to rename the Wyrme of Deth in honor of Edmund the Explorer. I would call it *The Explorer.*"

Bartholomew nodded. "A good thought, Edmund. To be truthful, the idea of adventuring in a ship named the *Wyrme of Deth* was not very appealing to me. It's settled then – tomorrow morning we leave on *The Explorer* to search for the Queen's Treasure Chamber. If fortune favors us, you'll soon be holding the Seventh Key in your hand."

The next morning Thunder and Lightning came careening out of their tent, almost colliding with Edmund. Lightning was laughing wildly. "Hey, Edmund, today's the day we find the Queen's

TREASURE Chamber! This is going to be our first big find, and we'll be famous treasure hunters!"

Thunder nodded vigorously. "Famous and RICH treasure hunters!" He noticed Edmund was carrying two cloth sacks. "What are the sacks for, Edmund?"

Edmund gave a mysterious smile. "Bartholomew shaped them for me. They're for you and Lightning."

"For us?"

"I thought during our voyage to the lost city you could rummage through the mounds of ore in *The Explorer*. I happened to notice quite a large number of gold nuggets and Nirriimian white crystals there. Piles of them as a matter of fact."

Thunder and Lightning's eyes grew wide. They simultaneously screeched, snatched the bags out of Edmund's hand, and dashed off towards the ship. Lightning looked back at Edmund and hollered out, "Thanks, Edmund!! You're the best!"

Edmund grinned. "That should keep them busy for a while."

After breakfast they cleaned up the campsite and packed their supplies into *The Explorer*. Edmund could hear Thunder and Lighting in the back of the ship shouting and laughing each time they found a gold nugget or Nirriimian white crystal.

An hour later Edmund stood at the controls of *The Explorer*. Bartholomew was next to him, pointing to a small dark area on Edmund's holomap. "It's right here. We'll have to go down beneath the desert five or six hundred feet. If the Mintarians were the ones who built this ship, she'll hold up under the pressures we'll experience at that depth. That's a big if, but I think the odds are in our favor."

Edmund nodded. "I agree. Some of the controls here would indicate they had underground docking facilities specifically for their mining vessels. That will be our doorway into the city. I have been discussing it with Oliver, and he thinks the city was built solely to support the Mintarians' vast mining enterprise here. The city may well have been built underground to hide their activities from the local residents. The Nirriimians would not have been thrilled to know the Mintarians were plundering their natural resources."

"I never thought of that. That's quite plausible. There could be ancient Mintarian cities hidden all over Nirriim."

Edmund adjusted his adventurer's hat then said, "Strap and roll, rabs! We're moving out!" He pushed one of the slider bars forward and inched the silver control rod to the right. *The Explorer* snaked around and headed back out into the desert.

They cruised along the surface of the sand at close to twenty miles per hour. Once everyone was comfortable with the peculiar swaying motion of the ship, Edmund increased the speed to thirty-five miles per hour. It would take another six hours to reach the city, over two hundred miles away on the far side of the desert.

The Explorer was displayed as a moving green blip on Edmund's holomap. He simply had to guide the blip to the area Bartholomew had designated.

Bartholomew spent several hours disposing of the disabled ore crushing machine, blinking it piece by piece to the bottom of the desert. The removal of the huge device opened up a sizable section of the craft which Bartholomew filled with several comfortable couches and a number of cushiony stuffed chairs. It wasn't long before he and Oliver were relaxing with glasses of a tasty white wine.

Thunder and Lightning emerged from the back of the craft, each one dragging a heavily laden sack filled with gold nuggets and Nirriimian white crystals. They could not have looked more pleased.

Bartholomew grinned at them. "How'd the treasure hunting go?"

"I'm going to buy my parents a huge mansion right next to the water!"

Thunder chimed in. "I'm going to buy them a giant boat they can sail around the lake and go fishing as much as they want."

Lighting flopped down on a long couch, resting his head on a pillow. Moments later he was sound asleep, one paw resting on his bag of treasure. Thunder quickly followed suit.

Edmund was keeping an eye on his map, watching as the green blip drew closer to the city. He pushed the control stick forward and the ship responded without hesitation, veering down beneath the sand. He had deactivated the ore intake doors so there was no longer any danger of anyone being injured by flying chunks of metal. The ship descended deeper and deeper beneath the desert, the hull making groaning sounds as they approached four hundred feet.

Oliver and Bartholomew were asleep in their large stuffed chairs when the alarm went off. It was both piercingly loud and immensely startling, instantly waking up all four of the sleeping adventurers. Oliver staggered to his feet in a state of confusion. "Great heavens! What? Is there a fire? Who's there?"

Lightning mumbled, "Is it time to get up already?"

Bartholomew blinked to the front of the ship. "Edmund, what is it? What's happened?"

"I've lost control of the ship! It's moving by itself and going deeper into the sand – we've passed five hundred feet and we're closing in on six hundred."

"Can't you override the autonomous function?"

"I've tried, but it just switches back on. If it goes down too deep we'll be crushed, buried alive!"

Thunder and Lightning entered the control room just in time to overhear the conversation. "What??!! We're going to be buried alive?"

Bartholomew held up his paw. "Everyone, please relax. No one is getting buried alive. Oliver and Edmund are the best two engineers on the planet. They will figure out what is happening to the ship."

Oliver strolled into the control room, gave a great yawn, tapped one of the dials, then noticed the looks on everyone's faces. "What? What's the matter? Oh dear, did I not tell you about the alarm? I set it to go off when the ship approached the city. Nothing to worry about, I assure you. If I am correct, and I usually am, the ship will take control of the docking procedure."

Everyone else looked dubious. "You're sure about this?"

"It's slowing down!" Edmund pointed to one of the dials on the control panel. The craft's velocity was decreasing and it had leveled out. They could hear loud clanging noises and screeching, grinding sounds echoing from outside the ship.

"What's that noise? Is the ship breaking up?"

Oliver tapped another dial on the control panel. "No need to fret, I'm quite certain this is all just part of the docking procedure. I believe the ship is being drawn into the landing bay by some external mechanical conveyance. We should be able to exit the craft shortly. Nothing to be concerned about."

Sure enough, less than a minute later there was a shrill whining noise and the two large semicircular doors at the front of the craft slid apart, revealing an impenetrable darkness beyond.

Bartholomew was filled with growing apprehension, but did his best to sound cheery. "All ashore who's going ashore! Welcome to the lost city of the Mintarians!"

Chapter 39

The Ghost of Mintar

The five adventurers stepped into the stagnant darkness of the forgotten city.

"Hold on." Bartholomew extended his paw, concentrating deeply. A dazzling stream of tiny sparkling lights shot out into the gloom. Thousands of the lights spread across the ceiling above them, growing brighter with each second, illuminating the room.

To their left was a long hallway lined with doors identical to the one they had just exited. This was mining on a grand scale, several dozen Wyrmes harvesting thousands of tons of ore on a daily basis.

In front of them stood row upon row of rusty green lockers, each one roughly ten feet tall and two feet wide. Many of the locker doors hung loosely on one hinge, and some had fallen to the floor, transformed into barely recognizable piles of rust and decay. Lightning dashed to the closest locker. "There could be treasure in here!" He unlatched it, and with a painful squeal the ancient door swung open. "It's just old clothes." A dingy pair of decrepit canvas coveralls hung inside the locker, a pair of crumbling boots beneath them.

Oliver made his way over and peered inside. "Mining gear, almost like the gear we wore in the ferillium mines. These lockers must have been for the Wyrme crews. It's astonishing the Wyrme of Deth survived for these hundreds of years. It seems clear the Mintarians ran short of raw materials on their own world and were plundering other worlds, taking whatever they needed."

Edmund nodded. "How do you think they sent the ore back to Mintar?"

"I have no idea. It would be almost impossible to transport such vast amounts of ore in ships, and they would have been spotted by the Nirriimians. Perhaps they had spectral doorways similar to the one you opened. I suppose we'll never know for certain."

They walked on past the endless rows of lockers to the far side of the room, where they found four sets of wide descending stairs.

Lightning pointed to the ceiling. "The lights are following us! How did you do that, Bartholomew?"

"Just a little trick Clara taught me, one she learned from Bruno Rabbit. They'll follow us until I blink them off."

Their legs were aching by the time they reached the bottom of the stairs. The Mintarians were far taller than rabbits or mice, which translated into eighteen inch tall steps.

Thunder moaned loudly. "Whew! That was rough. Hey, Edmund, next time can you carry me?"

"Look! It's a city!"

Bartholomew's lights had soared up over a thousand feet, dispersing rapidly across a gigantic dome made of an unknown bronze colored material. The lights multiplied, increasing in brightness until the entire city was ablaze in light. In front of the adventurers stood hundreds of buildings, many ten to fifteen stories tall. The city was crisscrossed with dozens of paved streets, now a spider web of cracks and fissures due to the unstable, shifting ground.

"It's gigantic! How could they make buildings that tall?! They look weird, kind of like plants." Thunder and Lightning stood gaping at the strangely organic cityscape. This was the first large city they had ever seen.

Bartholomew led the way down the wide rutted streets, stepping carefully across the multitude of fractures and crevasses, occasionally stopping to peer inside one of the darkened buildings. Oliver was the first to spot the skeletons. "Look over there! What do you suppose happened to them?" He was pointing to a group of four skeletons lying on the sidewalk in front of a badly damaged building. A few of the skeletons were partially covered by torn and shredded metallic debris. Their skulls resembled that of a snake, with two rows of curved, vicious teeth.

Bartholomew said, "When I visited the city using the Traveling Eye I saw these skeletons strewn across the entire city. I'm in the dark as to what happened here. Perhaps it was a deadly plague, or some kind of poisonous gas."

Edmund pointed to the side of the building. "Look closely at the outer walls. I've seen this before."

"What? I don't see it."

Edmund strode over to the building and touched a smooth round hole in the outer wall. Then he pointed to another, and another after that. Once they noticed the holes they could see hundreds of them on the surrounding buildings. "There was a vape gun battle here. Probably more of a massacre than a battle. It looks as though someone invaded the city and killed everyone in it." He looked down at the pile of skeletons, slowly shaking his head. "There's no doubt these are Mintarians. They were thieves on a monumental scale, but they didn't deserve this."

The adventurers walked on in silence down the ancient boulevard. "There's no end to the bodies." Edmund stopped. "Look. Here's our answer."

Lying in a shadowy doorway was a massive skeleton with two long curved tusks. Next to it lay a silver tube covered with dust and fragments of metal blasted from the building. "That metal cylinder is a Model 14A Heavy Particle Beam Projector. It uses the same basic technology as our vape gun. The 14A beamer was the main battle weapon used by Anarkkian soldiers during the war. This city was invaded by Anarkkians. I saw enough of this during the war to know exactly what happened here."

Bartholomew asked cautiously, "You mean Edmund the Explorer saw it?"

Edmund blinked. "Yes, that's what I meant. Edmund the Explorer told me many stories of his wartime experiences, but it's evident to me now how deeply it must have affected him. This is not something you quickly forget."

The mood of the group grew somber as they passed

the never-ending piles of skeletons. Thunder and Lightning stopped talking about treasure and were looking uncomfortable. Their lost city of treasure was transforming before their eyes into a lost tomb. Thunder and Lightning had little desire to disturb the Mintarian bones, much less search the remains for treasure. They spotted a few more Anarkkian skeletons along the way, but for each Anarkkian they found, there were a hundred Mintarians. This had been a brutal slaughter.

Bartholomew didn't have to read Thunder and Lightning's thoughts to know the city would have a powerful and lasting effect on them. It was painful to watch their reaction, but he knew understanding and accepting the existence of evil was a necessary part of growing up, and ultimately awakening to their inner voice. He sensed that Thunder and Lightning would bring great good to the world. Still, it was difficult for him to watch them now.

They walked silently through the streets for many blocks until finally Bartholomew spoke. "That huge building down at the end of this street is the main palace. I believe it's where we'll find the Queen's Treasure Chamber. When I was using the Traveling Eye I discovered a throne room and a large set of golden doors behind the two thrones. It's my guess we'll find what we're looking for behind those doors, unless Edmund's Blue Spectre was wrong about the Queen's Treasure Chamber."

A half hour later the party of five adventurers stood facing the Mintarian palace. This was by far the most magnificent building in the city, more fluid in form than the others, and covered with complex and elaborate architectural detail and carving. The steps leading up to the main entrance of the palace were wavy and irregular, but Bartholomew couldn't tell if it was the result of shifting ground or if that was the original intended design.

Bartholomew felt a growing unease as they made their way up the stairs. If they didn't find the Seventh Key here they would have to start over from square one, and he wasn't sure he even knew where square one was anymore. He couldn't bear the idea of losing Edmund the Rabbiton.

Reaching the top of the stairs they found themselves standing in front of three sets of massive doors, the center set nearly forty feet tall.

Oliver was the first to reach the doors. "I daresay we'll need all of Edmund's strength to open such an enormous door as this." He touched his paw to the forty foot tall door and it silently swung open. "Good heavens, that was rather unexpected."

Bartholomew flicked one paw and the lights covering the dome streamed down and flew into the palace through the open doorway. Oliver cautiously peered into the building and was met by the sight of more skeletons scattered across the palace's cavernous foyer. He stepped inside, gazing up at the vast ceiling. "These organic architectural forms are quite unique with their odd root like appearance. It's unclear to me what has a structural function and what is simply decorative. Perhaps it is a combination of both. Quite magnificent in its own peculiar way."

Bartholomew took the lead, doing his best to remember the location of the throne room. It was much harder to find it now that he couldn't fly through the walls. They passed through room after room with no sign of the two red doors he was searching for. Most of the rooms appeared to be offices, and though the furniture was dissimilar in form to Lapinoric furniture, it appeared to serve the same function. Thunder and Lightning stopped and poked through a few drawers here and there but found nothing which appeared to have any value.

After an hour of wandering through the maze of the hallways and rooms they nudged open a door and found themselves in an enormous marble room. In the center of the far wall stood a set of ornate red doors. There were hundreds of intricately carved figures and symbols on the doors, but none that Bartholomew recognized. When he touched one of the red doors it silently swung open. They were in the throne room.

Thunder and Lightning both shrieked, dashing across the pure white marble floor to the thrones. They stopped short. On the floor behind the thrones were two Mintarian skeletons. A crown lay next to one of them, a bejeweled sword in a sheath next to the other, both inlaid with delicate white and black marble designs.

Thunder and Lightning stared at the crown and the sword. Neither one wanted to be the first to touch them. Finally Lightning said, "If we don't take it someone else will, and maybe it will be someone who won't take care of it like we will. Or maybe it will just sit here for another ten thousand years until the entire city collapses on it."

Thunder nodded. "I'll take the crown."

"Fair enough." Lightning reached down, carefully retrieving the sword. This was not the way he had imagined it would feel to discover treasure. Part of him felt as though he was stealing from the former inhabitants of the palace. He knew he wasn't, but it was a hard feeling to shake. He decided to treat the sword as an artifact from an ancient civilization rather than pillaged treasure, and that made him feel better.

Thunder was ecstatic over his new crown. It was quite spectacular, with eight gleaming golden spires equally spaced around it, each with a uniquely colored gem mounted on top. Thunder immediately put the crown on his head. "Bow down before the great and terrible King Thunder!" Unfortunately, the crown was extremely large and slid down onto his shoulders, diminishing quickly his intended dramatic effect. "Creekers, these Mintarians had big heads!"

Bartholomew, Oliver, and Edmund stepped around the two marble thrones. Even Oliver laughed at the sight of Thunder wearing the huge crown on his shoulders. "Ah, a kingly figure if ever I saw one."

Bartholomew grinned, turning to face the towering golden doors behind the two thrones. "I think this is it. It only makes sense that these doors lead to the Queen's Treasure Chamber. It also makes sense that gaining access to the Treasure Chamber will not be a simple proposition." He backed away from the doors and held out one paw, a pale green ray scanning across them. Then a brilliant red beam shot out, holding steady on a single point for almost half a minute. Finally, a massively powerful white beam streamed out from both his paws, blasting the door head on. The doors glowed brightly for a moment, but were otherwise unaffected. Bartholomew frowned. "Nothing. The doors are impervious to shaping – they simply absorb the energy.

Edmund tried next with equally disappointing results. He pushed, pounded and even smashed into the door at a full run with no effect. They tried blasting through the surrounding walls of the chamber and again were unsuccessful. The walls were as impregnable as the doors.

Bartholomew stood in front of the chamber scratching his head. "Wait, I have an idea. I can use the Traveling Eye to enter the chamber and examine the inside for structural weaknesses." It was an excellent plan but proved as unsuccessful as the others. Even when he was a field of conscious energy his passage through the doors was blocked. He returned to his body and stood up. "Perhaps we should look around the palace for clues. I can't think of anything else to try right now."

Oliver studied the doors for a while then headed off with Edmund to explore other sections of the palace. He hoped they might find some Mintarian or Anarkkian technology on the lower levels which might be of use to them, or even a secret passageway leading into the Queen's Chamber.

Bartholomew set off to explore the upper regions of the palace. It was possible the answer to opening the golden doors might be found in the private chambers of the King and Queen.

Thunder and Lightning decided to stay and hunt for treasure in the numerous alcoves and ante rooms they had not searched already. After poking around in dark corners looking for secret doorways or hidden stairways they finally gave up. Lighting went exploring in the adjoining rooms while Thunder stayed in the throne room waiting for the others to return.

As Thunder sat idly in the huge room he eyed the great white marble thrones, imagining what it would be like to be an all-powerful king. He picked up the crown and ambled over to the largest throne. He climbed onto it and took a seat, putting the crown on his head. Giving his best attempt at a regal voice, he cried out, "It is I, the great and fearsome King Thunder, ruler of the world! You there! Bring me cake and ale! And treasure!!" He started laughing and wished Lightning was there to see him. He was laughing right up to the moment he saw the ghost.

It appeared on the opposite side of the room and was drifting slowly towards him, a barely visible white vaporous cloud. It began gaining substance and form, turning a peculiar rust color, and appeared to be walking, but Lightning noticed its feet weren't touching the floor. As it drew closer he could see its shape was that of a Mintarian, with a snake head and the hideous double row of teeth. It was also wearing a crown – a crown identical to the one Thunder had resting on his shoulders. "Uh oh. I don't think I should be in this throne. He looks mad." Thunder hopped down, dashing around the side of the throne, then peeked out at the meandering ghost. The apparition took no notice of Thunder and continued trudging along through the air towards the throne, finally standing directly in front of it. Rather than sitting in it, however, the ghost gave a great weary sigh, circling ponderously around the throne towards Thunder's hiding place.

"Eek!" Thunder skittered backwards out of the ghost's path. He almost stumbled and fell as he dashed around to the opposite side of the throne. He was now sincerely terrified. His experience with unearthly ethereal beings possessing two rows of curved vicious teeth was limited to the one he was now looking at – the one who appeared to be chasing him in torturously slow motion. He decided to apologize to the ghostly King. "I'm sorry for sitting in your throne, sir. I just wanted to see what it felt like to be a king. Even though I know you are the king, and not me."

The translucent floating King never acknowledged Thunder's words, instead making its ungainly way back to the two golden doors.

Thunder relaxed, watching curiously as the King removed his crown, holding it high in the air with both scaly hands. His grisly claws were almost as frightening as his teeth. The King walked towards the chamber doors, crown held above his head. When he was only inches from the doors, he turned the crown so the eight spires faced them, then pressed it against the doors. He repeated this action over and over, finally lowering the crown and placing it back on his head. He turned to the right, his feet shuffling several inches above the ground until he reached the far wall. Thunder was still watching when the ghost simply faded away to nothingness.

"Creekers. What *was* that??" Thunder began to shake. He thought he was going to either throw up or cry, and quickly glanced about to see if anyone was watching. Before he could do either, something began to nag at him. "What was the ghost King doing? Why was he pushing his crown against the door like that?" It took him only a moment to realize the crown he held in his own two paws was the key to opening the golden doors. When he fully grasped this he began shaking again, becoming quite light headed. He leaned against the throne until his dizziness had passed.

He stepped in front of the two magnificent golden

doors, examining closely the area where the king had pressed the crown. "Great Nirriimian Nadwokks! There's a circle of eight small holes in the door!! Yes! I think this is it!!" Stretching as tall as he could, Thunder still couldn't reach high enough to insert the crown. His eyes darted around the room until he spied a large wooden chair hidden in a dark alcove.

He dashed over and dragged the chair back to the doors. He was giggling uncontrollably now. "I'll be the one to open the chamber doors! I'll be the one!" He leaped up onto the chair. "Ha ha! Yes, I'll be the one! I am the famous treasure hunter Thunder!" Raising the crown above his head he positioned it so the bejeweled spires aligned perfectly with the circle of eight holes. He pushed the crown in with all his might. With a soft clicking noise the two massive golden doors swung open. Thunder began laughing hysterically, leaping about in a wild impromptu dance of manic joy. He gave a short yelp when his foot became caught between two chair rails and he lost his balance, tumbling to the solid marble floor below. His world quite abruptly turned a very dark shade of black.

Chapter 40

Life is but a Dream

Thunder never really knew how he wound up in the jungle, but there he was, with something dreadful chasing after him, doing its best to prevent him from finding whoever it was he was supposed to find. He didn't know what was chasing him, or who he was supposed to find, but he did know he'd better not let the dreadful thing catch him.

Each time he had the dream it was exactly the same. It began as he ripped his way through the thick, thorny foliage, slipping in between the coarse vines and branches. He stopped to listen for any sound of the thing chasing him, but heard only the harmless squawking of the feathered jungle denizens flying overhead. "Maybe it gave up and quit chasing me." He raced ahead through the jungle anyway, just to be safe.

Then came the river. He was only a mouseling, barely two feet tall, and he didn't know the first thing about swimming. Like clockwork, the crashing noises in the jungle started up again the instant he sat down to rest. He looked at the rushing river, saw the log floating past, heard the splintering trees behind him and made the leap. He plunged into the churning water, clawing madly at the log, barely managing to hold on. The thing chasing him let out a hideous rasping shriek as the log was carried rapidly downriver. First came the whitewater, then a small falls, then the jagged rock, then darkness, then he woke up face down in the mud.

It was dark then, and he'd forgotten his name. He grasped the medallion hanging from his neck because it made him feel safe. Crawling painfully into the slippery wet jungle he found a hollow beneath a massive vine covered tree and dragged himself down into it, falling asleep instantly.

The morning sun woke him, his stomach aching horribly from hunger. He felt weak and shaky. He didn't eat the berries he found because someone he couldn't remember had told him never to eat wild berries. He pushed through the prickly foliage until he emerged into a clearing. That's when he saw the two mice carrying metal buckets filled with orange berries. The grown-up mouse looked surprised to see him, his face full of warmth and concern. The mouseling next to him looked about his age and was staring at him with wide eyes.

The grown-up mouse said, "Are you lost? Do you know where you live?"

Everything spun about wildly as he tumbled to the wet jungle floor. The ending was always the same – cold, wet, darkness.

* * *

"Thunder! Thunder! Wake up! What happened? Are

you all right?" Thunder moaned slightly when Bartholomew shook his shoulder, but his eyes remained closed. Bartholomew touched a paw to Thunder's face, a swirling cocoon of pink light spreading out around his head and upper torso. The pink cloud was drawn into Thunder, and moments later his eyes blinked open.

"Uhh... is it time to get up already? It didn't get my medallion. I'm so hungry."

The concern on Bartholomew's face grew. "Thunder, what are you talking about? What was trying to get your medallion?" Bartholomew glanced around the room but saw no one. "How did the chamber doors get opened? What happened here?"

Thunder finally returned to the waking world. He stood up, but quickly sat back down in the wooden chair. "I opened the doors, Bartholomew! I put the crown in the circle of holes and pushed it and the door opened! I saw a ghost do it with his ghost crown and then I did it and it worked!"

Bartholomew was getting more and more confused by Thunder's story. "You saw a ghost and it was chasing you to get a medallion?"

"No, I saw the ghost, opened the doors, then fell off the chair and had my dream about the monster chasing me. I don't know why I said it wanted my medallion. It wants to stop me from finding someone too, but I don't know who. The dream is about when Lightning and his dad found me in the jungle when I was a mouseling. They took me in to live with them. I dream about that day all the time, and it's always scary."

Bartholomew's curiosity was piqued. "Clara says having the same dream over and over is your inner voice telling you to do something. Can you show me the medallion?"

Thunder removed a chain from around his neck, holding it up for Bartholomew to see. Attached to the chain was a plain hexagonal silver medallion, about one inch wide and as thick as a 20 credit copper coin. It looked entirely unremarkable until Bartholomew flipped it over. It had a single eye engraved on it. "Where did you get this?"

"I don't know. I had it when Lightning's dad found me. What's the eye? Is that bad?"

"No, Thunder, it's not bad at all. The single eye is the image found on Shapers Guild rings." He held out his paw, letting Thunder examine his Eleventh Ring.

"Do you think I got the medallion from a shaper? Do you think my... other parents were shapers?"

"I can't say. I've seen the eye on Shapers Guild Rings, the World Doors, and at the Blue Monk Monastery, but never on a medallion like this. The symbol is far older than the Shapers Guild. No one knows how far it goes back, or to what. Not even the Blue Monks know. Someone was chasing you in the dream?"

"Yes, but I never see them. It's big and sounds like a monster. I didn't know until now it was after the medallion."

"Well, I'm glad you're feeling better. You were lucky Lightning's father found you, although I suspect it was no accident that he did. I would imagine in time you will unravel the story behind your medallion and learn how you came to be in the jungle. But, as Clara would say, many events must first unfold at a pace determined by the universe. She says it's a process that cannot be rushed. We learn from each event we experience, even if sometimes we're only learning patience."

Thunder was looking at the golden doors. "Can we look in the Queen's Treasure Chamber now? Do you think it will be filled with gold and jewels? Do Lighting and I get some of the treasure?"

"If there is treasure, it will be shared equally by all of us, but we should wait until Lightning, Oliver, and Edmund return. We have no idea what manner of traps or terrors may be lurking inside the chamber."

"Or what manner of *treasure*!"

"Great heavens, Bartholomew, you opened the doors!" Oliver's booming voice echoed out from across the room. Lightning and Edmund were right behind him.

Bartholomew held both paws out towards Thunder. "Thunder is the hero. He discovered his crown was the key to unlocking the doors."

"That's because I saw the *ghost* of some old King trying to open it. I saw a ghost! A REAL ghost! He almost grabbed me!"

Lightning's eyes grew very wide. "He almost grabbed you? Holy creekers, I wish I'd been here! We didn't find anything. Edmund thinks the Anarkkians ransacked the city and took everything. What's in the treasure chamber? Did you find the Seventh Key?"

"We haven't gone in yet. Bartholomew said we had to wait for you to get back. There might be traps waiting inside."

"Traps, shmaps, let's go find some treasure!" Lightning made a dash towards the doors.

"Wait!" Bartholomew grabbed the back of Lightning's coat, stopping him in his tracks. He stepped in front of Lightning and faced the open doors, moving his paws in a circular motion. The cloud of small lights overhead streamed down from the ceiling and swarmed through the golden doors into the Queen's Treasure Chamber.

Bartholomew peered into the chamber. A defensive sphere popped up around the party of adventurers. "Stay inside the sphere until we know it's safe in there. Lightning, Thunder, this is not a game. Have you forgotten already about the vape rifle in the blinker? Many a treasure hunter has lost their life by acting in haste. There are times when you are forced to take risks, but you must think carefully before you act."

"We promise. It's just... this is our first real treasure."

"The treasure will wait for you. Everyone follow me." Bartholomew stepped through the doors, then held out one paw, a wide violet beam spreading out across the massive room. He moved the beam about until he was satisfied there were no traps. "It looks safe to me. Everyone look for the Seventh Key. Edmund said it was in a long canvas pack, but it could have been removed. We're looking for a heavy gold key with the image of a single eye on it, and a small blue shimmering cube."

Oliver studied the room. The Queen's Chamber was round, approximately two hundred feet in diameter. Within the room were three concentric rings of what appeared to be treasure chests, each about four feet long and three feet tall. The outer ring had forty-eight chests, the central ring had twenty-four, and the inner ring had twelve, for a total of eighty-four chests. Oliver was the only one to note that eight plus four add up to twelve. The number twelve must have been significant in the

Mintarian culture, probably having some connection to the twelve worlds.

In the center of the rings was an ornately carved white marble pedestal with a crystal sphere seated on the top of it. Inside the sphere was a small gleaming object, but Oliver couldn't make out what it was. He stepped through the rings of treasure chests and approached the crystal sphere. The object encased within the sphere was a large gold ring. Engraved on the ring was the Mintarian symbol of a spiral being pierced by an arrow. "Bartholomew, look at this. It's a Mintarian ring encased in a crystal sphere. It must be an extraordinary object to be placed in the center of the Queen's Treasure Chamber."

Thunder and Lightning were running about, madly flipping open the treasure chests. "Hurry up! Open them all! Creekers, another one filled with these dumb white marbles! This isn't worth anything! Keep opening them – maybe there's one filled with gold and gems and Nirriimian white crystals!"

Bartholomew stepped over to the marble pedestal and examined the Mintarian ring. "You're right, Oliver. There has to be something special about this ring. I'm guessing it's far more than just a ring, probably bestowing upon its wearer some form of power."

Thunder and Lightning raced on, opening treasure chests as fast as they could. "There's nothing here! Just white marbles! What kind of treasure chamber is this?!"

Bartholomew was still contemplating the ring inside the sphere. "It's worrisome to me that the ring is encased in crystal. I don't think we should try to remove it. In fact, I am sensing we should leave it where it lies. There's something... I'm not certain... but something is going–"

"GHOST!!" Edmund was pointing frantically at the golden doors.

"Creekers! It's him again! It's the ghost King!"

Lightning grabbed Thunder, dragging him over to the far side of the chamber. "Look out! He might get us! Edmund, clobber him! Clobber the ghost!"

Bartholomew kept his eyes on the ghost King, but felt none of the fear Lightning did. "Everyone be still. I don't think he means to hurt us. He is after something in the treasure chamber."

The adventurers were motionless, watching mutely as the ghost King shuffled along inches above the chamber floor in an awkward combination of drifting and walking. He passed directly through the treasure chests standing in his way. His form was ethereal. "He's a field of awareness, not physical matter. I don't think he could hurt us even if he wanted to."

The ghost King reached the center of the room, floating in front of the pedestal which held the crystal sphere. A warm golden light spread through him as he raised a scaly hand and placed it gently on the sphere. The golden light was pulled into the sphere, causing it to dissipate, leaving the ring floating several inches above the pedestal. The ghost King carefully retrieved the ring, sliding it onto his long clawed finger. An instant later he was no longer a ghost. He was solid, part of the physical world again.

Lightning shrieked out, "He's real! He's going to get us! Edmund!"

Bartholomew flicked his paw rapidly, defense shields popping up around each of the adventurers. "Don't move! Stay in your sphere. I still don't think he means us any harm. He just wanted the ring."

The ghost King looked at Bartholomew curiously, then at Edmund. Finally he turned and looked directly at Thunder.

"Why is he looking at me? Because I sat in his throne? I'm sorry, King! Bartholomew?"

The King held up both hands in a universally understood display of peace, showing clearly that he held no weapons or malice. He walked across the room, stepping around the treasure chests until he reached Thunder. He spoke for almost a minute to Thunder in a very peculiar language, one that made Bartholomew think of a horse with a mouthful of flies. The language was bizarre, but something about his words was disarming, and their fear of the King vanished.

Bartholomew called out to Thunder, "I think he's thanking you for opening the doors!"

The King motioned for Thunder to follow him, moving to the second ring of treasure chests. He held out one scaly finger, moving it from one chest to the next, apparently counting them. When he reached the seventh chest he walked over to it and pointed directly at it, repeating an incomprehensible phrase several times. He backed away from Thunder, his eyes roaming about the chamber as though having one last look. He nodded again to Thunder, touched the gold ring to his forehead and vanished in a brilliant flash of light.

Thunder blinked in surprise. "Did you see that? He's gone!" Then he dashed over to the treasure chest the King had pointed at. "This has to be the one!" He flipped open the lid and gave a loud yelp. "What?? There's just more of those white marbles? He tricked us!"

Soon the entire party of adventurers stood around the treasure chest, all of them talking at once.

Oliver's voice boomed out above the others, "There could be something buried beneath the marbles. Scoop them out and check."

Thunder looked dubious, but pushed his arm down into the chest. He pulled out a large pawful of the white spheres. "It's just more stupid marbles!" He flung them across the floor in frustration.

As the marbles bounced and skittered across the room Bartholomew once again heard the voice of the Cavern of Silence. "Every atom, every molecule, and every bouncing marble is exactly where it should be at every moment in time."

Bartholomew called out, "Wait! Everyone be quiet!" The only sound was the marbles clinking across the stone floor. Then there was silence, followed by the sound of twelve white marbles rolling towards the pedestal at the center of the room, gaining speed as they grew closer. When they reached the pedestal they disappeared with a soft tinkling noise.

Bartholomew ran to the center of the room. "Look, the marbles rolled down these holes next to the pedestal. There must be something below us. Maybe that's what the ghost King was trying to tell Thunder. Oliver was right, we need to scoop out all the marbles."

After several frantic moments of pawing out marbles Oliver cried, "The trunk has a false bottom! The marbles are sitting in a tray only eight or ten inches deep."

Edmund reached in with both hands and lifted out the huge tray of white marbles.

Lightning shrieked, "There's a big hole with a ladder

going down!"

Bartholomew clapped his paw on Edmund's back. "This is it, Edmund. I know it is. I'm certain we'll find the Seventh Key in the room below."

Edmund gave him an anxious look. The only time Bartholomew had seen him more apprehensive was when ants were involved.

"I hope you're right." Edmund nervously adjusted his adventurer's hat, then confounded Bartholomew again with his unpredictable behavior. Edmund stepped up onto the trunk and called out, "Strap and roll, rabs, it's treasure time!" He didn't bother with the ladder, but simply jumped into the hole, disappearing into the inky darkness below.

Chapter 41

The Queen's Haystack

"It's dark down here." Lightning's voice had a quaver to it.

"Hold on." A stream of sparkling lights swept out from Bartholomew's paw and floated up to the ceiling. They grew brighter until the entire room was blazing with light.

"Oh, my. This is quite astonishing. What do you suppose all this is?" Oliver waved his paw at the endless mounds of boxes and crates and sacks and chests and strangely wrapped objects filling the gigantic rectangular room.

Bartholomew gave a sigh. "I suppose we could call it the Queen's Haystack, and we're looking for the needle."

"Is this treasure or just more junk?" Thunder was looking dubious.

Edmund stood atop a huge mound of objects. "It's treasure if it's valuable to you. Were the chests in the

Queen's Treasure Chamber filled with treasure?"

Lightning snorted. "They were full of garbage. The Queen must have been a whopping nutcake to have all those marbles. I think maybe she *lost* all her marbles!" He gave a cackling laugh and began singing,"The Queen lost her marbles, the Queen lost her marbles!" Thunder immediately joined in.

Edmund waited patiently until they were done singing. "Suppose on Mintar the rarest substance was not diamonds or gold, but was pure white marble. Did you notice how many objects in the palace are made of white marble, and how few are made of gold? The city's King and Queen were displaying their vast wealth with objects made from white marble. They were more than likely going to take the chests back to Mintar where they would be worth trillions of credits. If you traveled to a planet where diamonds covered the ground like leaves in the fall, would you be rich there?"

Thunder shook his head. "I get it. It's only valuable if it's rare."

"It's only valuable if someone thinks it's valuable. It's treasure if you think it's treasure. You are the one who places a value on the things in your life. Which is more valuable, a sack full of Nirriimian white crystals or your friendship with Lightning?"

Thunder looked at Lightning. "The Nirriimian white crystals!" They both burst out laughing.

Oliver interrupted. "Yes, yes, that's all quite interesting, but we need to be looking for this Seventh Key of yours. We'll have plenty of time for chit chat on the way home."

Bartholomew smiled. Oliver was ever Oliver. Edmund however, was a far different story. Where in the world had he learned about placing a value on the things in his life? Where had that come from? His inner voice?

Bartholomew held up his paw. "I have an idea. Like Ennzarr the Red Monk, Clara has the uncanny ability to find lost objects. She says if I close my eyes and completely relax, then free my thoughts, I can ask the universe to guide me towards a lost object. Clara said the universe guides her with feelings and images, not words."

Thunder snickered, "Hey, can you find my favorite beater bat I lost when I was a mouseling?"

Oliver shushed him with a stern disapproving look. Lightning snorted.

Bartholomew held up a paw. "Quite humorous, indeed. Okay, I'm new at this, so I'll need quiet. Clara can feel the universe almost instantly, but it will take me a good deal longer."

Bartholomew walked to the top of a small mountain of objects. He stood silently, his eyes closed. Almost a full minute later he turned to the left and began walking cautiously across the piles of crates and boxes. He veered to the right, eyes still closed, then walked another thirty feet. He stopped and kneeled, reaching down as far as he could between two irregular shaped objects wrapped in a dark gray cloth. When he pulled his paw out he was holding a small wooden bat. He opened his eyes.

Lightning guffawed loudly. "It's a beater bat! Great job, Bartholomew! You found Thunder's beater bat!"

Bartholomew looked chagrinned, but tossed the bat to Thunder. "Will this one do?"

Thunder picked up the bat with a smirk. "It's perfect,

it's just–" He stopped, his teasing grin replaced by a look of stunned surprise. "How did... it's not possible. This *is* my old beater bat. It's the one I lost. It has my initials carved into it right here. How did you do that??" His voice was tinged with fear.

The Cavern of Silence spoke to Bartholomew. "Of all the objects in the world, why do you suppose Thunder asked you to find his favorite old beater bat?"

Bartholomew thought carefully. "Thunder, why did you ask me to find your lost beater bat?"

"Uhh... I don't know. It just popped into my head. It was funny."

"Popped into your head from where? Where did that thought come from?"

"From inside my head?"

"It came from the universe. I believe you sensed the beater bat was here, and I simply located it for you."

Thunder gave a nervous laugh. "The universe didn't tell me anything, Bartholomew, I just made it up to be funny. It's just a weird coincidence, that's all. Anyway, we need to look for the Seventh Key, not talk about this dumb bat."

Bartholomew understood clearly what Thunder was saying. "Okay, let's move on." He closed his eyes again, turning slowly, one paw outstretched. Cautiously he began stepping over the mounds of objects, making his way across the vast room. He stopped twice, veering to the right, then to the left, then straight forward. When he was nearly three hundred feet away from his friends he stopped and opened his eyes. He was only a few feet from the far left corner of the room. "It's over here! I'm going to need some help. It feels as though it's deeply buried."

Three hours later the party of adventurers had cleared away a twenty foot wide section of the room around Bartholomew. Lying on the ancient stone floor in front of them was a seven foot long dilapidated green canvas pack covered with flapped pockets and a long broken strap. The once rugged pack looked as though it would crumble to dust if someone were to shake it.

Edmund lowered himself to his knees in front of the pack. He hadn't said a word when they uncovered it, just nodded to Bartholomew. He ran his paw gently across the worn canvas. "The last time I touched this pack Edmund the Explorer was alive." No one said anything, but everyone knew what he was thinking.

There was a tenderness to the way he moved his paw across the pack's surface, bringing it to rest on a large pocket. The flap fell off in his hand when he pulled on it. He reached into the pocket. Time slowed to a crawl. The silence in the room was profound. When Edmund withdrew his hand he was holding a large gold key. The key had a single eye carved into it. He reached into the pocket again and pulled out a small shimmering blue cube. He made an odd gulping noise. His hands were shaking. They had done it. They had found the Seventh Key and they had found the time throttle.

Bartholomew put his hand on Edmund's shoulder. "It's time to go home, old friend." Of all the adventurers in the room, it was Thunder who turned away and cried. Lightning watched, but said nothing.

Chapter 42

The Long Road Home

Oliver and Edmund were standing on the marble steps in front of the Mintarian palace. "I daresay you should put that key in a secure place where you're certain not to lose it."

Edmund stared at Oliver, uncertain if he was joking, but decided he was sincerely concerned. "A good thought, my friend. I have already placed the key and the time throttle inside my chest panel. Where I go, they go."

"Excellent." Oliver turned to see Bartholomew, Lightning, and Thunder chatting in the main foyer of the palace. "Bartholomew! We should go – we don't want to be late!"

Again Edmund stared at Oliver. "Late for what?"

Oliver looked befuddled. "Well... late for anything, I suppose. It's always best to be on time. And, well, I do have many pressing scientific matters to attend to upon my return. I have quite a surprise in store for you and

Bartholomew and Clara back at the Fortress." Oliver chuckled to himself. "Yes, indeed, quite a surprise in store for all of you."

Bartholomew walked up behind them. "Okay, Oliver, we're ready to go. We'll leave the same way we entered. Let's walk across the city and take *The Explorer* back to the edge of the Timere Forest, then head back through the jungle to the Island of the Blue Monks."

Oliver nodded. "An excellent plan. Let's get cracking everyone! No dawdling." Oliver headed down the steps.

Bartholomew grinned at Edmund and whispered, "Better get cracking, Edmund!"

Edmund laughed out loud. Sometimes Bartholomew's jokes reminded him of Edmund the Explorer.

The party of adventurers found a comfortable pace as they made their way across the Mintarian city, again walking past the groups of skeletons scattered about the streets. Lightning couldn't take his eyes off them. "It's creepy to look at the skeletons and think they used to be walking around telling jokes and stories."

Thunder replied, "Or chomping down on mice with those giant teeth they have. And the claws – look at those claws!"

"I know, but still... they used to be alive and now they're not. I never thought treasure hunting would mean I'd have to look at bunches of dead skeletons."

Bartholomew strolled up alongside Lightning. "They're somewhere else now, in a different form – maybe an energy field like the ghost King, maybe in another body, born into another world. It's like a snake shedding its skin. It leaves it behind and moves on."

"I never thought of it like that. The ghost King seemed alive enough. That's not so creepy."

"Clara knows much more than I do about these things, and she always says we'll find each other again after we both die. She said Edmund the Explorer and Emma are probably together again by now." He glanced over at Edmund to see if he was listening.

He was, and he gave Bartholomew a smile. "I hope so. Nothing would make me happier."

Several hours later they were back on *The Explorer.* Oliver and Edmund made their way to the control room, while Thunder and Lightning dashed back to where they had hidden their sacks of gold and Nirriimian white crystals. They both stopped short. Lightning stammered, "Huh? Where'd all the ore go? Oliver! All the ore is gone!"

"Our treasure! Is it still here?" Thunder and Lightning ran to a panel near the rear of the craft and flipped it open. "It's here! The sacks are still here!"

Oliver and Edmund had heard the shouting and made their way to the stern of the ship. "Most interesting. The Wyrme must dump all the collected ore each time it docks. There must be cargo bay doors in the floor that drop down and the hairs move all the ore through the opening, probably into a vast storage chamber beneath the docks. The Mintarians more than likely transported it from there back to their planet.

Lightning grabbed Thunder's arm. "Let's count our treasure and see who has the most crystals!"

Bartholomew sat down in one of the soft cushioned chairs he had shaped. He could finally relax. They had found the Seventh Key and the Mintarian time throttle.

Edmund would be safe. A moment later he was asleep.

Oliver made his way up to the control room and pushed a green lever, switching the ship over to autonomous control. *The Explorer* came alive, backing out of the dock and heading off into the desert. Flipping it back to manual control he brought *The Explorer* up to the surface. He realized he had no idea whether it was day or night. They hadn't seen the sun in almost a week. The ship broke through the surface to a bright and beautiful day. "Ah, excellent. Quite marvelous to see the old sun back where it belongs."

Edmund walked back to find Thunder and Lightning. They were hunched over, counting out piles of Nirriimian white crystals and gold nuggets.

"Lightning! Thunder! Up front now, on the double! Strap and roll!"

"Huh? Are we in trouble? Did we do something?"

"Far from it. I'm going to teach the two greatest treasure hunters in all of Nirriim how to run *The Explorer*. That way you'll be able to come back and hunt through the mysterious and valuable treasures in the Queen's Haystack whenever you want. Who knows what you'll find there."

"We get to drive the ship??"

"Of course you do. You wouldn't be real treasure hunters if you didn't know how to drive a two hundred foot long ancient Mintarian mining vehicle that looks like the biggest worm you ever saw." Edmund laughed all the way to the front of the ship. Thunder and Lightning stuffed their treasure back into the sacks and dashed after Edmund.

It took a full day of training for Thunder and Lightning to become proficient in the ship's operation.

Oliver helped to instruct them and was a stickler for detail, making them memorize and recite over and over every aspect of the ship's controls and power systems. "I have no desire to pick up the morning paper and read about two young treasure hunters disappearing beneath the Nirriimian sands in a great worm creature. I am quite fond of you both, even though you still have a great deal to learn about proper manners and decorum."

Lightning looked puzzled. "What's decorum?"

"Oh dear, it's far worse than I thought."

Lightning laughed his cackling laugh. "Just joking, Oliver. You're the smartest rabbit we've ever met, and we've learned a lot from you. Even Thunder is starting to like science, and that's something I never thought I'd see.

"Ah, now this is good news indeed. I believe you would make an excellent scientist, Thunder. Both of you would, for that matter, being as curious as you are about the nature of this world."

Edmund called out from the control panel. "I can see the Timere Forest in the distance. We'll be there in about twenty minutes. I'm going to take her down just below the surface and we can exit through the overhead escape hatch. That way the ship will be hidden, but Thunder and Lightning will know where to find her when they decide to return to the lost city."

By the following morning the group of adventurers was strolling through the magnificent Timere Forest on their way back to the jungle. It was a long walk, and Edmund wound up carrying Thunder and Lightning's sacks of treasure.

Bartholomew found himself walking along next to Thunder. "I see you still have your beater bat. It holds sentimental value for you?"

"Uh... a little, I guess. I kept it because it was weird the way we found it. You know, when you said maybe I somehow knew it was there. I thought I'd keep it to remember that."

"Ah, a good reason indeed. Clara and I sense things like that almost every day. She's much better at it than I am though."

"I didn't want to say anything in front of everyone, but, um... I've known things before that I shouldn't have known. Sometimes I know what's going to happen before it does. I told my dad and it worried him, so I never mentioned it again."

"It's a gift, Thunder. It's a gift to be able to listen to the universe, to be part of it, to understand that all things are connected. The specific information your gift reveals to you may not be especially important, but being connected to the universe is."

"Do you think I should tell my mom and dad?"

"Only if you want to, but do it in a way that doesn't frighten them. The truth is we all have this inner voice, but some of us listen more closely to it. I'm certain the Thirteenth Monk would be happy to teach you more about your gift, if you're interested."

"I would like that, but... if I look at him won't I turn to stone?"

Bartholomew laughed. "I don't know where those stories came from. Edmund said he is the kindest, most understanding mouse in all of Nirriim. I will ask Edmund to tell the Thirteenth Monk you might be paying a visit. Bring your beater bat and tell him how and where you found it. He will understand the true meaning hidden beneath the event. Events often occur for far different reasons than the ones we imagine. I have a strong feeling the Blue Monks will play an important role in your life."

"Okay. But... just for now please don't say anything to Lightning about it."

A relaxing journey of three days found them at the Tree of Eyes. They arrived late at night, and soon were fast asleep in comfortable tents and cots shaped by Bartholomew. They had decided to stop and rest for several days before the arduous trek through the jungle. Bartholomew also thought Edmund might like to ask the Tree of Eyes a few more questions about Edmund the Explorer.

While everyone was sleeping, Edmund went for a long walk in the forest. Both moons were out and it was peaceful, the days when gigantic ants roamed the forest a distant memory.

Edmund took the Seventh Key out of his chest panel and studied it closely, then held it out as though showing it to someone. "We found the lost key, Edmund. We found the time throttle too. As soon as we take Thunder and Lightning home we'll cross the desert to the World Doors and return the key to Bruno Rabbit's house in Pterosaur Valley. That's what they call it now. We'll find a way to get the time throttle back to the Elders. You would like all my new friends, especially Thunder and Lighting. They're a lot like you were." Edmund was silent, then said, "Well, that's about it. I hope you found Emma. My friend Clara says I'll see you again sometime." Edmund put the key and time throttle away and headed back to the Tree of Eyes.

Like Edmund, The Tree of Eyes never slept, and it greeted him when he returned. "We trust you had a pleasant stroll through the forest?"

"Yes, it was quite lovely. I imagined Edmund the Explorer was there and I told him we had found the Seventh Key. I hope he heard me, wherever he is."

"I am certain he heard you. Our thoughts reach many destinations outside our current awareness. Some rabbits mistakenly think if they have not personally experienced a realm it must not exist."

"Do you know if he has found Emma?"

"I can now tell you he will find her again within one year, but she will not immediately recognize him. It will take time for her memories to return."

"That is a great relief to me. There are times when I feel... responsible for his death. If I had seen the ant before he had... I could have..."

"Edmund, what happened was part of the great and perfect Infinite Chain of events. Your actions cannot diminish the perfection of the universe because, although you may not realize it now, your actions are themselves perfection."

"It didn't seem very perfect to me when the ant killed him." Edmund gave a deep sigh, then perked up. "Oh, I had a question. Do you get tired of standing in one spot? I wondered about that during my walk. Trees never get a chance to walk through the forest."

"We are able to travel as Bartholomew does using the Traveling Eye. Our physical body remains here, but our awareness journeys incalculable distances through space and time."

"I had no idea. It must be amazing to see the wonders of the universe and witness events that occurred long ago, and events which will occur in the distant future. Oliver said his fondest desire is to see the world when it was filled with prehistoric beasts like the pterosaurs."

"We will show this sight to Oliver on his next visit if he wishes. We might add that we have come to know simple awareness as our greatest joy. To exist is to know bliss. Our happiness would be no less if we lost this ability to roam across space and time."

Edmund and the Tree of Eyes chatted until dawn when Oliver emerged from his tent, the first adventurer to rise. Next came Bartholomew, followed several hours later by Thunder and Lightning.

Ever the culinary enthusiast, Oliver prepared a scrumptious breakfast for everyone using supplies shaped by Bartholomew.

Lighting called out, "These are the best flapcakes we've ever had, Oliver. You're the greatest chef in all of Nirriim!"

"Here, here! I second that!" shouted out Thunder.

Oliver beamed. "Perhaps I have underestimated you two. For a couple of rough and tumble treasure hunters your highly refined culinary sensibilities are quite remarkable." He gave a great laugh.

The following day they bid farewell to the Tree of Eyes and headed south towards the jungle. Thunder and Lightning were eager to get home.

"I can't wait to show my mom and dad our treasure! We could buy them a hundred new houses with just my sack of gold and white crystals."

Bartholomew was shooting orange beams of light from his paw, cutting a path through the dense foliage. "What are you going to do with all that treasure? What will you buy? I doubt your parents will need a hundred new houses."

Thunder frowned. “I keep changing my mind, and now I don’t really know. A lot of the things I was going to buy I realized I didn’t really want. I guess I’ll give most of it to my parents. Really, the best part was finding the treasure.”

Edmund joined in the conversation. “Edmund the Explorer said those very same words to me when he talked of the treasures he brought back from his expeditions. He said Emma was the only treasure he truly needed. He gave most of what he found to museums and charities. He always said it was better to lead a simple life, and it didn’t hurt that it kept him out of trouble. Then he’d laugh.”

Bartholomew nodded. “He was a wise rabbit, Edmund. I wish I could have met him.”

The days rolled on and the Island of Blue Monks drew closer. Finally they broke through the dense trees and vines and saw the lake in front of them. “There it is! There’s the lake! We’re home, Thunder!”

Edmund blew the gold whistle the Red Monk had given to him and soon they were riding the long graceful boats back to the island. When the mice began to sing, each of the adventurers wished the crossing would never end.

“Bartholomew, Thunder and I would like to stop at the monastery on our way home. Would you and Oliver and Edmund go in with us? We have something we would like to tell the Thirteenth Monk.”

Bartholomew looked at Lighting curiously. “We would be happy to go. Edmund has an open invitation to visit whenever he wishes, so we will be welcomed there.”

They made their way to the outer gates of the

monastery, where Edmund raised the great iron knocker and let it fall three times. The two massive doors groaned open.

Edmund greeted the two red-robed monks who stood before them. “I am Edmund the Rabbiton, and I am here to visit my old friend the Thirteenth Monk.”

One of the monks gave a smile. “Thank you, Edmund, your presence is quite unmistakable. Please follow us. He has been expecting you.”

The party of adventurers followed the two monks into the garden where they found the Thirteenth Monk sitting on a wooden bench with five empty chairs in front of him. “Edmund, friend of Edmund the Explorer, it is always a great pleasure to see you. I hope you are well.” The Thirteenth Monk motioned for the adventurers to sit, then said, “I trust your search for the Seventh Key was successful? I sense a certain satisfaction not previously present.”

Edmund smiled. “Yes, we found it in a long forgotten underground city once inhabited by the Mintarians. It was in a secret room below the Queen’s Treasure Chamber. I would like to introduce you to our two new friends, Thunder and Lightning. They are highly skilled treasure hunters and their assistance was invaluable during our search for the key. Without them we would not have found it. Also, please give our thanks to Ennzarr for his suggestion that we visit the Paw and Dagger Inn. That is where we met Thunder and Lightning.”

The Thirteenth Monk smiled. “Ah, Klanndirr and Binndirr, it is lovely to finally meet you. I have been quite looking forward to it and I welcome you both to the monastery.” He looked directly at Thunder, who glanced nervously down at his feet. "But perhaps Thunder already knew I was looking forward to meeting you both?" He laughed quietly and put his paw on Thunder's shoulder. "I will not turn you to stone. You are far too gifted a seer to meet such a ghastly fate as that."

"I'm a gifted what?"

"We shall continue this conversation on another day, Thunder. Edmund, is there another reason why you have chosen to visit at this time?"

To the surprise of the other adventurers, Lightning answered the Thirteenth Monk's question. "Sir, Thunder and I would like to give half of all the treasure we find to the Blue Monks. We would like you to use it to help the island mice. I know there are many houses in need of repair, and food can be scarce during the long winters."

It was the first time Edmund had seen the Thirteenth Monk show surprise. The blue-robed monk looked first at Lightning, then at Thunder. He appeared deep in thought. For almost a full minute he said nothing.

Lightning finally stammered, "Uh... if that's okay with you, of course."

The Thirteenth Monk smiled, "Forgive me, there is more to this than is readily apparent. I am overwhelmed by your sincere generosity. That such young mice would put others before themselves is quite remarkable and says much about your nature." From his pocket he withdrew two golden whistles, giving one to Thunder and one to Lightning. "The doors of the monastery are always open to both of you. You have helped to forge an unbreakable link on the Infinite Chain, and for this I am sincerely grateful."

"The infinite what?"

Bartholomew took pity on Lightning. "We should take our leave now. It has been a long adventure and Thunder and Lightning are anxious to see their parents."

The Thirteenth Monk rose, warmly shaking the paws of the adventurers, again thanking Thunder and Lightning for their generosity. He walked them to the main gate, and as they were leaving he put his paw on Edmund's arm, saying, "Have patience, my old friend, your long journey is almost over."

Edmund nodded, but the meaning of the monk's words was unclear to him. "Thank you, the quest for the Seventh Key was a lengthy one, and I look forward to seeing the Fortress of Elders again. We should arrive within a week."

The Thirteenth Monk's eyes were twinkling. "Until the next time we meet, then."

Bartholomew, Edmund, and Oliver walked Thunder and Lightning home and were greeted warmly by their parents. They watched as Thunder and Lightning emptied their bag of gold and Nirriimian white crystals onto the living room floor. The look on their parents' faces was a sight Bartholomew would never forget.

The following day as they bid their farewells, Bartholomew said, "We will be back again to visit you. Quite soon, as a matter of fact. I will be returning with Clara, to show her the Timere Forest. It is one of the most beautiful places I have ever seen and I know she will love it. Now that we have the Seventh Key, blinking here will take almost no time at all."

Thunder and Lightning hugged everyone, thanking Bartholomew for hiring them, and thanking Edmund and Oliver for teaching them how to operate *The Explorer*.

After a three day trek through the jungle, Bartholomew, Oliver, and Edmund were again gazing out across the vast desert.

"Edmund, perhaps you might walk in front of us, just on the off chance we run into one of those dreadful Wyrme of Deth creatures. Especially since we know they have a taste for fresh Rabbiton." Oliver roared with laughter at his own joke.

Edmund rolled his eyes, just as Edmund the Explorer had taught him to do so very long ago.

The desert crossing was relatively uneventful, and to no one's disappointment they did not see a single Mintarian Wyrme of Deth. They were held up for almost four hours by a flock of wild creekers, but Bartholomew flicked up a large defense sphere as soon as Edmund spotted the beasts flying towards them. After two more days of walking and many long discussions on all manner of topics, Edmund led them to the area where the World Doors should be located.

Bartholomew reached into his pack and withdrew a pair of World Glasses, handing them to Oliver. "Look through these and see if you can spot the door. It will appear as a dark rectangle. I'm going to test an idea of mine. I don't know why, but I have a feeling the Eleventh Ring will allow me to see the World Doors without World Glasses.

Less than an hour later Oliver and Bartholomew simultaneously shouted, "I see it!" Bartholomew's hunch had been correct. When he wore the Eleventh Ring he had no need for World Glasses.

Soon they stood in front of the floating door, which

was quite invisible to Edmund. "You're certain it's really there? I see nothing at all."

Bartholomew pulled the door open, revealing the hallway with the six doors on each side and the door to the Isle of Mandora at the opposite end.

Edmund stepped up into the hallway. "It has been over fifteen hundred years since I walked through this doorway with Edmund the Explorer." He flipped open his chest panel and withdrew the gold Seventh Key.

"Ah, excellent, you didn't lose it." Oliver chuckled loudly.

Edmund stepped down the hallway to the seventh door. As the key drew closer, the keyhole appeared. He inserted the key, then gently twisted it. There was a click and the door opened. The noxious odors from the Swamp of Lost Things flooded into the hallway. They were dreadful and wonderful at the same time. Oliver grinned like a bunny as he pointed up at the sky. "One moon! Hurrah!"

They were home at last. A great wave of relief washed through Bartholomew. The Seventh Key would soon be back in Pterosaur Valley.

Chapter 43

Augustus C. Rabbit's New Job

Augustus C. Rabbit, former president of the Excelsior Electro-Vacuumator Corporation, was standing in a rather stark office, watching patiently as his new boss perused the most recent round of technical drawings. Augustus cleared his throat, then asked, "What do you think? The third prototype functions flawlessly, and we're set to begin production as soon as you give the go ahead."

"I like it. You've outdone yourself to have gotten so far in such a short time. This is excellent, Augustus. May I say again, I am ever so happy you decided to join me in this remarkable new venture."

"Thank you, Oliver. I wouldn't have missed this opportunity for the world. This miracle of technology you have created will change the way rabbits work and live. This is truly a first for the world of rabbits and muroids."

"Truthfully, it's been done before, but a long time

ago. Why don't we take a stroll down to sub level three and you can give me a tour of the production floor. How many Rabbitons do we have working for us?"

"Right now there are close to three hundred, but we can expand that as the company grows."

Oliver T. Rabbit and his new chief of operations, Augustus C. Rabbit, walked down the long hallways of the Fortress of Elders until they reached the set of stairs leading down to sub level three.

Augustus pressed a violet disk on the wall and two wide doors slid open.

"Great heavens, this is enormous! I didn't realize sub level three contained a room this large."

"We are finding more and more hidden areas in the Fortress. We believe this was a storage area, but it makes a perfect factory floor."

Oliver could barely hear himself talk as they stepped into the new production area. Hundreds of Rabbitons were scurrying about in a vast maze of gleaming machinery, much of which Oliver did not recognize.

"What is this technology? Where did it come from?"

"The Rabbitons brought it up from sub level four. No one even knew there was a sub level four until they showed up with these machines. Apparently this is what they used to produce their own vehicles back when the Elders lived here. I have no idea what sort of vehicles they had then, and the Rabbitons have been less than chatty when it comes to sharing that information with us."

"Hmmm... quite amazing." Oliver knew very well what vehicles the Elders had produced but said nothing. The world was not ready for blinkers and scouting ships and interworld transports. Those things would come later. Most rabbits didn't even have electricity in their homes.

"How do you like the sign?" Augustus pointed to a huge painted banner on the far wall that read:

The Pterosaur
Flying Carriage
Company

Above the company's name was the silhouette of a flying pterosaur.

"Magnificent, Augustus. You've thought of everything. And you know, with these new updated vacuumator engines the flying carriages will be even quieter and faster than the *Adventurer II.* Perhaps one day there will be a Ptersosaur in front of every home in Lapinor and Grymmore."

"Better than that, Oliver. We already have orders for well over a thousand Pterosaurs, from six different countries. It appears we are a success even before we have begun production."

"Good heavens. You have my blessing to begin production immediately. I'll get out of your way now, Augustus. I have a few errands I must attend to."

After fifteen minutes of walking up and down stairs and through the massive hallways of the Fortress, Oliver found himself in a small office facing an A9 Engineering Rabbiton.

"During my recent travels I came upon a damaged blinker ship in the Timere Forest of Nirriim. Would it be possible for a group of Engineering Rabbitons to bring it back to the Fortress so I might examine it?"

"This task is one which could easily be accomplished. Is there something in particular about this blinker ship you wish to examine? Perhaps you are seeking to determine the cause of its malfunction?"

"No, I am simply trying to understand the technology behind its power source and the anti-microgravitator motors which drive the craft. These systems could be utilized in future generations of Pterosaurs."

"Would it not be more practical simply to examine one of the many blinker ships on sub level four?"

"There are blinker ships on sub level four?? Great heavens, lead the way, my good Rabbiton!"

"As you wish. Just have this MAH092075 form signed and we will proceed." The Rabbiton pulled a long sheet of paper out from a slot on its arm and handed it to Oliver.

Oliver looked down at the form in his paw. "What is this? This must be signed? By who?"

"In order to access sub level four your MAH092075 form must be signed by an Elder with a minimum R9 security clearance."

"An Elder? That's rather silly, isn't it? There has not been an Elder here for over fifteen hundred years."

The Rabbiton's glowing red eyes blinked off and on rapidly. "One moment please, and I will have your response." Minutes later Oliver was still watching the Rabbiton's eyes blink.

Finally the Rabbiton spoke again. "Your MAH092075 form must be signed by the Master of Rabbitons."

"Edmund the Rabbiton must sign this form? My old friend Edmund?"

"Your MAH092075 form must be signed by the Master of Rabbitons."

"You are well aware of the fact that he is my old and dear friend. Why must I –"

"Your MAH092075 form must be signed by the Master of Rabbitons."

Oliver shook his head and gave a long sigh. Even the Elders had not managed to escape the cumbersome hand of bureaucracy. "Oh dear, I suppose now I must travel to Pterosaur Valley and have Edmund sign the form. Well, I will treat this as a welcome chance to visit with Bartholomew and Clara and see how they are settling in after our recent adventure."

Chapter 44

The Scream

Oliver sat in his comfortable chair gazing out across Pterosaur Valley. "No matter how many times I see Pterosaur Valley from this marvelous vantage point I am still quite awed by its spectacular beauty."

"I feel the same way, Oliver. Bartholomew and I love it here. In fact, we have decided to make this our permanent home. I can easily blink back and forth between here and Penrith. The Guild does keep me busy – membership has doubled over the last year."

Edmund stepped out of a side room and approached Oliver. "Here is the signed form, and I do apologize for the Rabbitons. I have tried to update the Fortress systems, but old habits die hard, even for Rabbitons."

"It's no bother, it was a lovely trip and it is wonderful to see my old friends again. Have you showed Clara the Seventh Key and the time throttle yet?"

"I have not. We have been busy making Bruno's old home more to the liking of Bartholomew and Clara." Edmund flipped open his chest panel and withdrew the gold key and time throttle, handing them to Clara.

"So this is the infamous Seventh Key." Clara turned it over in her paws. "It's amazing to think this was lost for all those years. Who knows how it found its way to the lost Mintarian city. It certainly must be important if Bruno Rabbit was so concerned about it." Clara closed her eyes, holding the key close to her. "There is something. It's hard to feel exactly what it is, but there is... an event, something new. Something blossoming... or something being born? That's all I can get now." Clara opened her eyes again and handed the key and time throttle back to Edmund.

"I will return the Seventh Key to its proper place among the other World Keys, just as Edmund the Explorer promised Bruno Rabbit." Edmund turned and walked towards the alcove containing the massive obsidian block and the other eleven World Keys.

Bartholomew called out, "We'll be right there, Edmund, just as soon as we finish this delightful wine Oliver was kind enough to bring us."

Oliver chuckled. "Well, you know me well enough by now to know when it comes to wine I never–" Oliver never finished his sentence. He never finished it because he was interrupted by two sounds. The first was an almost paralyzing scream, a dreadful melding of surprise and terror. Clara's glass of wine fell to the floor, shattering. The second sound was a clanking, groaning sound that echoed through the cavern. Following these two sounds came a deathly silence.

Clara was the first to respond. She was leaning forward, her paws covering her ears. "It's Edmund! Something has happened to Edmund!"

Bartholomew disappeared in a blink of light,

reappearing outside the alcove. He saw Edmund lying in a tangled heap on the floor. He was not moving. Clara and Oliver dashed up behind Bartholomew, both seeing Edmund simultaneously.

"What happened to him?"

A chill shot though Bartholomew. "What is *that*??"

Clara and Oliver looked to where Bartholomew was pointing. The huge block of obsidian which held the twelve World Keys had vanished, and all twelve keys appeared to be floating in mid air. Below them, hovering eight inches above the floor, was the ten foot long body of a rabbit. Its eyes were closed and it appeared to be dead.

"Good heavens, it's a huge rabbit. It's... is that an Elder? Did it do something to Edmund? What is it?"

Bartholomew said, "This was triggered when Edmund placed the Seventh Key on the obsidian block."

The three of them spun around. Edmund was moving. They watched as he rose to his feet, looking at them with a dazed, bewildered expression.

Clara said, "Edmund? Are you all right? What happened?"

Edmund gazed at her. "Who are you? What is this place? What have you done to me?" He held his hands out in front of him. "*What have you done to me??*"

Oliver tried to calm Edmund. "Edmund, it's fine. You're fine now. You must have fallen when you saw the rabbit's body in the block. Do you know who that is? Do you recognize him? Did he do something to you?"

Edmund looked at Oliver as though he was dim. "Of course I recognize him. It's me, Edmund."

"What do you mean, it's you?"

"I mean it's my body. I'm staring at my own body."

In a single brilliant flash Bartholomew saw the strings running beneath the fabric of the world. The intricately woven web of interconnected events lay open before him. Once again he stood before the universe in awe of its incomprehensible perfection. "You are Edmund the Explorer."

"I am Edmund the Explorer. I am married to Emma. I should not be in this A2 body, I should be in that body over there."

Oliver whispered loudly to Bartholomew. "Has he gone daft? He really thinks he's Edmund the Explorer?"

Clara put her paw on Edmund's arm, then stepped back. "He *is* Edmund the Explorer. I can sense his life force now, trapped in Edmund the Rabbiton's body."

The alcove was abruptly filled with a bright blue flickering light . "Ah, hello, Edmund. Not very pleased with your shiny new Rabbiton body? I have to say, you're far better looking now than you ever were before." The voice gave a great laugh.

Bartholomew whirled around to see a tall shimmering blue rabbit, parts of it sharp and clear, parts blurry, eerily glowing and shifting about.

Edmund backed away. "It's you – the Blue Spectre! I... I saw you... in the Swamp of Lost Things. I think I did. I feel like I've been dreaming forever and I just woke up. Are you real? Is this real? Where am I?"

"You don't recognize me do you? I suppose I shouldn't be surprised. I look a bit different from the last time you saw me. Edmund, it's me, your old friend Jonathan the Explorer. You and I had scores of adventures together. I doubt another Elder ever saw as much of the twelve worlds as we did."

"Jonathan? I remember Jonathan and you're not Jonathan. That's not possible. You don't look anything like Jonathan. You do have his voice though. I don't know. Maybe this is still a dream." Edmund closed his eyes tightly then opened them again. "You're still here and I'm still stuck in this A2 body. Wait, if you're Jonathan, tell me what I got Emma for our first anniversary."

"Easy. Dimmer that you are, you didn't get her anything. You forgot your first anniversary. I've heard Emma tell that story a hundred times."

"Creekers. Could be a lucky guess, but probably not. What happened to you? Why are you blue? Are you dead? Are you a ghost? Am I dead?"

Jonathan laughed. "Do I sound like I'm dead? Do you feel dead? This sparkling blue form standing before you is one of the new bodies the Elders were working on about the time you got squished by a big ant. You were probably yammering on and on about Emma instead of paying attention to what was going on around you."

"Now I know you're Jonathan – just a big old furry ball of sympathy, aren't you? Well, not so much of the fur now, but you get the idea."

"That's the thanks I get after everything I've done? Fifteen hundred years of watching you simmer inside the A2, waiting for you to pop out of the oven?"

"You're as incomprehensible as ever. Fifteen hundred years? What are you rambling on about?"

Oliver rubbed his eyes. "Good heavens, this is without a doubt the strangest conversation I have ever been witness to. Will somebody please tell me what is going on here, and who is talking to who about what?"

Bartholomew grinned. "Jonathan, shall we go have a seat in the main room and you can explain all this to us?"

"Gladly. I'll even use small words so Edmund will be sure to understand me." He laughed loudly, clapping Edmund on the back. "I've missed you, my old friend. More than you can possibly know."

For the next hour, Jonathan told the story of how Edmund the Explorer had come to occupy the body of his A2 Rabbiton. When the A2 brought Edmund the Explorer to the Tree of Eyes, it was too late for the Tree to simply repair his body. In a desperate attempt to save his life, the Tree transferred Edmund's thoughts, memories, and his remaining life force into the A2. This was supposed to be temporary, but when the A2 lost power, things got complicated. The essence of Edmund the Explorer was deeply buried in the A2, and nobody had the slightest idea when he would emerge from his metallic cocoon.

"The Tree of Eyes contacted Bruno Rabbit, who then contacted me. Bruno brought Edmund the Explorer's body back to his home here in the valley and eventually managed to repair it. He placed it inside the obsidian block and froze it in time, knowing the Seventh Key would not be returned until Edmund the Explorer was awake enough to find it, fulfilling his promise to return the key. Bruno used the Seventh Key as a trigger to reveal Edmund the Explorer's original body inside the obsidian block.

"The scout ship brought the A2 Rabbiton back to the Elders, and eventually it was refurbished as a Model 9000 Rabbiton with the Series 3 Repositorian Module.

But, somewhere inside that metal shell lay the dormant life force and memories of Edmund the Explorer. I made certain it was programmed to remain in the Fortress and not leave with the Elders. We were convinced that one day Edmund the Explorer would wake up, but we had no idea when that day would come.

It wasn't until Oliver T. Rabbit met the A2 in the Central Information Repository that things began to percolate inside him. Having friends to talk to was exactly what he needed, and gradually over the next year Edmund the Explorer's personality began to emerge. It must have been frightening for Edmund the Rabbiton to have a new personality keep popping up inside him like that."

Oliver interrupted Jonathan. "We thought he was going mad! Sometimes he was our old friend Edmund, and then out of nowhere he'd start hollering, 'strap and roll, rabs!' or go storming into some disreputable tavern. It all makes sense now. Great heavens, I would never have dreamed such a thing would be possible." He stopped abruptly. "What about our dear friend Edmund the Rabbiton? Where is he? Is he lost? Oh, dear, this is most distressing." Oliver clapped his paw over his mouth, looking close to tears.

Jonathan quickly reassured Oliver, "He'll be perfectly fine now. Once I've finished what I came here to do, you'll have your old friend Edmund the Rabbiton back again just as he was before. The danger was that his personality would be eclipsed by Edmund the Explorer's personality, and the Edmund the Rabbiton you know would simply disappear. That will not happen now. Plus, since some of Edmund the

Explorer's residual universal life force will remain in the Rabbiton body, your friend Edmund will be the only truly living Rabbiton in the world."

Edmund the Explorer said, "Whatever you came here to do, I hope it involves a couple of pints of ale. Hey, isn't this Bruno Rabbit's house?"

Jonathan snorted. "Hold off drinking any ale while you're in that Rabbiton body or you'll fry all your neuronic synapses and we'll never get you out of there. And yes, this used to be Bruno Rabbit's house. Now, give me twenty minutes and I'll have you back in your old body. Times have changed, and so has our understanding of the universal life force. We can't light the candle, but we can move the flame to a different lantern. Take a few days before you head for the nearest tavern. Which, by the way, will be quite a hike considering where we are."

"Let's get busy then. I can taste that ale already."

"You know, there is another option besides returning to your old body. I could pop you into one of the new bodies, just like mine. They're a combination of light and particles, completely indestructible, and allow instantaneous travel anywhere. And it won't be long until they crack the time wall."

Edmund the Explorer didn't hesitate. "I like my fur. And when I find Emma again, I want her to recognize me."

"It doesn't really work like that."

"Maybe not, but I'll stick with my old furball of a body anyway."

"Well, you're not the first Elder to turn down the new bodies. I'll be right back."

Jonathan returned several minutes later with

Edmund the Explorer's former body floating in front of him. With a wave of his paw it settled down onto the couch. "Sit down next to your old body and put your hand on its forehead."

"Now this is just plain weird. I'm touching my own furry head with these Rabbiton hands."

"Quit your jabbering and do what I say."

"Lovely bedside manner you have. Have you ever thought of *not* becoming a doctor?"

Jonathan grinned and began to move both paws in a slow circular motion. A swirling blue cloud emerged and was drawn into Edmund. Edmund's color gradually changed until he was a brilliant sky blue. Jonathan flicked a paw, and like a ghost leaving its old body, a blue form floated out from Edmund the Rabbiton and entered into Edmund the Explorer's old body.

"Okay, my old friend, here comes the real magic. We start your clock ticking again." Jonathan pressed his paws tightly together. A brilliant purple sphere of light appeared above them, growing brighter and brighter until everyone in the room had to shield their eyes with their paws. Jonathan whispered, "Go!" and the light blasted into Edmund the Explorer. His body glowed brilliantly for a moment, then faded back to normal. "Any moment now."

The first thing Edmund the Explorer said after he opened his eyes was, "Holy creekers, now this is more like it!" He tried to stand up but collapsed back onto the couch.

"Hey, I said take it easy. Lie down, it'll be a day or two before everything is working properly. I'll stay here and keep an eye on you. No ale until we're sure your tiny little brain is functioning properly. Not that it ever functioned properly before."

Edmund the Rabbiton's gleaming silver body quivered for a moment, then rose to its feet. "Oh my, this is much better. I'm feeling like my old Rabbiton self again. It was quite crowded and confusing in here for a while. And all that business with the ants was quite disturbing. I mean really, who is afraid of ants? I certainly hope you didn't think *I* was afraid of ants. Ha ha ha ha!" His eyes moved over to the couch where Edmund the Explorer lay. Edmund the Rabbiton made a great gasping noise then whispered hoarsely, "Edmund the Explorer! It's you! Oh my, it really is you. Clara said I would see you again. She said I would. Do you remember me? I was–"

Edmund the Explorer's smile lit up the room. "Hey, A2, remember that time we were being attacked by creekers in the Nirriimian desert and I had to fight them off with my bare paws? And then the deadly poisonous snow spiders popped up from under the sand and I had to carry you because you were too scared to run?"

"Ha ha ha ha! Snow spiders in a blazing hot desert? I was too scared to run?? Ha ha ha ha!" Edmund the Rabbiton was on the verge of hysteria.

"Of course I remember you, A2. You were always my toughest audience and my favorite one. I've said it before, and I'll say it again, you are one of a kind. It was my lucky day when I plunked down those credits and brought you home. Come give me a hug, old friend."

Chapter 45

Edmund's New World

Bartholomew and Clara invited Edmund the Explorer to stay with them for as long as he wanted. They were thrilled to be in the presence of a real Elder, having many conversations with him about life in the Fortress when he lived there. It turned out the Fortress was even larger than they had previously thought. There were two additional sub levels beneath the vehicle production and storage level, making a total of six sub levels.

Oliver broke the news about his new Pterosaur Flying Carriage Company, which of course required Bartholomew to shape numerous glasses of a fine vintage champagne. As they toasted Oliver, he promised each of them a shiny new Pterosaur once the production lines were rolling. Edmund the Rabbiton got all sniffly, deeply moved by Oliver's great generosity. Edmund the Explorer, who decided champagne wasn't as good as ale but wasn't as bad as water, said to

Edmund the Rabbiton, "Hey, are you forgetting that time I got you a bottle of silver polish? Now *that* was a generous gift."

Jonathan the Explorer spent a great deal of time talking with Edmund the Explorer, knowing full well his transition from the world of fifteen hundred years ago to this new world would not be an easy one, even for someone like Edmund the Explorer, who usually landed on his feet.

"It's a new world out there since the Elders moved to Mandora. It's not better or worse, but it is different. All the rabbits you knew and loved are gone, except for the ones who switched to the new bodies. Life is different in the light bodies. In some ways it's much better, in some ways not. I miss the warm breeze blowing through my fur. But I like traveling to other worlds in the blink of an eye. I know I don't need to tell you that Emma is gone."

Edmund the Explorer couldn't look at Jonathan. "What happened... when I didn't come back? What did Emma do?"

"Bruno Rabbit told her what happened to you and how you had sacrificed your life to send Neilana safely home, and that your sacrifice would eventually bring an end to the war. Bruno is a strange one. He has no time for explorers, but he said you were an exception. He liked you. That's why he repaired your body and froze it in time until the Seventh Key was returned. It was all his idea. He tried to bring you back while Emma was still alive, but even he couldn't wake you. I was in on the plan from the start. In fact, I was the one who helped your A2 open the spectral doorway to Nirriim. I told him I was his inner voice and convinced him he was the one creating the doorway. Can you imagine me being an inner voice?"

"Did Emma... you know..."

"Marry again? No, she didn't. She said you were the only one for her, and she would find you again. She lived to be almost one hundred and eighty, and I don't think a day went by that she didn't mention you."

Edmund looked at his old friend Jonathan. "How do I find her? How do I know if she's back here again?"

The glittering lights within Jonathan's spectral body sparkled and danced. "If I knew anything specific I would tell you. This new body has a few other interesting benefits besides immortality and instant travel. It connects us more deeply with the universe. I can tell you this much – I have sensed that Emma is back and is looking for you, although she probably doesn't know exactly who she is searching for. Don't run out like the mad rabbit and try to find her. You know well enough how the universe operates. Go on about your life, but keep your eyes open and pay attention to your feelings. It won't take long. You'll recognize her when you see her, even if she doesn't look the same, and even if she doesn't know you."

"Okay. Thanks, Jonathan. You're not quite as dim as you look."

"Finally, after all these years you pay me a real compliment. It was worth the wait. Speaking of which, I'd say you're healthy enough for a few small sips of ale. You have to be sensible though, so no more than four or five pints."

Edmund the Rabbiton spent many long days getting reacquainted with Edmund the Explorer. He told Edmund the Explorer all about the Thirteenth Monk and how he had relived his lost memories of the ants in the Timere Forest.

"You forget, A2, while you were reliving your experience I was there with you, half asleep in your Rabbiton body. I saw everything through your eyes, although it seemed like a dream to me. When I saw the ant grabbing me, my only thoughts were of Emma. I'll have to tell her that when I see her. You know, I'm probably the only rabbit in history who's gone back and watched himself living his own life. It taught me one thing. It's the little things we do for others that make a difference, not the big grandiose gestures. It's mopping the floors for Emma, or buying a few pints for Jonathan. A whole lifetime of that can change the world."

Edmund the Rabbiton smiled. "The kindness and friendship you showed to me when I was a young A2 Carrier Rabbiton changed my life forever. I am quite certain you will find Emma again. Clara said you would, and she is extremely gifted in matters such as this."

"Thanks, A2. Hey, did I ever tell you about the time I was swallowed by a gigantic Nirriimian Wyrme of Deth who–"

"Um, that was me, not you."

"Oh. You're right. How about the time I..."

* * *

Oliver looked through the glass wall to the vast factory floor below his office. The production lines were rolling, and they were shipping out eleven flying carriages a day. Orders for the Pterosaurs were piling up and Augustus C. Rabbit already had plans in motion to double their output. The Pterosaur was a far greater success than Oliver had ever envisioned, but he frowned at the sight of the paperwork piled up on his desk. It seemed all he did was sign papers and pore over technical drawings. He was beginning to wonder if there was any difference between this and his old job at the Excelsior Corporation.

"Good heavens, there really is no reason for me to be moping about like this. As president of the Pterosaur Flying Carriage Company, I hereby decree it is time for a delicious snack." He rose up, stepped to the back of his office and opened a clear glass case. Inside the case were eight pink boxes filled with Madame Beffy's éclairs. With the help of Bartholomew and the engineering Rabbitons, Oliver had cracked the technology behind Bruno Rabbit's time bending food storage system. The éclairs were as fresh as the day they were made, almost three months prior. He gingerly removed one and returned to his desk. Just as he raised the éclair to his mouth he was interrupted by a soft knocking on the door. He set down the éclair and called out, "Enter!"

The door slid open and familiar face peeked in. "Hello, dear Oliver!"

"Clara! How lovely to see you again. I trust you and Bartholomew are enjoying your visit to the Fortress?"

"We are having a lovely time. I have developed a certain fondness for the food synthesizers, and your flying carriage factory is quite astonishing. You really are a brilliant rabbit, Oliver."

"Oh dear, you mustn't say such things to me, Clara. I might have to steal you away from Bartholomew."

Oliver chuckled loudly, always his own best audience.

"It's interesting you should say that, Oliver. I have a puzzling letter addressed to you that arrived in today's post."

Oliver looked at her curiously. "A puzzling letter for me? If it's from someone who wants a Pterosaur, I'm afraid they'll have to–"

"I don't think that's it, Oliver." Clara pulled a pink envelope out of her pocket, a mischievous smile on her face. "It's quite a lovely envelope, and smells distinctly of lilac scent. Who do you suppose it's from?" Clara blinked her eyes innocently.

Oliver's usual composure vanished. "Great heavens, I have not the faintest idea who would send me such a letter. Just throw it on the pile with the rest of my correspondence and I'll get to it later."

"Mmm... the return address says it's from someone named Madame Beffy in Grymmsteir. Isn't she the one you buy all your éclairs from?"

"Madame Beffy... well, yes, of course, she makes the very best éclairs in all of Grymmore. Her pastry shop is quite well known. She is also a very lovely rabbit. We have become rather good friends over the last year, though I have no idea why she might be sending me a letter. Perhaps it is simply a note to thank me for all the éclairs I have purchased."

Clara smiled as she handed the letter to Oliver. "I'll stop teasing you now and let you read your letter. Oliver, I'm truly happy you have found a dear friend in Madame Beffy. You deserve all the happiness in the world."

Oliver T. Rabbit had met his match and he knew it. He dropped all pretense, taking the letter from Clara.

"Thank you, Clara. I am quite fond of Madame Beffy and it is my intention to spend more time with her if she is so inclined."

"If she searched for a thousand years she would not find another rabbit as wonderful as you, Oliver."

"Oh dear, I really should get back to work now. Stacks of papers to sign and drawings to approve, you know."

"I understand. We'll stop in again before we leave for the Timere Forest. Bartholomew says it's the most beautiful place he has ever seen. It sounds lovely."

"Yes, quite lovely indeed. Especially now that the giant ants are gone." He was still chuckling after Clara had left.

Glancing back to make certain the door was closed, Oliver set Madame Beffy's letter down in front of him. He ran his paw gently across the envelope, the memories of his last visit to Madame Beffy's Pastry Shop flooding back to him, his senses filled again with the delicious aromas of éclairs and lilac and freshly baked cinnamon rolls.

He picked up Madame Beffy's letter, studying it closely. At this very moment in time, the content of her letter was a cloud of infinite possibility. The letter could say whatever he wished it to say. Madame Beffy could confess that Oliver was her heart's fondest desire. She could also say he was simply a cherished friend or a valued customer of the pastry shop. Once he opened and read the letter, this luxury of imagination would come to an abrupt end. The cloud of infinite possibility would be distilled down to a single focused reality, becoming a new truth in his world, a turned page in the story of his life. He leaned the envelope up against his table lamp with a sigh.

"Tomorrow. I'll open it tomorrow."

* * *

Edmund the Rabbiton stood gazing at his reflection in the mirror. A smile slowly spread across his face. "I am Edmund the Rabbiton, and I am alive. I am alive."

* * *

Bartholomew and Clara strolled paw in paw through the majestic primordial Timere Forest, dappled sunlight fluttering across the soft forest floor.

Clara gazed up at the glorious beams of light filtering through the forest canopy. "It's far more beautiful than any description you could ever have given me. It is ancient and timeless. I hear the song of the trees more clearly here than anywhere else I have ever been."

"That's what it was! That's why it seemed so beautiful to me. I was hearing the song of the trees but wasn't consciously aware of it."

"It's breathtaking. I'm so glad we decided to come here."

"I hope Edmund the Explorer finds Emma, just as you and I found each other."

"You really have become quite the romantic. It's a big change from the last time we were married, but I like it."

"The last time we were married?"

"Yes, before we were rabbits."

"What does that even mean?"

"We haven't always had these rabbit bodies. It's like Edmund the Explorer moving from a Rabbiton body back to his original rabbit body – our consciousness simply moves from one vehicle to another."

"Oh. I didn't have scales back then did I? I don't think scales and claws would be a good look for me."

"You know perfectly well none of that matters. The only thing that matters is us being together."

"I would agree one hundred percent. I happen to know the Blue Monks wrote on a small piece of paper over five thousand years ago that the greatest treasure in this world is love."